MW01520827

CHAMPAGNE
COWBOYS

Also by Leo W. Banks
Double Wide

CHAMPAGNE COWBOYS

LEO W. BANKS

BRASH
BOOKS

Copyright © 2020 Leo W. Banks. All Rights Reserved.

The characters and events portrayed in this book are fictitious. Any similarity to real persons, living or dead, is coincidental and not intended by the author.

No part of this book may be reproduced, or stored in a retrieval system, or transmitted in any form or by any means, electronic, mechanical, photocopying, recording, or otherwise, without express written permission of the publisher.

ISBN: 1-7324226-4-8
ISBN-13: 978-1-7324226-4-3

Published by
Brash Books, LLC
12120 State Line #253
Leawood, Kansas 66209
www.brash-books.com

CHAPTER ONE

I drove through the neon kingdom of Speedway Boulevard blowing smoke from my six-dollar cigar and listening to the wail of cop sirens.

It was morning in Tucson, the top down on my Ford Bronco, the desert wind in my hair, sun shining, palm trees waving, the walking-dead drug addicts begging with cardboard signs from the sidewalks.

At a red light, a guy with a tat mask and an unlit cigarette dangling from his lips split the lanes of traffic on his bicycle. I could smell him going by.

He was struggling to balance a twelve-pack of Bud Light bottles on the handlebars.

Everybody has dreams. I was rooting for him.

My phone rang. Roxanne Santa Cruz.

"Morning, Rox. Isn't it a beautiful day in the jewel of the Southwest?"

"I wouldn't know. Just got pinged on a bank robbery. Where are you?" Roxy was a minor celebrity in a town that couldn't produce any other kind. She worked as a reporter at KPIN-TV telling the "real story," as the slogan went.

"On my way to breakfast with Cash," I said. "After that we're going to visit Charlie at St. Joe's. He fell off his ladder."

Cashmere Miller sat right beside me. He was a tenant of mine at Double Wide, the trailer park I owned. He had a narrow ghost face. He stared straight ahead, lost in the coffeeless wilderness of early morning.

"I need a favor," Roxy said. "Could you run out to Ash Sterling's house and check on him for me?"

"Right now? I'm hungry, Rox."

"If you're going to the hospital, you're already on the east side."

"You've spent a lot of time with that guy and gotten nothing out of it."

"A war hero comes home from Afghanistan, forms a band of ex-marine thieves and makes a bundle cleaning out rich people's houses? Yeah, I'm willing to work to get that story."

Roxy had told me about her dealings with Ash Sterling.

Once a week for several weeks running she'd been driving out to his house. No notebook, no camera, no hard questions. Just a patient reporter sitting in a man's living room trying to get him to open up.

A rich, dying man. The end was near. Heart failure.

In his initial call to Roxy, Sterling said he'd watched her on TV, admired her work, and wanted her to tell his story after he was gone. He told her of his wartime experiences and a few random bits about his life as a highly successful thief.

But he kept the details in his pocket, and every time Roxy pressed, he backed off.

"Sounds like he just wants a beautiful woman's company," I said.

"Today's different."

"All I want right now is bacon and hash browns."

"It's not that far. I'll make it up to you. Please, please, cherries and all that."

Roxy's voice got me. It was the voice of an angel with an abominable past. Soft, but a touch raspy, a mix of vanilla ice cream and Chivas Regal neat.

I can resist many things, but not that voice.

"All right," I said. "What's different about today?"

"Last night on the phone I told him, 'Look, I'm canceling for tomorrow. I can't keep driving out there and have you clam up on me.' And he said, 'You want to know about that double murder in the Foothills, don't you?'"

The breath caught in my throat. I jerked the steering wheel and swung into the parking lot of a carpet store. A Truly Nolen exterminator truck had been riding my bumper and the driver had to mash his brakes to avoid hitting me.

He sang me a crazy song with his horn.

The roach chemicals can't do those fellows any favors.

Roxy said, "Then he goes, 'Would you like to solve it?'"

"Did he ever mention the Foothills case before that?"

"No. But I was beginning to suspect he was involved. I tried hard not to spill my nightcap and very politely said, 'Why, yes, I do want to solve it.' We set it up for noon today and now I can't reach him. I've been calling and it's straight to voice."

"You think something happened?"

"He sounded really weak. Just see if he's okay. I can make it out there later."

I puffed my cigar and watched the morning traffic zip by. The Foothills murders had been a huge weight on me since they'd happened. The victims were Paul and Donna Morton, close friends of mine.

Roxy and I had been investigating it together and getting nowhere. If Ash Sterling knew something, it'd be our first real break.

"Give me directions."

I drove northeast onto Tanque Verde Road, hit the Catalina Highway, and kept rolling north until all the important cultural landmarks were behind us.

That was another way of saying we'd passed the last Circle K.

Before starting the climb to Mount Lemmon, I hung a right onto an unmarked dirt track, and soon there was nothing on either side of us but open desert.

The Bronco's tires drummed on the corduroy road for three miles until I reached Sterling's earth-colored Santa Fe–style mansion.

It sat halfway up the side of a canyon, perched there by some architectural magic, in multiple sections on different levels, each flat-roofed with pueblo-style ladders leading from one to the next.

The front was rounded and mostly glass. A fieldstone driveway led to the main entrance. I stepped from the Bronco and heard a sharp metallic click.

Cash had pulled out his .45-caliber Ruger and racked a round into the pipe.

It was eight o'clock in the morning, so of course he was carrying.

I said, "You were figuring on trouble at breakfast?"

"Sometimes I hear footsteps on my back trail."

"Hearing anything now?"

"Don't like that front door being open. Rich folks don't leave doors open. Table's tipped over in there, too."

Distracted by my hunger, I hadn't noticed. My breakfast plans had gone to hell.

"All right, then," I said. "What're you waiting for? Go clear the house."

Cash was rehab thin and had rubber legs and a wide-stepping walk. But now he drew everything up tight, the veins in his forearms bulging as he readied himself for the task.

Arms straight down, double-gripping the Ruger, he sidestepped toward the open door.

CHAPTER TWO

I had an idea what Cash would find inside, and I was right.

"Got us a body in here."

"I'm right behind you, Cash. Coming in."

The front doors were huge and turquoise. The left one was carved with the letter *A*, the right with an *S*. They led into a tiled entryway as cool as the desert morning.

Mail littered the floor.

Sterling had likely set it on the small table that an intruder had knocked over along with two heavy carved-wood chairs of Mexican design.

The main part of the house was rustic and brightly decorated. The floors were terra-cotta, the ceiling exposed pine beams. I passed under a brick archway into a dining area with a kiva fireplace and through double oak doors to the living room.

The walls were thick adobe and had cutouts that held miniature statues of helmeted conquistadors. They looked downright grumpy. Someone had tossed the room.

I stepped over a fallen conquistador and around a large framed oil of Apaches on horseback pursuing a wagoner who looked frantic, wondering if this was his last day.

The painting didn't show how the chase turned out, but I could guess.

It fit the morning's theme.

About twenty feet farther on, I saw the body.

He lay near floor-to-ceiling glass doors leading to a grand balcony. The bullet had come from the canyon, shattering the glass, and the body lay amid the shards.

The sun poured in through the opening, bright and hopeful, indifferent to what it illuminated. Out beyond the balcony, the mountain split as if by cataclysm to form a yawning gap filled with tumbles of rock and wiggling canyon air.

Looking down at the corpse, Cash said, "I'd ask how your morning's going, sir, but I reckon I know."

The man looked to be in his early fifties and withered by a disease that had nothing to do with what killed him. That would be the hole in the center of his chest. His skin was yellow and pressed tightly to the bones of his face.

He lay on his back, eyes open. Death had taken whatever light had been in them, leaving them dull, like frosted glass.

He had on gray twill pants and a white pullover shirt gone red with blood.

"Get a load of the slippers," Cash said. "Who wears leather slippers? I take it this is Mr. Ash Sterling?"

"Never saw the man."

"Gotta be. Nobody goes visiting in slippers."

"I wouldn't think so."

Cash moved closer, careful to stay outside the blood circle on the floor. The dead man's right hand was palm up in the blood puddle. The thumb and forefinger were missing, making an ugly claw of it.

"Why mutilate him?" Cash said. "Trophies?"

"To do what with?"

"I knew a guy took trophies. Warrior shit. Beginning of time, man."

"In a war zone, but why here?" I thought it over. "Unless they wanted to get into his phone. Fingerprints. For a touch code."

"Something's on Sterling's phone."

"Maybe pictures, a recording. Something big for sure."

"Cutting off a man's fingers, that's what I call motivation." Cash glanced out at the canyon. "Had to be a four-hundred-yard shot."

I looked at Sterling, saw plenty, didn't need to see more, and stepped back. "He had no clue what was coming. Suppose there are worse ways to go."

"Fact of the matter," Cash said, "if today had to be his day, going out like this was a gift. One shot, center mass. Off to see the wizard."

"You sound impressed."

"It's good work. Clean."

"You missed something." I pointed to a small hole in the white adobe wall behind me.

"Round passed clear through. Very good, Mayor." Cash dug his finger into the hole. "No bullet. Shooter hiked down and dug it out maybe?"

"More likely there was somebody in the house working with him."

Sterling wore no socks, and the slippers were off his feet, lying loose. A shot fired from four hundred yards meant a powerful rifle. The sudden violence of the round striking him had knocked him out of his slippers.

His feet were white as chalk and the toenails needed trimming.

The house sat alone on the last private land before the Coronado National Forest. The shooter had hiked a long way to get into position, which told me he was determined, acclimated to the outdoors, patient, and certainly a good shot.

We searched the house looking for any clue that might tell us what had happened. Cash took one side and I took the other, and the story was the same in every room.

Everything that could be tipped over had been.

No sign of Sterling's phone.

The last room I checked was the kitchen, and it was wrecked, too.

The floor was a scatter of tourist magnets and family photos, all of which looked to have been knocked off the refrigerator in the frantic search.

Something caught my eye, another photograph, postcard size, on the floor between the refrigerator and the floor cabinet. I slipped two fingers into the crack and pulled it out.

It showed three men, soldiers in full battle gear in front of a Humvee. The shot wasn't posed. It looked as if they were headed out on patrol, someone had called to them, and they turned as the shot was taken.

Across the top was scribbled, "The Cowboys."

On the back was the date July 21, 2013, and the words "last mission."

I slipped it into my pocket.

An open door at one corner of the kitchen led into a large pantry, at the back of which was another open door. Inside that room was a walk-in safe with a five-spoke handle and a steel-plated door with a black nickel finish.

The door was two inches thick and swung wide open. The safe had been emptied.

I called Roxy. She knew something was wrong from my voice.

"Don't tell me," she said. "Sterling's dead, right?"

"It wasn't his heart."

I told her about the rifle shot, the mutilated hand, and the empty safe.

"He kept stacks in there, like a million dollars' worth," Roxy said.

"Did he tell you that?"

"He showed me. Sterling was proud of his work. Did you call the cops?"

"It's too early in the morning for cops. I'll let you do it."

"I'll start over there in a little while and call when I get there," Roxy said. "They'll be pissed I got there before them, and you know how much I like that."

Cash grabbed a banana from a fruit bowl on the kitchen counter. I gave him a what-do-you-think-you're-doing stare. Never eat a dead man's fruit. Cash had no idea what my problem might be. He shrugged and peeled.

On the counter beside him sat a yellow carry box containing a maid's cleaning supplies. The name "Bella" was written on the side in black laundry marker.

"Looks like the maid left her stuff here, but there's no maid," I said. "Bella, right?"

"She was there all the time," Roxy said. "I'm sure she was more than a maid."

"That's not good. Whatever Sterling knew about the Foothills murders, she might know it, too."

On my phone I punched "Bella" and "maid" into Google and found a business named Extra Clean Maids. Bella Kowalik was proprietor and sole employee.

"There's an address listed," I said. "I'll hop over there and see if she's okay."

"This story is a stand-up in front of the bank and three sentences from the FBI mannequin du jour. Soon as I'm done, I'll drive to Sterling's."

CHAPTER THREE

Driving from the east end of the Tucson valley to midtown is always a stop-and-go proposition. Gas it to fifty miles an hour, travel a half mile to the next red light, and jam the brakes.

Just as your spine adjusts to the whiplash, the light switches to green, so you gas it to fifty again, and repeat. Throw in bomb-crater potholes and you need to see the chiropractor after every crosstown trip.

At the red lights along the way, Cash held his phone across the seat and showed me the website for Extra Clean Maids, which said that Bella Kowalik was twenty-six and a Polish immigrant.

Her photo showed a flat face, thin lips, a sloping nose, and short, untended hair. She was plain-looking and her expression resolute in that way peculiar to immigrants willing to do anything to make it.

I made passage across town in forty minutes.

Bella lived south of the University of Arizona in an old neighborhood that catered to students who could afford the rents and have money left over to pound Jack and Cokes at the Buffet Bar.

On Eighth Street, I crossed a bridge with a view on both sides to a north-south cement drainage below. After a quick turn south on Tyndall Avenue, I came to Bella's house. Like all the houses along her street, it backed up to the drainage.

It was modest, brick and painted white with hedges along the sidewalk. A metal, candy-striped awning over a cement slab made a makeshift porch.

The front door was wide open.

"We're two for two on open front doors," I said.

"What do you suppose we'll find inside?"

"I'd settle for a happy individual going about her day."

"We might need a second option in case that don't work out."

"You take the drainage behind the house," I said. "I'll give you time to get back there."

"Anyone inside's gonna bolt out the front when I come in the back. That makes him all yours. Bring your Glock?"

"To breakfast?"

"A blunder if I do say. Uh-huh, uh-huh."

"If there's shooting, you bingo outta there and we'll meet at headquarters tonight."

Headquarters was the Waffle House on the west side of Tucson, at Grant Road and Interstate 10.

Cash walked down the sidewalk. If I looked out my window and saw Cashmere Miller kicking along, head swiveling, arms swinging like he was swatting flies, I'd call the cops just to get a head start.

When he was a short distance past Bella's place, he disappeared between two houses.

If this blew up, it'd be best not to have the Bronco parked in front of where the blowup occurred, so I drove ahead four houses, parked, and walked back.

The shooting started just as I reached Bella's house.

There were two quick reports followed by a break of three seconds, then a burst of four shots fired in rapid succession. I recognized the sound of Cash's Ruger. More shots boomed from a second gun, and Cash fired back.

He was chasing someone through the drainage.

Gunfire in a quiet neighborhood is an indecent and ugly sound.

I hustled up the front walkway and planted myself beside the front door, back against the brick wall. "Bella Kowalik! I'm a friendly. Are you inside?"

No answer.

I peered quickly through the open door. Nobody shot a hole in my head. I looked again and saw an ugly green carpet on the living room floor, fake wood paneling on the walls, and a large and tattered Polish flag on the wall above a maroon couch.

A small glass-topped coffee table had been tipped over and there were magazines on the floor, along with assorted items from the table's undercompartments.

I took another fast look. The living room and the kitchen behind it formed one large open space with two bedrooms to the right split by the bathroom. I heard whimpering in the kitchen.

"Bella. Is that you?"

The shooting in the drainage had become more distant, and I decided it was safe to go inside. Bella was lying on the kitchen floor beside the refrigerator with a bloody knife just beyond her right hand.

She'd been shot in the stomach and was pressing her left hand against the wound. I said her name and her eyes focused and searched to find my voice.

On my knees beside her: "What happened? Tell me what happened."

She didn't speak. Her eyes were there and not there, filling and emptying again. Her breathing was shallow.

"Tell me who did this."

She whispered several words, but I could only make out one: "Alive."

"I'll do the best I can. Hang tough." I reached and grabbed a towel off the oven door. Utensil drawers had been jerked out and dropped onto the floor. I had to step over a litter of knives and forks and other items.

The shooting in the drainage had stopped, and the quiet of the morning resumed.

I pressed the towel against Bella's wound.

"Who did this? Give me a name."

"Protect her."

"I will. Give me a name."

She tried to speak but couldn't. Blood bubbled off her lips.

"Stay with me, Bella."

At the sound of her name, her eyes cleared again.

"I'll find out who did this, I promise. Who do you want me to protect?"

"Sister ... Sister."

"I'll protect your sister. Tell me who did this."

She never spoke again. Death walked in and took her before she got the chance. Watching her die reminded me how close living is to dying, only a thin membrane of struggle and blood separating the two.

Sirens sounded in the distance. I wanted to look around and had barely a minute or two to do it. One of the bedrooms remained just that, a bedroom.

The other had been converted to an office. I concentrated on that.

The room had one window facing the backyard, and the window was open. Blood drops dotted the floor in front of the desk. They wouldn't be Bella's. She couldn't have made it into or out of the office with a bullet in her stomach.

It had to be the attacker's blood. She'd fought and used the knife to good effect.

The drawers had been rifled and a small trash bin emptied. The center space atop the desk was bare, marked only by a dust square the size of a laptop, as if the killer had scooped it up and made off with it.

The sirens got louder. Time had run out.

I stepped back into the kitchen and looked at Bella again, on the floor in that pose of perfect stillness that can never be misunderstood.

Leaving her didn't feel right. But if I stayed, I'd have to explain the shooting in the wash, and I couldn't do that without giving up Cash. They'd toss him in the hole for being a felon in possession of a firearm.

I climbed out Bella's office window, bolted through three backyards to the Bronco, and drove away slowly, eyes straight ahead, hands at ten and two.

The black-and-whites screamed past me as I went.

CHAPTER FOUR

Cash belonged to a network of former combat marines. They fixed things for one another, right or wrong, legal and otherwise. The brotherhood.

They'd shelter him through the daylight hours, and he'd emerge again after dark.

He arrived at the Waffle House at 7:30 p.m. and looked the same as he had that morning. He wore his Arizona Feeds ball cap, blue flannel shirt untucked, the T-shirt underneath untucked, loose jeans stained with paint, and black-and-white Pro-Keds sneakers.

He slid into the booth across from me and motioned to the waitress for coffee. The Waffle House had a good evening crowd, tired travelers off the freeway looking for a late feed.

"Shooter got away, Mayor. Big guy. Could run."

My ownership of Double Wide had earned me the title of Mayor. It wasn't merely honorary. We had actual elections, but all it meant was that whenever one of my tenants had a problem, personal or otherwise, they were at my door asking for help.

I was expected to serve coffee until we found a solution, which never happened.

"Was he carrying anything?"

Cash shrugged. "Couldn't tell you."

"Bella's laptop was missing, and the house was trashed."

"Like Sterling's. Has to be connected."

"Two people who were tight getting murdered an hour apart? Yeah, it's connected."

"Killer was looking for Sterling's phone," Cash said.

"They don't find it at his house, figure he gave it to Bella and take his fingers along to get into it."

We spoke over the clank and rattle of plates and silverware.

"I seen a kid with a bike on the Eighth Street bridge," Cash said. "Looking down into the drainage."

"That's something. Describe him."

"Long blond hair. The bike had red wheels. Boy or girl I couldn't tell you."

"That's it?"

"I caught a fast glimpse before the shooting started. After that I was *occupado*."

"Looks like Bella used a knife on this guy," I said. "Did he run like he was in pain, bent over, anything like that?"

"Moved along good."

"You're sure no laptop or phone?"

"He could've been carrying a piano and I wouldn'ta seen it. I was watching the gun."

"Whoever he was, he's a murderer."

Cash nodded, expressionless. He would've had the same reaction if he'd been chasing a tailor. He measured me across the table. His hound-dog eyes never stayed fixed on anyone for longer than three seconds before they began roaming.

At the end of their trip, he might be looking at you from the side, or he'd be aiming them a mile over your head.

"You don't look so good, Mayor."

"I promised Bella I'd find the shooter."

"You gotta quit doing stuff like that. You're like a humanitarian or something. It's a real problem. Uh-huh, uh-huh."

"You didn't see what I saw," I said.

Cash tapped his finger on the table and looked out the window at the elevated freeway. Only the tops of the cars were visible. They made streaks of light against the sky as they passed.

"I'm just saying life'd be simpler if you got out of the rescue business," Cash said. "But you being you, I suppose that ain't gonna happen."

"Nobody's asking you to come along."

"You're lucky my calendar's open. Ever since I got back."

"You don't have a calendar."

"This is true."

He studied the menu. His fingertips were red from eating pistachios. The act of peeling pistachios calmed his nerves and kept him out of his head. Without something to do with his eyes, he was back on night recon in the Hindu Kush hearing the *pop, pop* of rifle fire.

"I'm gonna order me a stack. You?"

"Nothing's gone right today."

"Think about Sterling. He builds a big old safe thinking his fortune's protected, and guess what? Plus which he's, you know, dead."

"My plan was to live a quiet life in the desert."

Cash chuckled. "Yeah, well." He stuck the menu into the holder. "I'm leaning toward the chocolate chip waffles. Getting shot at and missed is better than TV, but not as good as chocolate chip waffles."

"I haven't thought about food since this morning."

"The world tracks you down no matter where you go, Mayor. Might as well enjoy yourself. Between the calamities."

I watched Cash eat. I didn't want to, but it was like driving past a wreck. At least he was quick about it, in a refugee sort of way.

When he was done, I paid up and Cash got a toothpick and smacked and dug all the way over Gates Pass to my trailer park.

CHAPTER FIVE

Double Wide is west of the Tucson Mountains. On the east side of those mountains, there's the Tucson valley and hordes of people bumping shoulders.

On the west side there's nothing at all, unless you count millions of saguaros on open desert, me and Bundle, my black Lab, and eight trailers set around a patch of enchanting dirt.

I bought the place after my baseball career tanked amid a cooked-up cocaine scandal in Mexico. I wanted a place to read, think, and heal my wounds while the world spun around me.

I had all the stars and moon a man could ever need, and between the occasional rents my tenants paid and a chunk of money left over from baseball, life looked okay.

What I didn't count on was so many misfits showing up at my door looking for a place to live. Someday a woolly-headed professor of this or that will write a paper about why the Sonoran Desert produces more wanderers than any other landscape in America.

Nobody will read it, and the desperate and the dispossessed will keep coming.

My place was an Airstream trailer, a 1979 Ambassador, twenty-eight feet long and shining with a new coat of silver paint. If you remembered to change the oil, there was no better living.

I called Roxy and told her I was sending along the photo of the Cowboys. It was the first of several times we'd talk that night.

Sometimes she'd call me and sometimes I'd call her.

She couldn't sleep either.

Two murders will do that.

"These conversations with Sterling," I said, "tell me more about how they went."

"I'd get there first thing in the morning and we'd sit around talking about whatever. You bought shoes at the mall, how fascinating. Tell me more. When you're working a source, that's the game. Waiting. When he decides to trust you, that's when it all comes out. We got there eventually, but the shooter beat me to him."

I was lying in bed with my feet high up on the opposite wall. "Somebody takes him out right before he's set to talk about the Foothills murders. Do we believe in coincidences?"

"What about the phone?" she said. "What do you suppose is on it?"

"The answers. If we can get our hands on it."

I walked out to the kitchen. In an Airstream that's a journey of twelve feet. I'd learned to walk with my six-foot-two-inch frame set as low as it could go, and still my hair dusted the ceiling. I wasn't winded upon arrival.

I got out the fixings for a peanut butter sandwich. Recognizing the fascinating sounds of sandwich making, Bundle stormed into the kitchen to investigate.

His nose twitched as he tried to determine what was on the menu.

Peanut butter has a distinct aroma, and Bundle was very interested.

"I'm looking at this photo of the Cowboys," Roxy said. "You think it's Sterling's crew?"

"It doesn't help us to assume they're not."

"How do we ID them?"

"I'm already on it."

The first thing I'd done after getting home was click around on my laptop until I found a blog called *Battle Rattle* that mentioned the Cowboys in several entries.

No names were given, Sterling's or anybody else's.

Otherwise the accounts were detailed and well written. The writer went by the handle Sergeant Major Zero. I'd emailed him the photo and he'd responded, saying he'd get back to me with the names.

"Zero tells firefight stories," I said. "Bullets-flying, face-in-the-dirt stuff."

"Sounds like these guys were deep in the shit."

"The blog says they were the best. When a Taliban fighter needed to go to heaven, the Cowboys got the mission."

"They bond in combat, can't adjust at home, and take up burglary to make money."

"Money's always good, but I'm thinking they missed the adrenaline rip, too."

I walked back through the accordion door separating the kitchen from the bedroom. Bundle sniffed at my heels the whole way. I sat on my bed and took a bite.

Bundle stared with moon eyes. He hadn't eaten in a thousand years.

While I ate, I took a closer look at the picture.

The soldier on the left had fat cheeks, expressive eyes, and a dark Hispanic face. A red do-rag covered his head. He wore a flak jacket with no undershirt and was turned sideways, showing a heavily-muscled right arm decorated with a tattoo of a huge sword that could've belonged to Genghis Khan.

The man on the right wore military-issue boots, camo pants, a black sweatshirt, and a campaign hat with a pull-string under the chin. His face was square and handsome, even behind smears of grease paint.

He was built like a linebacker and gripping a rifle.

The middle soldier, staring straight at the camera, was Ash Sterling. He stood above the others with a boot in the open door of the Humvee. He had a rifle balanced on his hip and an expression of total confidence and daring.

I didn't say anything for a while, and neither did Roxy. We knew each other well enough that silence didn't matter, and the sounds of our breathing were enough. I heard ice cubes banging around in her glass. She never missed evening cocktails.

"I wonder if Bella was seeing dollar signs," Roxy said.

"You think she was working Sterling?"

"Look at it this way. She starts out as his maid and pretty soon she's polishing more than the silver. When he gets sick, she stays around to take care of him, and every time she's in the kitchen she eyes that safe and thinks, 'How many years would I have to work to pile up the money that's in there?'"

"I don't get grifter from her."

"A million in cash money twenty feet away can turn into love real fast."

"Did Sterling mention any other names we can follow up on?"

"He had a daughter, Jackie Moreno. She's a nursing student at UA."

"We need to talk to her."

The night banged on. We traded more calls, and there was a certain energy to them, a feeling of excitement that we were finally making some movement on the Foothills murders, no matter how uncertain.

CHAPTER SIX

Shortly after midnight, I fed Bundle and let him out for evening patrol. The coyotes were cutting an album somewhere out in the desert. I fixed supper and ate with the television on above the kitchen table and didn't feel like sleeping.

I grabbed one of the novels on the shelf behind my bed. I read the same ones over and over, the great detective stories. I have a rotation system. After a couple of reads, I put the book in storage and replace it with another.

How long a book stays on the shelf before losing its place and which one replaces it can become matters of raucous internal debate.

I grabbed *The Real Cool Killers* by Chester Himes and sat at the kitchen table. Himes's Harlem detectives Coffin Ed Johnson and Grave Digger Jones walk though their rotten world doing all the rotten things they need to do to keep the rottenest among them from taking over.

That night I understood Coffin Ed and the Grave Digger better than ever.

But I couldn't concentrate. My mind wouldn't stop spinning.

I was thinking about Paul Morton.

We met the first time when I was barely past twenty years old and pitching for the AAA Tucson Thunder. He was a young lawyer who did work for the ball club. When one of our guys got into a scrape, Paul handled the case.

He didn't know Donna then. She was in college and liked hanging around the ballpark with her friends hoping to meet players. I was one of them.

We went out briefly, but it didn't amount to much. We saw each other plenty of times afterward, and the encounters were always pleasant.

But we didn't keep in touch.

Paul and I did, usually when I'd land in a nearby city and he'd travel there to watch me pitch, and afterward we'd go out. Paul liked to drink back then, wear a lampshade and howl, until Donna straightened him out.

They invited me to their wedding. I'd rather go to a blind dentist than a wedding, but I went to theirs. I didn't dance. Paul couldn't stop dancing.

Sweating, his shirt hanging out, he never looked more foolish, or happier.

He started as a prosecutor, switched to criminal defense, and did extremely well. His practice included pro bono work.

He and Donna had two boys younger than ten, Mike and Cody, two rowdy springer spaniels, a swimming pool the dogs wouldn't stay out of, a psychotic cat named Ron, and frequent backyard barbecues.

The cops had nothing resembling a motive for their murders and weren't talking. But Roxy had a source telling her it might've been nothing more than terrible luck. The Mortons had interrupted a burglary, and somebody panicked and started shooting.

The fortunate part was that Mike and Cody were at their grandmother's house, and unharmed. It was date night for Paul and Donna.

Their faces stood out clearly in my mind, along with powerful memories. It's easy to think back on earlier times as the best in your life, the days you'd like to have back.

Feel them again. Live them again, just one more time.

But those days with the Thunder, the very start of my career, really were special, and the Mortons were a big part of it.

Bundle scratched at my door. I let him in, got into bed, and fell immediately into a surface sleep busy with a vivid dream. I was being held prisoner in an empire ruled by bird-watchers and plotting to kill them all when my phone woke me.

"You Stark?"

"What time is it?" I rolled over and put my feet on the floor.

"Burnside here, aka Sergeant Major Zero." His voice came out of a spidery tomb. "Would've called sooner but I had to research you, make sure you're not an asshole."

I rubbed my forehead and yawned. "How'd I do?"

"Got a pen?"

I reached for one on the counter opposite the bed. "Go ahead."

"On the left, Private Titus Ortega. The other one, greased up, Lance Corporal Vincent Strong."

"Thanks. Know where I can locate these guys?"

"Negative. I have a message for you, Stark."

"Yeah?"

"When you find Cap's killer, zero him out for me. Got that?"

I went back to bed. Burnside's voice was still echoing in my head when the first light of a cool October morning showed at my little bedroom window.

There was a racket in the kitchen, like a bear tearing through a campsite.

"I'm trying to sleep in here." I used my Mayor's voice to project authority through the ridiculous accordion door.

"I'm on early shift this morning and I'm starved."

The voice belonged to Opal Sanchez. She was seventeen, a runaway from the Tohono O'odham Reservation.

Knowing my attempts at sleep had ended, I struggled to my feet.

"Well, shit."

"Language, Mr. Whip."

CHAPTER SEVEN

By the time I got to the kitchen, Cashmere Miller was there, eyes crusty, yawning, greasy hands wrapped around my Chicago Cubs coffee mug like the Airstream was the local diner.

"Do you two ever eat at home?"

Cash looked at Opal and shrugged, and Opal shrugged back. That cleared it up. No, they never ate at home.

Opal stood at the oven cooking. She'd taken a job as a waitress at the Waffle House and was wearing the uniform, black slacks and a blue short-sleeved shirt open at the collar, a black tie hanging loose. The apron was black, too.

For someone slightly more than five feet tall, she took up a lot of room. She had short, all-terrain legs, wide hips, and straight black hair parted in the middle and hanging to her waist. She had a sweet, big-eyed baby face that looked younger than seventeen.

She came to the table and stood with her hands folded in modest waiting.

"Is there anything I can get you gentlemen?" She pressed her lips together to suppress a giggle.

We needed more coffee. She poured. I asked how the job was going.

"Not so good. Kinda bad really. Yesterday I got ketchup all over a guy."

"How'd you manage that?"

"I dropped a bottle. Like on the floor? And when I tried to pick it up, I stepped on it and the ketchup squirted everywhere."

"I'll bet that was a mess."

"Totally. It was a massacre in there."

"Sounds like it. Did you clean it up?"

"This is where it gets bad. I went to pick it up again and fell down. Like, right into the ketchup. Splat!" Opal spread her arms like an umpire calling safe. "Gary got all trippy, said he was going to fire me, and I'm like, 'Hey, I didn't do it on purpose. Sometimes a girl falls down, okay?'"

Cash piped in. "It's human nature."

"That's exactly what I said. Now Gary wants me to practice my skills. I was thinking, how about I make pancakes and I'll serve them to you guys?"

"Already had a doughnut," Cash said. "I'm sure the Mayor can help you. Public service and all."

I looked at Cash. He was grinning behind the Cubs coffee mug.

Opal said, "Please, please, Mr. Whip."

"All right, give it a shot."

"I promise it won't suck."

"If you ever open a restaurant, there's your slogan."

Before the Waffle House job, Opal made money doing pencil sketches on the sidewalk in downtown Tucson. She brought along some of her oils, too. Her work attracted the attention of a New York couple who wanted to fly her east to meet their influential gallery friends.

Lloyd and Grace Gelman were due to arrive at Double Wide in less than a week to pick up the paintings for shipment. Opal wanted me to help her select them but kept putting me off, like she was unveiling a lost Renoir.

Her pancakes weren't awful. I could still walk and talk after eating.

The work had her running late, so Cash drove her over the mountain into town.

For the remainder of the day, I worked the laptop for whatever I could find about Ash Sterling, and a rough profile emerged.

He was from Ferndale, in northern California. He played sports in high school for the Ferndale Nighthawks and earned coverage in the local paper for his football heroics. He was the quarterback. Teammates and coaches called him Captain America.

He got more coverage when he graduated from Cal Berkeley, when he enlisted in the marines, and at his commissioning ceremony. Sterling's postings around the world, in Germany, Africa, South Korea, and a dozen other places, earned a few paragraphs, as did his return visits to Ferndale.

The paper said he'd shipped out to Iraq in 2003 and earned two Bronze Stars, a Silver Star, and a Purple Heart for fighting there and in Afghanistan.

After he came home in June of 2013, no new mentions of Sterling turned up.

The same for Titus Ortega and Vincent Strong. They appeared in a few hometown stories, but no hits after returning stateside.

Becoming an online ghost was hard to do. But for high-end thieves, the Internet was synonymous with wearing handcuffs, so it made sense they'd work at being invisible.

Jackie Moreno was another story. Getting her address was easy.

If somebody's on the grid, you can find them in five minutes on Spokeo, two if you don't stop for another peanut butter sandwich.

I called Roxy and we arranged a visit.

CHAPTER EIGHT

An hour before dark that day, I pulled up outside Jackie's house. Roxy was waiting by her car and smiled when she saw me, and I smiled back. Most of the best things in my life have happened at ballparks, and that included meeting Roxanne Santa Cruz the first time.

She interviewed me at Hi Corbett Field. I was accidentally charming, she was preternaturally beautiful, and we went out for Mexican.

We'd been together ever since, with the normal intervals of doubt and distance thrown in.

On the sidewalk, she kissed me once, and when I thought we were done, she bounced up on her toes, grabbed a fistful of my shirt, and yanked me close for another, this one much longer.

"In broad daylight?"

"You object, Prospero?" Only two people called me Prospero, my father and Roxy.

"No, ma'am. Just wondering why I'm so lucky."

"Maybe I'm a tart and don't care who knows it."

"You might be onto something."

Roxy was tall and lean in places where lean was good, and full in all the others. She had long black hair colored with blond streaks, good cheekbones, and wide oval eyes. Her skin was olive. She wore a black-and-pink polka-dot shirt and a black pencil skirt.

Her shoes, normally the outfit maker, were only mildly spectacular.

They were black suede boots with a zipper up the back and a block heel, not too high. She could move gracefully in those heels, or heels of any height, and her beauty was such that her appearance at a news event usually attracted gawkers.

Not a mob, but the name drew admirers, and as many women as men.

The reason puzzled me. After careful pondering, I'd concluded it was her shoes.

Jackie Moreno's neighborhood was just west of the University Medical Center. The houses were modest, solid, and well kept. Hers was a single-story duplex, sandstone colored and long and wide with driveways on both ends.

The front lawn wasn't grass but decorative stones that had been spray-painted bright green to give them that highly prized artificial look.

Parked in the right driveway was a black Dodge Ram truck. Beside it was a jacked-up Toyota RAV4, and there was a yellow Camaro convertible in the left driveway.

As Roxy and I approached the left-side apartment, the right-side door opened and a man with a blond buzz cut stepped out. He held a steaming coffee mug. He had a pug nose and a pudgy face and had to be six foot six.

He went in the left-side door, which was Jackie's address, without knocking. Seconds later, he jerked the door open and sneered at us, studying the ID lanyard around Roxy's neck and the notebook in her hand.

"She don't want to talk to you people. No comment."

He slammed the door.

Roxy said, "He's been waiting to say that his whole life."

We stood at the closed door, letting a few easy moments tick away. I asked how it went with the cops at Sterling's house.

"Fine. They were pissed, of course. How'd you get here first and all that. Danny got footage of the body before they showed up."

"You're not going to put him on TV like that."

"We'll do a tasteful edit. It'll make a nice promo for the ten o'clock show."

"I couldn't do what you do."

"You're my favorite person on the planet," Roxy said. "But it's a Twitter world and you're like a transistor radio or something."

"When I was a kid, I listened to ball games in bed when I was supposed to be sleeping."

"That was the extent of your youthful larceny?"

"I was up pretty late, and my parents never knew."

"That might be the cutest thing you've ever said."

"It's what I do." I pointed at the door. "We don't know who this guy is, right?"

"Let's find out."

She hammered on the door with her palm the way cops do when they have a warrant. She giggled and shook her hand as though it hurt.

The big man jerked the door open. Behind him, a female voice said, "It's all right, Donny Jim. I don't mind."

He said, "I told you she ain't talking. Beat it." He slammed the door again.

"Doesn't he know I'm a famous TV personality?"

"You must get that all the time."

"I talk to doors a lot. And backsides. He's a large fellow."

"Definitely a load."

Roxy turned her head and raised her eyebrows at me in challenge. "A broken-down ballplayer like you, do you think you can handle a guy that size?"

"Broken-down but smart," I said, and walked to the Dodge truck.

Dirt streaked the doors and the tires were caked in mud. I removed the valves on the driver's-side tires and fingered the air out of them.

When Roxy attacked the door again, Donny Jim shot out like he was escaping a fire. "What'd I just say to you?"

I threw a thumb over my shoulder. "Is that your ride, Jimbo?"

"Damn." He ran to his tilting truck.

I made an after-you gesture to Roxy. She gave me an impressed face, and we stepped into Jackie Moreno's apartment.

CHAPTER NINE

Jackie was slim and pretty, maybe twenty-five. She stood about five foot six and had black hair in a ponytail and a dark complexion. She had bright black eyes and cuff earrings consisting of a constellation of stars that got bigger and more sparkly as they climbed her ears.

Upon our entry, she walked toward us looking down at her iPhone. She slipped it halfway into the front pocket of her snug-fitting jeans and drew a harried breath.

"I wish you'd called. I've got to be at school." She wore a rust pullover with crocheting at the low-cut V-neck and a tassel tie at the waist. No shoes and her toenails were purple.

She pointed to Roxy's lanyard. "You're with the press or somebody?"

Roxy introduced herself and me. Hearing my name, Jackie alerted. "The baseball player. I've heard of you. You're working in TV now?"

"I'm helping Miss Santa Cruz. We're investigating your father's murder."

"I'll tell you what I told the police," she said. "Ash Sterling's death has no impact on me. I've had no contact with the man for years, and nothing in my life will change now that he's gone." She laughed uneasily. "That sounded cruel, didn't it? Look, I don't know how I can help, but come on in. I've got just a minute."

As we followed her inside, I noticed a small, vivid tattoo of a tiger's growling face behind her left ear.

The living room had two couches set at ninety degrees in front of a large-screen TV. The dining room behind it was lit by outside light streaming in the back window.

There were four chairs around a table.

We all sat. A mountain bike hung from the ceiling in the corner.

"Even if you and Sterling weren't close," Roxy said, "it still must've been a shock."

"The police told me what happened." Jackie's phone buzzed, and she excused herself to read a text. Distracted, looking at the phone: "Getting shot at his house that way, yeah, that was a shock." She shrugged. "But it's karma, right? He was a soldier and died the way he lived."

Jackie finished with the phone and put it on the table as Jimbo swept in the door, his face flushed with excitement.

He stalked toward me looking as if he wanted to have a go.

Jackie intercepted him with an impressive leap over an otto-man and steered him to the couch, where he sat, reluctantly and spring-loaded, as if the slightest provocation would send him airborne in my direction.

"You haven't been properly introduced," Jackie said. "This is Donny Jim James, my neighbor, protector, and all-around teddy bear. He lives next door with his girl, Holly."

Jackie pointed at me. "Do you know who this is, Donny Jim? This is Prospero Stark, the famous pitcher. You know, Whip Stark?"

I gave him a beauty queen wave.

"I know who the hell he is," Jimbo said.

"And this lady, she's Roxanne Santa Cruz, the TV reporter."

"Why mess with my truck, bro?" Jimbo said. "Let the air out of my tires? Seriously?"

"AAA can fix it in no time," Jackie said in mild annoyance. "Try not to explode."

Jimbo drew back at her reproach, and when his temper cooled, Jackie returned to the table and sat. On the dining room wall hung a banner with red lettering that said, *Bear Down*, the university's athletic slogan.

Roxy asked if she knew what her father did for a living.

"Do you mean did I know Ash went around breaking into houses? Sure, I knew. After a job, they'd get together on Ash's balcony and drink a toast. They called themselves the Champagne Cowboys."

Roxy jotted notes. She was left-handed, so her arm formed that awkward question mark around the notebook. I pulled the Cowboys photo from my pocket and showed it to Jackie.

"That's them," she said. "They were around, but I never knew their names."

"But you knew they were burglars?"

"My stepmom, Val, she came out and told me."

"Just like that?"

"I wasn't supposed to know, but she and Ash were splitting up at the time, so I think telling me was like revenge for her. Did-you-know-your-father's-a-thief kind of thing." Jackie read the words at the top of the image. "The Cowboys. They must've added the 'champagne' part after they came home."

"Celebration of a job well done."

"Whatever. But he only bothered rich people and that's better than being a regular thief, right?" She handed the photo back. "If you want to know more, try Val. Valentine Constantine. Her husband owns Constant Lexus in Scottsdale."

A woman walked in the front door and stood behind Jackie with her palms flat on Jackie's shoulders.

"This is Holly, my neighbor," Jackie said, and patted one of Holly's hands with hers. "Say hello, Holly."

Holly gave us a fast nod devoid of warmth or welcome. She had close-cropped brown hair and silver crescent moon earrings. She wore a gray work shirt with *Handy Dandy Plumbing* in red stitching over the pocket.

She had a tattoo sleeve on her left arm. All I could make out amid the splash of colors was a red heart. The rest of the image disappeared under the cuff of her shirt.

"You need to be getting to school, Jack," Holly said. "You don't want these two making you late for your meeting."

She gave Roxy and me another icy stare and walked over to Donny Jim. "Let's go outside and wait for the AAA guy."

When Donny Jim didn't budge, keeping up his death stare, Jackie motioned to Holly to take him out, and she did, pulling him by the arm. Jackie watched them go.

"Donny Jim works with Holly in her plumbing business. She's done really well. I'm so proud of her." She looked at her phone. "I should be going."

Roxy said, "A couple more questions. Did you know your dad was dying?"

"No. How would I?" Jackie showed no surprise or even interest.

"He didn't have much time and wanted me to run a story about him after he was gone."

Jackie snickered. "That sounds right. Captain Sterling thought the world was his and everybody else was just passing through."

"The story wasn't about him," Roxy said. "There was a double murder in the Foothills a year ago. Ash knew what happened and wanted to unload."

"I don't know anything about that," Jackie said.

I broke in. "There's a second murder that's part of this, a woman named Bella Kowalik. She was his maid."

"Never heard the name." Jackie checked the time on her phone again. "Sorry, but I've got to change for my meeting."

We walked to the front door. With her notebook put away, Roxy asked about Sterling's fortune. I'd seen her use the technique before. Interview seemingly over amid pleasant good-byes, then, in a friendly tone, the gold-mine question.

"One more thing, Jackie. Were you aware that Ash kept a million bucks in a safe at his house?"

"I was not." Nothing in her face changed. She had as much expression as a cat.

"He must've made arrangements for it after his passing."

"I have no knowledge of that, okay? And no interest in it."

Roxy tried again. "You're his only heir. Are you sure he didn't contact you?"

"When I said I hadn't seen or heard from Ash Sterling in years, that's what I meant." The words came out quick and hot. Jackie paused and forced a smile. "I can't imagine why he'd want to give me anything. I doubt he could pick me out on the sidewalk."

"He must've had other plans. A million bucks is pretty sweet."

"It's important to me to make my own way in the world," Jackie said. "I have no interest in my father's dirty money."

"Of course not," Roxy said.

CHAPTER TEN

I walked Roxy to her Audi convertible. The darkness was still incomplete but progressing in its inevitable way. The university's massive medical complex loomed above us, the buildings like mountains in shadow and, as always, under renovation.

Dump trucks crouched alongside piles of debris outside green-fenced work areas. Silver clouds had rolled in. The construction cranes reached for them.

Roxy was leaning against her Audi convertible reapplying her lipstick. "Interesting bunch," she said. "We're supposed to believe Jackie has no interest in Ash's money."

"That wasn't the part that bothered me."

Looking into her compact, the words warbling out through pooched lips: "I can't understand not wanting a million bucks. Really?"

"Jackie didn't like it when you pressed her on contact with Sterling."

"You think she was lying?"

"There's no reason to get pissed if you're telling the truth."

Roxy tilted her head as she looked in the mirror. "The blond giant with the butch cut, he's got a temper, too."

"I'll bet he's got some arrests," I said.

"I've got sources I can try."

"Didn't you used to date a guy in burglary?"

She snapped the compact closed and put it in her purse and took out a hanky and pressed it against her lips, doing whatever it was women did with hankies and lipstick. "Honey, please. There's burglary, ag assault, fraud. I've got a whole list. The hostage unit."

She tossed her head and laughed, and when I raised my eyebrows, she realized what she'd said and rubbed my arm in a reassuring way.

"Don't worry, that was a long time ago. Pre-Prospero. Besides, I've heard plenty of stories about you ballplayers."

"That was the other guys. I went back to the hotel to read Cornell Woolrich."

"Because you like your novels chipper and full of hope for mankind." I was staring at Donny Jim's pickup and Roxy noticed.

"What's on your mind?" she said.

"He's got a rifle rack in his window but no rifle."

She looked. "Hmm. What have you been up to, Jimbo?"

"Hang on a sec, Rox. I've still got enough light."

I walked over and snapped a picture of his tires. The dirt on his truck and on the tires told me he'd been off-roading, and given the amount of public land around Tucson, it could've been anywhere, including in the national forest behind Sterling's mansion.

The AAA guy arrived. Jimbo stepped out of his apartment to meet him and glared down the sidewalk at me. He paced around and glared some more.

Helping Holly in her plumbing business didn't seem to be his calling. He was too big to fit under a sink. He belonged working the door at a nightclub with a sticky floor and tax problems.

When Jimbo's kettle began to whistle, he stalked over to me on his tree-trunk legs, his head thrust forward. His face was red.

"I know all about you, Stark. They run your ass outta Mexico for cocaine and your old man's a stinking murderer."

"I can't believe they let you have a computer."

"Your daddy's on death row. How's that feel?" Anger curled his lips. "Yeah, Whip Stark, the famous baseball player. You're all over the Internet. The big star gets booted out of entire countries. How do you even do that?"

"Calm down, Jimbo. You look like a tomato."

Holly used her outdoor voice from the driveway. "Donny Jim! Got us an emergency call. Let's get a move on."

That broke the spell. Jimbo jabbed his finger at me. "You and me'll meet another time, Baseball," he said and stomped away.

He and Holly drove off in the big black Dodge.

"That's Google," Roxy said. "Any clown can dial up every mistake you've ever made."

"You used to be able to hide from the world."

"There's no redemption anymore. Google remembers all."

"I can take it for me, but I worry about my father rotting in that damn hole."

The temperature was dropping fast, the way it does in the desert at sunset. Construction workers in yellow hard hats walked past us to their cars.

"What's going on with Sam?" Roxy said. "Finding anything useful?"

My father, Sam Houston Stark, was on death row at the Arizona State Prison in Florence. I'd been looking for new evidence to appeal his conviction for first-degree murder.

"Cash and I are going to Tempe to look for someone. We're going to stop in Florence to see Sam."

"He hanging in there?"

"At least he's off the junk. I'm glad for that, but it's going to be a long road."

"Give him my love."

Sam was the finest Shakespeare teacher who ever lived. His victim, as the law incorrectly asserted, was a prostitute named Cristy Carlyle. I say "incorrectly" because he didn't kill her.

I knew that in the deepest part of me.

The trouble for the defense was that Sam, a renowned professor at Arizona State University, and Cristy Carlyle were together the night of the murder in Cristy's apartment, and Sam, my charismatic, kindhearted, and desperate father, was addicted to heroin, gone to hell on the drug when the police found him at a bus stop across from Carlyle's apartment.

He remembered nothing. He was covered in blood from a gash on his forehead where it had struck a table, and from Carlyle's wounds.

She'd been stabbed multiple times. Police found blood from a third donor at the scene, and that person remained unidentified.

The murder weapon, believed to be a knife missing from her kitchen, was never found.

The guilty verdict was a terrible shock. It took months to be able to think straight and decide what to do. When I was clear-eyed again, I hired another lawyer, filed an appeal, and started my own investigation focusing on the missing knife.

The previous lawyer's private investigator couldn't find it.

But I didn't trust his work or his dedication to proving my father's innocence.

If the knife was out there, I was going to find it. And I had a lead. It was thin, but thin was better than nonexistent.

I'd spent a month calling the homicide detective in Tempe to request a meeting. She'd finally agreed with a six-word text message: "I'll give you five fucking minutes."

Strange, but I don't think she found me charming. First time ever.

CHAPTER ELEVEN

Next morning, Cash reminded me that I'd promised to visit Charlie O'Shea at the hospital. He was another of my tenants. They were keeping him longer than expected. He was a house painter, and the injuries from his fall included a dislocated tailbone.

Cash couldn't figure out what that meant.

"Did his ass move somewhere else?"

"I believe that's exactly what happened."

I was eager to make the hour-long drive to Florence, so we skipped the hospital and drove over the mountain and north on Oracle Road, a major north-south boulevard, onto State Highway 77.

Up that way, the map fills with black-dot towns surrounded by a lot of dirt.

Catalina, Winkelman, Kearny, Hayden, Mammoth, San Manuel.

They're witness protection towns, born on the mineral dreams of bearded drifters with pickaxes and made-up names. When the mine shut down or the railroad rerouted, the town refused to die, though it had no particular reason to live.

The long quiet set in. The years passed, the decades.

Nothing much changed. Dogs still sleep in the streets.

Arizona has places the wind can't find, and Florence was one of them.

Driving into town, the first thing you see is the 1891 redbrick Victorian courthouse, its cupola dominating the horizon. The second thing is the Arizona State Prison Complex, which looked exactly as it should.

High walls, razor wire, guard towers, light stanchions, and weeping women walking back to their cars after seeing their men. I drove past it to the quiet downtown and dropped Cash at Nora's Café, planning to pick him up later.

At the prison, I parked and walked up a long ramp to the visitors' check-in office. There were two guards, a metal detector, and a dog to sniff out contraband. After being cleared, I walked down a short hall into a midsized room with bare, Navajo-white walls and a small table with a chair on either side.

Sam came through a door wearing an orange pullover shirt with *ADC* in black letters on the back, baggy orange pants, white socks, and flip-flops.

We hugged until a guard told us we'd used up our allotted contact time.

Sam took a long and wary look around the room and, finally comfortable, looked across the table at me.

"Let's get right to it. What have you been reading lately?"

"Well, *The Tempest* for one. It makes me think of you, Sam." He'd named me after the magician Prospero, the lead character in the last play Shakespeare wrote alone.

"I can't read it without feeling immense sadness," Sam said.

"He had his time and used it well. That's all any of us can do."

Sam nodded in solemn affirmation. "I don't fancy hearing it said, but it's a truth that will outlive us all. And here's another."

He held his hands to his bowed head, a gesture of reverence.

"Did you know that every year, thousands of letters arrive in Verona, Italy, addressed simply to Juliet?" His eyes thrilled. "Think about that, Prospero. More than four hundred years later and the love of Romeo and Juliet survives yet. It'll never die. Never!"

"You know it's my favorite of his plays, not *The Tempest*."

He dismissed that. "Made my peace long ago. In retrospect I couldn't have named you Romeo. Think of the ribbing." He smiled. Even a man with a dubious future can find a moment of pleasure. "It warms me to know those letters to Juliet will be arriving long after I'm gone."

A private thought intruded, and his face darkened.

"But for me, what is there left? I sit in this place day after day with nothing but my thoughts and the four walls. Do you know I'm not allowed to read late at night? Do you know what it's like to only see the sun three days a week?"

He laughed without pleasure. "Tell me it's still there, boy, shining over our fallen world."

They said Sam looked like me, and I suppose he did. He was tall and thin and still had a good hairline for a man of fifty-eight, a sandy brown mop mixed with some gray that had no part or pattern and went in whatever direction the wind blew.

He had an aquiline nose and thin lips. In the best of health his face had good color, a ruddy red. But heroin had grayed his skin and pulled his cheeks inward. His eyes were more deeply set as well, a weary blue, as though his nights were a long fight to quell his mind and sleep.

"I'm on my way to Tempe, Sam. I have a lead in your case."

If he heard me, he showed no sign of it. He lowered his head in preparation to say something, but the idea seemed to vanish. He found it again by shutting his eyes and pressing his thumbs against the bridge of his nose.

"Here's something you wouldn't expect," he said. "Some of the men I've met in here, why, they're fine fellows."

"Sam, tell me one more time what you remember about that night."

"Nothing. I've told you again and again." Suddenly animated, he bolted forward in his chair. "Everything about that night is gone, erased forever. I'm tortured as much by that as what happened."

I started to speak, but he cut me off.

"Sometimes I'll fall into a vivid dream and remember certain things. I'll see shapes and people. Her. I see her."

He meant Cristy Carlyle, but the name could never be spoken.

"I feel it all over again, the terrible shame. And before long I'm convinced that I committed the deed after all. Do you still want me to remember?"

"Don't say you did it. That's not true."

"I could have. How can you be sure I didn't?" Sam's voice rose as some of the old power returned to it. "I see the men in this place and they're good men. But they've done a horrible thing. Seized by one awful moment and their lives are over. I wonder if that happened to me."

I started to tell him about the lead. He turned away until I explained that it involved a homeless man nicknamed Tom Sawyer.

"Ah, the indomitable Mr. Clemens," he said, and set his head in a listening posture.

The private detective for Sam's previous lawyer had focused on a homeless camp in the wash adjacent to Cristy Carlyle's apartment complex.

Thinking the murderer might've come from there, the investigator interviewed some of the men and women from that camp. He zeroed in on a fellow he'd nicknamed Tom Sawyer, for his habit of storing his collected junk in shopping carts and in a sack carried over his shoulder.

The man was aggressive in the protection of his belongings, and the other homeless feared him. His real name remained unknown.

I'd been to that camp a dozen times and found a guy who knew him.

He said Sawyer had fled for California after the Carlyle murder and had only recently returned. What if this latter-day Tom Sawyer was the real killer?

What if his collected junk still included the missing murder weapon?

"It's hopeless, Prospero. You're searching for a unicorn, and I love you for it. If you were to succeed, you'd be a magician, and here you are, the namesake of the greatest magician in literature. I see the closing of a great circle."

"That's why you need to believe. This will happen, Sam. Believe in magic."

"You won't stop, will you?"

"No, I won't."

Tears rolled down his face. He put both hands against his lips and blew me a kiss.

I walked out of the prison struggling to breathe past the dump truck in my throat and trying very hard to stop thinking about what put it there.

CHAPTER TWELVE

On the drive from Florence to Tempe, I called Constant Lexus in Scottsdale. Valentine Constantine was all over the Internet, a well-known TV personality in the Phoenix valley hawking Lexus cars from her husband's dealership.

With big hair, big lips, and a beautiful Mexican face, she looked like a beauty queen and dressed like a siren in ads that encouraged customers to come talk to "Your Pal Val" about putting you in a luxury ride today.

But my pal wasn't taking calls. I left a message saying I'd be in Tempe the remainder of the day and needed to talk to her.

The next stop was the Tempe Police Department, headquartered on Fifth Street in a big gray building with black windows. I parked under the flapping flags outside the main entrance, and Cash and I walked inside.

A secretary led us into the office of Detective Wanda Dietz, who stayed seated behind her desk with a glum expression. She looked like she should be wearing an orange apron at Home Depot.

She had stringy hair and broad shoulders with no neck to speak of and meaty hands with fingers that looked chewed up. On the wall behind her was a framed photograph of Dietz cuddling with an Irish setter.

Beyond her cubicle telephones rang and computer keys clacked.

"Let's go, Stark, I'm busy. Start talking."

"If you'd sent me your investigative notes, this meeting wouldn't be necessary."

Dietz grabbed something off the corner of her desk, stuck it halfway into her mouth, and held it there with clamped teeth.

It was either a pumpernickel bagel or a hockey puck.

She picked up the file that had been underneath it and waved it at me. She put the file down, chomped the bagel with unselfconscious gusto, and spent the next thirty seconds chewing.

Done with that, she picked up the file again and gave it another wave.

"Right here," she said. "This was my case. What do you want to know?"

"Everything you've got on Tom Sawyer."

"That's easy, nothing."

Cash and I sat in the witness chairs in front of Dietz's desk. Cash wore his usual outfit, including his Arizona Feeds hat. He looked like the soup kitchen admiral.

I rattled off what our private investigator had found. His description said Sawyer stood five foot nine, weighed 150 pounds, had a bushy mountain-man beard, brown eyes, a frequent cough, and a nasty temper.

"Sounds like the guys in that homeless camp remembered him."

"They remember the moon landing, too," Dietz said. "Wanna know why? They were there when Neil Armstrong stepped out of the capsule."

"You're saying they made him up?"

"They make up shit all the time. For fun, for CI money, because they're nuts." Dietz's eyebrows made dark half-moons above tired brown eyes. The sacks underneath them looked like carry-on luggage. "Do you know how many hours I spent looking for this Tom Sawyer?"

Cash took a plastic bag full of pistachios out of his pocket and began cracking them open. He took off his hat, put it upside down on Dietz's desk, and dropped the shells into it.

In my life, I'd probably seen Cash without his hat five times. He looked entirely different.

The trip from his eyebrows back to his shrub-like hairline was long and arduous, marked by blotches, a rash or two, unnatural bumps of the kind caused by wonderful nights out and savage mornings, and finally, with the removal of his hat, a blood-red brim line across his forehead as if from a hatchet wielded in anger.

"Sawyer was a defense lawyer's invention," Dietz said, "and not too clever if you ask me. They were looking for something and they created this guy."

"You'll have no objection if I go down to that homeless camp and look around."

"Monsoon flooding washed it away this summer."

"That happens every year. They build it back up again in the fall, right?"

"You wanna waste time, be my guest."

"I found a guy that says Sawyer's been in California but he's back now. Thought you might want to know."

Cash rubbed a finger back and forth under his nose chasing an itch. He smacked his lips, peeled more pistachios and dropped the shells into the hat, and scratched his nose again.

Dietz stared at Cash, at me, and then at Cash again. She said, "He's lying to you like they all do. You won't find anything, Stark. I tried."

"My father's on death row."

"Where he should be. He killed that girl."

I felt my anger get up and march. But there was no point responding. Her reaction was predictable. Homicide cops enjoy being told they're wrong the way pitchers enjoy ninth-inning grand slams.

"I've got a chance to prove his innocence and I'm going to take it."

"The case is over. You and Huck here can do whatever you want."

I stood. Cash stood and wiped his hands over Dietz' desk.

"Excuse me," she said. "What the hell are you doing?"

Cash grabbed his hat and eyed the trash bin on Dietz's side of the desk. She edged a foot out and toed it closer to her chair.

With that option closed, Cash looked around for another, found none, and settled the matter by putting the hat on his head with the shells still inside.

Not a single one escaped.

He gave Dietz an I-fixed-you look, and we left.

CHAPTER THIRTEEN

Cristy Carlyle lived and conducted business seven blocks from Tempe Police Headquarters and less than that from ASU. The Brook Meadow Apartments consisted of three shabby stucco buildings on different levels of hilly ground off Apache Boulevard.

The front lawn was sprinkled with beer cans.

The grass was a patchwork of orange and scorched brown that badly needed watering.

All three buildings had missing roof tiles and clunker cars in the parking lot.

I parked the Bronco outside the main office. The desert across the boulevard had yet to be bladed and built up, so it looked as it had a hundred years ago.

Cash and I dodged traffic to get there and fought for balance as we boot-surfed down the steep bank to the bottom.

Washes are the arteries of the desert, zigzagging passageways of sand and rock that collect runoff from the summer rains. The rules and norms that govern the streets don't apply in washes. They're slices of frontier within sight and sound of civilization but still remote from it.

Everything is different in washes, even the weather.

At street level, the temperature was cool, but cool became downright cold down below. And there was shade and the breeze had become more concentrated by the high sheltering walls.

We ducked through the octopus branches of an ironwood tree out to the center of the wash. About a quarter mile to the west we saw a pile of dead and mangled trees and brush that looked too structured to be random and started walking toward it.

The recent storms must've been powerful, for they'd carved gouges in the walls of the wash and channels in the sandy bottom, where narrow bands of water still trickled.

Closer in, we saw six men clustered around the debris pile. Plastic bags covered the roof and there was a hole cut in the side to make a crawl-in space.

From a distance, I recognized one of the men as my source.

I said to Cash, "The one in the red lumberjack shirt is Squeaky."

"Is that his real name?"

"He's got a voice like a leaky tire."

As we approached, I said to the men, "Nice hooch."

All of them turned in my direction. Four gave me squinty looks before drifting away, in no hurry but definitely not sticking around. One of those who remained wore a black raincoat open over a ripped red T-shirt.

He had on greasy pants and a battered straw cowboy hat with a Confederate flag hatband.

Squeaky was the other. He wore jeans made for someone twice his size. His shoes were mismatched, and the sun had so dried his face that it looked mummified.

His lips collapsed into a toothless mouth.

I asked Squeaky where I could find Tom Sawyer. He shook his head quickly. Raincoat gave Squeaky a sharp glare, and if I had to guess, the message was "Keep your mouth shut."

They knew where Sawyer was.

I said, "Hey, Squeak, this is important. I need to find this man."

Squeaky put his hands over his ears and retreated into the brush. Raincoat stayed to give us the long eye. He didn't like being pushed.

He growled from the bottom of his throat and up through his nose, spat something yellow and glistening at our feet, and palmed the trailer off his chin. He held his narrow-eyed glare for another minute before joining Squeaky.

"I don't think he likes us," Cash said.

"We're from the world that tossed him out. He's not going to give us anything."

"Got a plan, Mayor?"

Squeaky and Raincoat were about thirty feet away. I could see them through the trees and hear their voices.

"Let's try again," I said. "This time you get in Raincoat's face. He'll get hostile, but stay with him and try to distract him."

"You think Squeaky will talk?"

"When you guys get loud, I figure he'll split. I need a minute alone with him, that's all."

We walked through the brush and up to where they were standing.

Cash raised his chin to Raincoat and said, "Come on, man, you know the dude we're talking about. Guy's got a bushy beard and keeps his stuff in shopping carts."

Raincoat stood perfectly still, his mouth drawn into a tight, lipless line.

"Is that what you want, friend? You want trouble?" Cash stepped closer.

Raincoat didn't back up and didn't speak. Cash kept talking in a loud voice. Squeaky put his hands over his ears, made varmint noises, and stepped away.

I followed until we were far enough away and took him by the arm.

"Look, I need to find Sawyer," I said. "You know where he is. I know you know."

Cash jabbered at Raincoat. Squeaky kept his hands over his ears. I grabbed his wrists and pulled his hands away.

"Sawyer? Where is he?"

Squeaky gave Raincoat a frightened look. He put his index finger to his lips in a shushing gesture. "Papa Joe's Pizza on University," he whispered, and nodded like he was shaking the hornets away. "Boss man feeds him real good out the back door."

When I let him go, he put his palms back over his ears and sang a nonsense song.

I whistled for Cash. He said to Raincoat, "Later, my man. Have a wonderful day," and we hustled out of the wash to the Bronco.

CHAPTER FOURTEEN

I swung out of the Brook Meadow parking lot into traffic along Apache Boulevard. The drive to Papa Joe's Pizza took ten minutes.

The restaurant looked like a popular hangout. Music blared from roof speakers. Sun Devil banners decorated the front windows and there was still a good-sized afternoon-pitcher-of-beer crowd on the canvas-covered patio along the sidewalk.

Cash hustled down the alley next to the building. I went in the front door and asked to see the manager. Sports posters covered the walls, and there must've been seven TVs playing various sporting events.

Elliott Duran was short and greasy-haired. He had a Confucius goatee with six or eight strands hanging down, just long enough to foul his pea soup. He wore a Detroit Tigers T-shirt and didn't want to talk about the homeless man he fed out the back door.

"All I need is a name and a way to find him," I said. "This doesn't have to involve you beyond that."

"Is he in trouble?" Duran looked to be in his early thirties.

Cash came in the front door and shook his head at me. No Tom Sawyer out back.

I explained that Sawyer might have the knife that killed Cristy Carlyle.

"You think he's involved in a murder?" Duran scoffed. "There's a thousand of these homeless folks around here this time of year and they never hurt anybody. How do we know we're even talking about the same man?"

"Does he carry his belongings in a sack over his back?"

Duran hesitated, looking surprised. "Maybe."

That confirmed I had the right guy.

"He's hungry, that's all," Duran said. "We have leftover food and I do what I can."

"He'll be back, right?"

"He was here two days ago. Could be he shows up in five minutes, could be a week."

"Next time he's here, call Detective Wanda Dietz at the Tempe Police. Can you do that?"

Duran made a sour face. "I'm not calling any cops. These folks trust me."

"Elliott, I'm talking about a homicide." I explained about Tom Sawyer's shopping carts and my suspicion that the murder weapon might be stashed in one of his carts.

"Sounds shady, mister," he said.

Duran needed prodding. Being in a sports bar with a fellow wearing a Detroit Tigers T-shirt gave me an obvious opening. I handed him one of my baseball cards, the first one issued after I'd made it to the major leagues.

I carried them for just such situations. They opened doors, and that was the flip side of that sack of nails I'd been carrying around since the cocaine arrest.

"Wait, you're Whip Stark?" Duran said. "That Whip Stark, the pitcher? No fooling!"

He gave me a two-handed handshake, like he was trying to pump water out of an abandoned well. "When you said Prospero Stark, it didn't register. Why didn't you tell me you were the famous pitcher?"

Duran had the kitchen make us pizza. Cash couldn't believe we were getting free food. Duran wanted to take pictures, and Cash said fine, and Duran said he meant pictures of me.

"Unless you played, too," Duran added, eager not to offend.

"How about for the New York damn Yankees. Is that playing enough for you?"

Duran took pictures of me alone and me and Cash together, Cash giving the thumbs-up and making muscles with bent arms. The kitchen staff came out to take pictures, too. I wrote my cell number on the baseball card and again asked Duran to call if Sawyer showed up.

"If you're not comfortable calling the cops, call me down in Tucson. Try to keep Sawyer around until I get here. I'll leave right away when I get the word."

Duran offered us more pizza for the road or maybe a ham and cheese sub.

We said no but took two slices of their chocolate cake.

We could've left with the furniture if we'd asked.

CHAPTER FIFTEEN

We got on the interstate back to Tucson at six that evening. The trip was a hundred miles and I never could figure out Picacho Peak, a rock formation shaped like a baying hound that dominates the horizon for most of the drive.

It was a chameleon, there one moment and gone the next, and no matter how much time passed or how fast you drove, it never seemed to get any closer.

I called Roxy to get the latest news. She'd done some digging into Donny Jim James, whose real name, to my surprise, was Donny Jim James.

His parents had a sense of humor, and Donny Jim had a record.

He'd been arrested twice, the first time for a bar brawl. A few months later, in the fire pit of summer, he was involved in a traffic dispute in which he'd pulled a man by his hair through the window of his car, not an easy thing to do.

He did a few months for assault and paid a hefty fine.

Roxy wanted to find out if he was a hunter or had been in the army, either of which could've given him the skills to make a long-distance rifle shot.

The news on Bella Kowalik was what I'd expected. Roxy had found no arrests.

She was a Polish bride, married an American who'd promptly died of a heart attack, leaving her with nothing in a new country.

"On her own," Roxy said, "she started the maid business and was making it go."

"She said something about her sister, wanting me to protect her sister."

"There's no record of any family in the States. After her husband died, she was alone. She's active in her church, St. Anthony's Church on Wilmot."

"What does she do there?"

"Volunteer. She's there all the time. Mass every morning, that kind of thing."

I wanted to learn whatever I could about her, what she did, where she went, who her friends were, and if she'd talked to them about Sterling. I called St. Anthony's and left a message for the pastor, Father Robert Rinerson.

Cash had promised Charlie that he'd get him out of St. Joseph's Hospital as soon as he could. They'd cooked up a spring-the-patient plan and were eager to pull it off.

That was where Cash wanted to go as soon as we reached Tucson.

But I'd been thinking a lot about the scene at Bella's house the night of her murder and wanted to go back. Cash said if we went to Bella's first, we'd never make it to the hospital.

"It'll hurt Charlie's feelings," he said. "He'll think we're ignoring him, we don't show up. Guarantee he won't like it."

Cash called Charlie and he didn't like it.

As I drove along listening to Cash talk, I thought about Elliott Duran and his reaction to meeting me. It made me uncomfortable. Celebrity always did, but ultimately, I knew it reflected the worshiper, not the worshiped.

Sounded reasonable. A penetrating insight. I allowed myself one of those a month.

You can pull a muscle thinking too much.

Also penetrating was the idea that if I drove seventy-five miles an hour toward Picacho Peak, it would eventually get closer. But it wasn't working out that way.

I flipped on the car radio to a sports station. The Major League Baseball playoffs were going on, and the hosts were talking about the pitchers scheduled to be on the bump that night.

The Mexico City Pirates won the Mexican League championship the year I pitched for them. I won the seventh game in Mexico City, where the elevation tops seven thousand feet.

There's no tougher place in the league to pitch. The ball flies like FedEx on the thin air.

But I held the Monterrey Sultans to three hits. The city went crazy. Pirates' owner Carlos Venable was so happy he offered to send me on a vacation anywhere in the world.

I was twenty-six and getting a second look by big-league scouts in the States.

Two years later, I was out of the game.

The cocaine story. Listening to the radio brought it all back.

I was sitting in the Mazatlán beach house I shared with Rolando Molina, my best friend and the league's best catcher, when Mexican cops burst in and found a stash of cocaine in his gear bag. They took me in, too, setting off a long negotiation with the Mexican judge over how much of a bribe it would take to get us out.

The irony always got me.

The bust has followed me like a hungry hound, and I never touched the stuff. Not once. All the stories printed and broadcast about me that said I did were lies.

After five months in jail and turning over a fortune in cash, Rolando and I walked free. As soon as we reached the States, I dropped him off at a rehab center in Malibu.

I drove away thinking, Okay, Whip, what now?

I'd started life at the top, really burning it up in the game at twenty-one, and now that it was over, I realized that might be the best I was ever going to be at anything.

How do you come back from that? What do you do then?

The first thing you do is turn off the radio.

Cash put his Pro-Keds up on the dash. He wasn't wearing socks and his ankles were filthy. He said, "Sure you wanna go to that dead lady's house?"

"What're you worried about? Cops are long gone. And it's Bella."

"There won't be any evidence. They clean those places up good."

"I want to look around, settle some things in my mind."

"Do we get to mess with the crime scene tape? That's on my bucket list."

"Sure, and afterward I'll buy you an ice cream."

"Sprinkles?"

"What, like I'm cheap?"

The wind had picked up and sent dust swirling across the interstate. Sunset awakened the shadow monsters and the tumbleweeds came out to dance with them.

I drove across the desert dreaming lavender dreams and wondering if the moon looked like this, and if the moon had Cracker Barrels and baseball teams, and did the ball carry a long way up there, and if Picacho Peak was a real rock or an illusion, a trick put there for the amusement of its creator.

It kept ducking behind the brown haze, reappearing larger and bolder than before and looking less like a baying hound and more like a hand with two mangled fingers.

After another stint behind an obliging cloud, the peak reappeared as a shrieking woman that looked a lot like Bella Kowalik.

CHAPTER SIXTEEN

We exited the highway at Speedway Boulevard and headed east toward the university and south on Tyndall Avenue. Early evening, 7:30 p.m.

We rolled past Bella's house to make sure it was empty and dark, and it was.

No activity that would impact us. No parties going on. No nosy dog walkers.

Yellow crime scene tape looped around the front porch.

Two blocks down, we parked and entered the shadows between two houses and doubled back through the cement drainage, trotting along in the dark underneath sheltering trees on both sides. We climbed the slope behind Bella's and jumped the chain-link fence into her backyard.

It was a quiet night with a helpful moon that allowed us to see the crime tape around much of the backyard.

The glass panel that should have been in the middle of the rear door had been replaced by a plywood sheet that sat crooked in the space. I grabbed one edge, bent it enough to pull it out, and reached in to turn the doorknob.

Cash stayed outside. I had a flashlight.

The kitchen smelled of bleach. Black fingerprint dust covered the white countertops. The bedroom had been cleaned out, all the clothes removed from the closet. The bureau drawers were empty, and the sheets stripped off the bed.

Atop the bureau stood a framed photo of Pope John Paul II and a set of rosary beads hanging from the lamp. The trash bins in the bedroom, the bathroom, and the kitchen were all empty, the contents no doubt taken by crime scene techs.

After fifteen minutes of poking around, I heard voices in the backyard and went outside. Cash was standing beside a man of about fifty with a suspicious face.

"He heard noises and came on over," Cash said. "Lives next door." Cash held the Ruger behind his leg, his body turned so the neighbor couldn't see it.

The man was bald on top except for some renegade strands trapped on a fast-disappearing median of scalp. He wore white socks, moccasin slippers, a wrinkled pullover shirt, and gray sweat pants.

"You're not supposed to be in that house," he said. "Don't you see the tape around it?"

"We're looking into what happened here," I said.

"What happened was somebody murdered Bella. Up and shot her." When I said I was a friend, the man's eyes narrowed. "Friends don't use back doors, mister."

"There's nothing going on here you need to worry about," I said.

"A lady gets killed next door to me, I worry about it. The cops asked me to keep an eye on things. Could be they want to know what you fellas are up to."

"Could be they don't," Cash said, and drew the Ruger slightly away from his leg. The moonlight struck the black steel and glinted.

The neighbor saw it and gestured toward the house. "Heck, I don't mind answering a few questions. Don't see no harm in it. No, sir."

Hoping to put him at ease, I asked his name.

"Ah, Bob." He sounded like he wasn't sure.

"Okay, Bob. Why don't you tell me what you knew about Bella?"

He looked back and forth between the two of us before beginning.

"Okay, well, she had her habits. Liked to do things the same way at the same time. Went to church every morning, had a bottle of Amstel Light with her dinner, and loved doing yard work. Kept her place spruced up nice, I'll say that."

"Sounds like you knew her pretty well."

"Not really. We talked, neighbors and all. That's about it."

"There's something I need," I said. "I'm looking for a kid who rides his bike around here. Red wheels, long blond hair."

"Sure, I've seen him around the neighborhood. He rides in the drainage, practices flips and turns and all that trick stuff they do on TV."

"He might be a witness to this thing. I need to find him."

"Don't know his name, but if you watch the drainage long enough, why, he'll turn up."

"You've sure been helpful, Bob," I said, and patted him on the shoulder.

He smiled with half his teeth and stuffed his hands into the pockets of his sweatpants. "Who are you guys, anyways?"

"We're crime fighters," Cash said. "Best in the business. What you just witnessed was first-class investigative work."

"I see," Bob said and rocked on his heels.

Cash made a show of stuffing the Ruger under his belt so Bob would notice. "I got me a question, Bob," Cash said. "You're not going to call the cops when we leave here, are you?"

"I already talked to the police."

"No need to talk to them again, right?"

"Funny thing. My phone just busted a minute ago."

"Good man. We'll say good-bye and trundle on outta here, how's that?"

That was fine with Bob, and we hopped the fence into the drainage and hustled back to the Bronco.

CHAPTER SEVENTEEN

I drove out of Bella's neighborhood. All was quiet and no need to hurry. Even if Bob called the cops, we'd be long gone by the time they got there. But I doubted he would, and the reason was fear. Experience told me fear worked better than trust.

I wanted to go to headquarters for supper, but Cash insisted we go to St. Joe's to free Charlie. At that time of night, it was a fifteen-minute drive to the hospital on Tucson's east side.

On the way, Cash ran into a Circle K and bought Charlie a Big Gulp and a pint of Gordon's gin, his brand, and mixed him a going-home cocktail. I told him to go light on the gin to avoid sending Charlie down the raging river.

Charlie's problem was a bad memory.

For six months of the year, he was a good citizen. He forgot about the bug juice and went about his business of painting houses and thinking life was grand. The steady work filled his pockets with folding money, and he was in love with humanity.

Then he'd remember that his daughter wouldn't let him see his grandkids because he drank too much, and he'd remember the end of his accounting career due to what he called "a potential embezzlement scenario," and humanity would start to suck again.

He'd repair to a bar stool in Tucson, and there, loud, pickled, and unloved, sit for days until the proprietor loaded him into the back of a pickup, tossed a blanket over him, and drove him over the mountain to Double Wide.

I'd know he was there when the proprietor would lean on his horn until I came out, and we'd help Charlie into his trailer. Sometimes he went right to sleep and sometimes he grabbed his gun and shot holes in the moon first, his version of reading to get sleepy.

Anyway, with Charlie you were always waiting for his memory to kick in.

Turned out, getting someone out of the hospital before they'd been formally released was more complicated than breaking out of a supermax prison.

Charlie's nurse, a stern woman in blue scrubs, protested vigorously. She said the doctor hadn't released him, hadn't left instructions for his medications, and would surely drop him as a patient if he insisted on departing the premises.

"The hell with him," Charlie said. "This place is uncivilized. They don't provide a man the necessities."

Cash handed him the Big Gulp splashed with gin. "This'll set you right up."

Charlie stood beside his bed gripping the side rail for support. He took a long sip and winked with satisfaction. "My good man, I'm renewed." He had a jowly face, good teeth, a head of wavy white hair, and ears like the handles on a pitcher of Kool-Aid.

In his excitement at finally leaving, along with a boost from the gin, Charlie peeled off his hospital gown, twirled it like a lasso over his head, and tossed it away. The result was something that should never be seen outside of a steam bath in Ukraine.

He had cascading folds of unnaturally white skin under his arms, a bobbing man-rack and a dumpster for a stomach. The latter made him look top-heavy on his bony bird legs.

He walked in short, teetering steps that produced cabaret-style jiggling on top.

The nurse didn't blanch at his naked glory. She'd probably seen it before, but that couldn't have been much comfort.

"I can't let you do this, Mr. O'Shea. It's for your own good."

She insisted that he sign papers acknowledging that he was leaving against medical advice. He ignored her. Cash gripped Charlie around the waist to prop him up and led him down the hall while nurses bellowed their protests, and Charlie responded by blowing extravagant kisses at them.

"Say good-bye to old Charlie O'Shea, you delightful people. He's outta here!"

By the time we got across town to the Waffle House, Charlie had finished his drink. Opal was working the late shift. We got a booth at her station.

Charlie ate a big meal and declared in a loud voice, "I believe I would like some pie now, Miss Opal." He elbowed me. "I hear it's tasty."

"Give it a rest, Charlie."

"What? I'm doing my bit for our girl."

"You're toasted."

"I object to your assertion, sir." He held up a finger as if to make an important point. "I'm merely interested." He leaned out of the booth and roared, "She's a delightful young lady on top of it."

The manager stared at Charlie, and not happily. Opal acted like she didn't hear a thing but gave a secret grin as she darted into the kitchen.

When she got off shift at 11:00 p.m., Cash walked her out to the parking lot and into his Malibu for the ride home. I drove the Bronco.

Charlie sang "Raindrops Keep Falling on My Head" in the seat beside me.

I followed Speedway west up the side of the mountain to its peak at Gates Pass and started down the winding road to Double Wide. Its lights shone over the dark desert ahead, and normally they were the only lights for miles.

But in my rearview, I saw headlights streak over the pass behind me. The vehicle followed the downslope a short distance before turning south onto a dirt road that wrapped around the middle of the mountain.

I knew that road. It was rough going, more of a horse path than a real road.

Then the headlights went dark.

At Double Wide, Cash helped get Charlie out of the Bronco and down to his trailer. I went into the Airstream and got my Glock out from under my mattress and told Cash to watch over things there while I went back to investigate.

I drove up the mountain and turned onto the horse trail. Down a short distance, I flipped on my high beams, got out, and walked to the end of the light.

No vehicle was in sight, and the road beyond the beams was as dark as the last day.

And quiet. No sound of vehicle or man.

Cash was waiting for me when I returned to Double Wide.

"Anything?" he said.

"Already gone."

"Can't think why anybody would be on that road this time of night."

"No good reason."

He nodded and stared up at the mountain. Nothing more was said. We stood together, Cash holding his AR-15 and me the Glock.

The desert was quiet but for a night breeze whispering through the saguaros.

CHAPTER EIGHTEEN

The next morning was fine and blue, everything an October morning in the desert should be. After breakfast, I stepped outside to smoke a cigar.

The mountains south of Double Wide, down toward the Mexican border, had lost that scorching-white look of June and begun to color up. The landscape held on to the green that sprouted with the summer rains, and it was finally, blessedly cool.

People elsewhere don't understand the euphoria that comes with late October in the Sonoran Desert. The cruel months have passed. The burn on the back of your neck has cooled, and you no longer sweat into your drawers and cuss in lost languages.

Month's end was days away.

Halloween marked the first night you needed the fireplace.

No one else in the world celebrated it, but October 31 was a beloved holiday in Tucson.

Opal stepped from her trailer dressed for work and gave me a sleepy wave, and Cash drove her to town in his ancient blue Chevy Malibu.

As always after the first few magical puffs, my cigar tasted like a gym sock.

I tossed it away, thought how much I hated cigars, thought again about quitting, thought about buying more to make sure I didn't run out, and hopped into the Bronco and drove back to Bella's neighborhood to look for the kid.

I parked at the curb outside Hughes Middle School and stared in at the playground, not quite sure what I was looking for.

Name? No idea. Male or female? No idea.

All I had was a red-wheeled bike and long blond hair.

I sat there and watched through the fence and thought about Donny Jim James. Was it a coincidence that his rifle was missing from the window rack in his truck?

Was it a coincidence that his truck was so muddied up?

He'd obviously been off-road, but where?

At recess, I stepped out of the Bronco and stuck my nose through the fence for a closer look. That lasted ten minutes. Then two burly security guys ran me off.

They had no sense of humor at all.

In the afternoon, after school hours, I drove to the drainage and stood on the Eighth Street bridge and looked down, seeing nothing. I waited awhile, then trolled the neighborhood, pulling alongside sidewalk strollers, rolling down the window and asking for help.

Then it was back to the bridge. The drainage was empty, and nobody knew anything about a blond kid on a bike with red wheels.

That night I spent a couple of hours on my laptop.

After the Mortons had been murdered, I'd developed a routine of checking Facebook, Instagram, and other sites for mentions of their names or of the case.

Some of Paul's fellow lawyers blogged, and his name turned up every week or so in some innocent reminiscence. Donna's did, too, usually in comments from other parents she'd met at the kids' school.

As I worked, Bundle barked furiously outside, and that meant either coyotes were afoot or a drug mule had wandered out of the wash behind the Airstream looking for water or a ride or something he could steal.

Northbound smugglers usually weren't a problem. They had loads on their backs and did everything they could not to attract attention.

But after making their drops and starting back south, those mules got dangerous, eager to steal a gun, a camera, or jewelry, something they could turn over for fast cash on the south side.

I opened the kitchen door and whistled for Bundle. I have an American flag on a forty-foot pole outside the Airstream, and Cash flies the marine corps flag outside his place.

Even a light breeze got the hoist chains knocking against the poles, and it made quite a racket. I whistled again for Bundle, louder, and this time he came running.

I closed and locked my door and went back to thinking about Donny Jim James.

Sitting on the edge of my bed with my phone in hand, I called up the photos I'd taken of his tires to have another look. They were a serious off-road brand, Nitto LT Grabbers. The tread was deep, with P shapes in the center and angled blocks on the shoulders.

I got one of my forest service maps out of a drawer and walked out to the kitchen and spread it out on the table.

As I leaned over the map, Bundle sat beside me watching everything I did with intense fascination. He knew the map meant a trip and that he might be coming with.

Oh, the unbridled joy. And the drool. He wiggled all over in anticipation.

Pressing my fingertip down on Sterling's canyon, I dragged it north across the forest boundary to find the only road into the area.

The double dashes meant a primitive, four-wheel-drive road.

It ended two miles back from the Sterling mansion.

The shooter had to hike the remainder of the way carrying a long rifle.

It hadn't rained since the murder and the area was remote. If Donny Jim had driven into that country in his Dodge truck, the tracks of his tires might still be visible.

I walked down to Cash's trailer and told him to get ready for a trip in the morning.

CHAPTER NINETEEN

Cash and I pulled out of Double Wide before dawn and drove across the valley to its far northeast side, right up against the mountains. That was the place to be in Tucson, a Shangri-la of sprawling houses on secluded lots with swimming pools, tennis courts, guesthouses, sundecks, and abundant wildlife.

Bear, deer, and bobcats often came around to pose for pictures, and the spectacular views had Realtors blowing their trumpets. The same wildlife liked to feed on small dogs and cats, turning the furry beloveds into wild-land scat.

But that part never made the sales pitches.

We drove on the Catalina Highway past the spur to Sterling's mansion and began the climb toward Mount Lemmon. Three miles up, we turned east onto a well-maintained forest road, and with the sun peering over the Rincon Mountains, we followed it back into the trees.

After a mile, the road gradually bent south below the forest boundary toward the back of Sterling's mansion.

When we entered the primitive section of road, Cash and I switched out.

He got behind the wheel and I walked ahead of the Bronco looking for Jimbo's tire tracks, and it soon became clear our mission was foolish.

Foot and vehicle tracks had made an unreadable mess of the dusty road. I hadn't counted on so many crime scene workers having the same idea, and they never did anything halfway.

If Donny Jim had driven that road, the evidence had been wiped away.

I had an idea.

"Let's hike into Sterling's canyon," I said. "It's about two miles down."

"Follow the killer's footsteps."

"I want to get within shooting distance. See what he saw."

"We got a ridge to get around." Cash checked the sky. "Might get wet, too."

Storm clouds had massed over the valley. Above us we had only blue sky, but the wind had picked up and the clouds would soon be on the move.

We hiked the road to its end and from there picked up a rocky trail.

Cash stayed behind me, and Bundle bounded ahead.

His job was to water the rocks and return to jump at our feet in celebration of a mission accomplished. With his tail in a constant whirlwind, he'd dart back down the trail and do the same thing all over again.

The grade was steeply down. It was good moving weather. October is different from other months in the desert. It's temperate, especially late. October isn't plotting to kill you with the heat of summer or the bone-rattling cold of winter.

We hiked through shadow and sunlight until the trees gave way to open rock and canyon, deep gorges, and thick stands of saguaros on the mountain's southern exposure. I stopped to sip from my canteen. The early sun touching the mountain made it horrible and glorious in the same glimpse, the Sonoran Desert's unique calling card.

Pressing on, we followed the tumbling ground between the mountain's big shoulders to a rock window that afforded a long look down to the Tucson valley. Rain was falling in the narrow slice of the city that we could see, the storm forming a gray curtain topped by bright sunlight.

Descending farther through the widening canyon, we saw a brown speck below. Sterling's mansion. The way forward was a zigzagging trail through a cut in the rocks all the way down the slope.

"You take the trail and try to find the sniper's perch," I said.

"You?"

"I'm going to rough it." I pointed immediately west toward a steeper slope marked by larger concentrations of boulders spaced by manzanita thickets. "Could be the shooter didn't take the trail in or out to avoid leaving too much sign. I'm going to have a look around that slope."

I climbed the rocks and began a slow crawl down through the difficult terrain.

At times I had to turn sideways and step down to the next level, using my hands to grip the rock I'd just departed. I'd done that three times when I saw something black on a sliver of ground between two rocks.

The object was a circular piece of black plastic, about two inches in diameter with the letter *L* on the back. I stuffed it in my pocket and continued down to the connecting trail, and Cash. He knew immediately what the object was.

"This here's the lens cap on a sniper scope. *L* is for Leupold. They make scopes."

"You sure?"

"Sure I'm sure. Seen plenty of 'em over there."

"Our shooter was probably military."

"Must've lost it getting back up those rocks."

We walked the trail a short way down to a tumble of boulders. He looked it over carefully, staring down at Sterling's place and back at the rocks around him.

"Believe we've found his perch, Mayor. The angle of the ground tells me it couldn't be anyplace else."

Cash climbed behind it and made a rifle of his arms, laying them across the rock.

"Yeah, this was it. No doubt about it." He took aim behind his imaginary gun. "I been around enough snipers to know how they work and how they think. To them, killing a man's a math problem."

He held up his index and middle fingers, three inches apart.

"You got to send this bullet four hundred yards across your battle space into some son of a bitch's heart. Figure distance and wind, figure whether it's uphill or down, figure the humidity, work out all your dope and do it real fast, like a math geek, and squeeze her off."

He closed one eye and spied through his hands to Sterling's house. "Shot's the easy part."

"Any thought of the target?"

He eyed me as if confused by the question. "He's the enemy. He chose to get up that morning and pick up a rifle to kill my friends."

"It's business. I get it."

"If there's a rogue sniper out there, Mayor, my buds might know. I'll ask my counselor at the VA, too."

"If our guy's working out his problems shooting people, he's not keeping appointments at the VA."

"I know other folks there, too. In the hallways and so forth."

"I thought you quit going to your counselor. Didn't do any good."

"Talking and pills, talking and pills."

"But you're going again?"

"She got a script pad."

I didn't say anything. Cash was sitting on a boulder. He threw a rock down the canyon and listened to it click down the slope.

"I got a lot of friends walking around that ain't right," he said. "They need help more than me, but they won't talk to nobody and they sure as shit don't want the feds mucking around in their business."

"You hand out the prescriptions?"

"Ain't much, whatever she gives me."

"Be careful. The cops are cracking down on that."

He spun on me, eyes snapping. "You want me to let them go to hell? Die like cowards on the bathroom floor? That your plan?" His loud voice echoed over the mountain.

"No," I said, surprised by the outburst. "Can't have that."

"Warriors don't die on the bathroom floor."

Cash stared straight ahead, seeming to laser in on another world behind the clouds. His anger had surged like a gust of wind and disappeared as quickly, leaving something on his face that looked to me like shame, the shame of the survivor.

I waited. He waited. Bundle panted. Cash pulled his hand down across his face to clear it of sweat, and looked up at a beautiful red-tailed hawk, soaring and watching.

Nothing more was said, and we hiked back to the Bronco.

At Double Wide, I left another message for Father Rinerson at St. Anthony's Church.

By late afternoon the next day, I'd concluded that the good father had no intention of calling me back, and it was time to annoy him by showing up.

CHAPTER TWENTY

I drove over the mountain into the noisy brown city. It took forty minutes to get to the east side and St. Anthony's Church on Wilmot Road, a north-south thoroughfare lined with restaurants, schools, small businesses, and medical offices.

The church stood out for its size and grandeur. It had arched entryways, bright white walls decorated with elaborate scrollwork, narrow stained-glass windows, and a golden dome bell tower topped by a white cross.

I walked into a courtyard with a burbling fountain in the center and a covered walkway supported by ornate stone columns on three sides. Offices and classrooms lined the walkway.

The massive church door stood wide open. I stepped inside and didn't see anybody. The quiet of an empty church is like no other. It smelled of candles recently extinguished.

As I turned to walk out, an elderly woman came through the door behind me.

"I didn't know we had company," she said in a gentle voice. "May I help you?"

She had white hair and was smiling through a face like old fruit. Glasses hung on a tether around her neck.

I said I wanted to talk to Father Robert Rinerson. When she asked if I had an appointment, I lied and said yes, and waited to be struck by lightning.

"The pastor is just coming out of a meeting. He's so busy these days."

"I believe that. Such troubled times."

"Wait here while I run and get him. What'd you say your name was?"

"Carl Yastrzemski."

"Just a moment, Carl."

Rinerson wasn't going to like me anyway, so why not make up a name? At least I picked one of baseball's great left fielders, and a Triple Crown winner.

A moment later Rinerson motored through the door. He was short and squat, probably in his midfifties, with a busy man's walk.

He had a puffy face and looked as if he could've boxed in his youth and had given that up for wine. He had a saddle nose marked by fine red lines making a nifty road map of it. His attitude and bearing were arrogant, and he looked annoyed at my impertinence in interrupting one so important.

"If we had an appointment, I'm unaware of it," he said.

"We didn't. But you wouldn't call me back, so I guess we're even."

"My schedule has been simply prohibitive." He breathed deeply. "What is this about, may I ask?"

"I'm looking into the murder of Bella Kowalik. She did volunteer work for you."

"I'm well aware of that." He looked me up and down as if I'd stumbled uninvited in the back door reeking of whiskey and soaking wet from a midnight rain.

I couldn't imagine what he might find objectionable. I had on jeans and my black cowboy boots and a mildly stained white corduroy shirt from the Yogi Berra collection. I'd even made sure my fly was zipped.

"Can you tell me who you represent?"

"I'm working with a TV reporter, Roxanne Santa Cruz."

"I certainly know that name. Indeed." He made no effort to hide the contempt in his face. "It's not appropriate for me to speak with you. My people and I have given what information we have to the police and won't be making further comments."

The white-haired lady lingered nearby with her ears on a wire.

"I'm not asking about police business. I want to know about Bella personally, who her friends were, where she went, what she did, that sort of thing."

"As I said, it's a police matter."

"Nobody gets hurt if you talk to me."

"You've taken up enough of my time." He dismissed me by looking at his watch.

"I'm just getting started, Padre."

Rinerson didn't like that at all. He had on a blue short-sleeved clerical shirt with the neck undone and a portion of the white collar hanging down. Anger turned his neck red.

"You should leave, and I mean right now. If you remain on church property, I'll call the police and you can talk to them."

The white-haired lady watched Rinerson depart and waited to make sure he was gone. "Bella was the most beautiful young lady inside and out. All of our hearts are broken, especially Sister Joseph Philomena."

"They were friends?"

"Sister is part of our ministry team. She and Bella were dear friends."

The word "Sister" hit me in the gut. As she lay dying, Bella asked me to protect her sister. Or so I thought at the time. But Roxy had learned she had no blood sister.

The person she wanted protected was Sister Joseph Philomena.

"Where can I find her?"

She drew back and her eyes got shy. "Really, Carl, I'd love to help, but I don't know if I should."

"That's a phony name, by the way. Carl. I used to play baseball. That's why I said it. My name is Prospero Stark."

The occasional magic of my name didn't work. She had no idea who I was.

"It's crucial I talk to Sister Philomena," I said. "She might be in danger from the same man who murdered Bella."

The white-haired lady put her hand to her mouth. "All of this has been so terrible." She looked around to make sure we were alone and lowered her voice: "Sister lives in an apartment in back. Number three. She should be getting back there momentarily."

"Thanks, and sorry about the fib."

"Promise you won't tell Father Bob I told you. He's forbidden us to talk about this, and he can be, well, difficult."

"Not a word," I said.

CHAPTER TWENTY-ONE

The church bells were chiming their six-o'clock song when I knocked on Sister Philomena's door. Her place was a simple stucco casita with big evaporative coolers on flat roofs. Five such apartments stood in a row behind the church, and they looked neglected compared with Rinerson's opulent residence next door.

Priests talked about the vow of poverty as they jetted off on their next vacation.

The nuns who kept things running never got the joke.

Sister Philomena had just finished teaching a class and was still wearing her full-length white habit, which looked like a curtain from a Holiday Inn liquidation sale. She wore soft, black, blocky shoes that went easy on the bunions.

She'd removed her black veil, putting into full view her thin face and black hair, which strained to reach her collar. She looked about thirty, had a dark complexion, full dark eyebrows, smart dark eyes, and a long nose.

After names and introductions, Sister Philomena said, "Why, yes, I knew Bella quite well. She was a marvelous individual."

"Do you mind if I come inside and ask you some questions?"

Her eyes leaped past me to Father Rinerson's house. "Does Father Bob know you're here?"

"He told me to leave or he'd have me arrested."

"But you stayed, Mr. Stark? You defied our pastor?"

"Tell you the truth, Father Bob strikes me as a resounding dick."

Sister Philomena's jaw fell open and she gushed out a laugh that started with a high yelp and kept repeating until, at the end, it sounded like gobbling turkeys.

"In that case," she said, "come right in."

The apartment had a main living area with a white couch and two ordinary chairs facing it. In front of the couch stood a foldout tray. Left of the front door there was a circular, cocktail-sized table, and beyond that an inset kitchen wide enough to fit one person, if she inhaled and walked sideways.

The room showed none of the disorder of ordinary life. It was clean, even antiseptic. The dove-white walls were unadorned except for a large black crucifix over the mantel.

Sister Philomena invited me to sit on the couch and brought me an iced tea.

I asked her to tell me about Bella.

"What words can I find? She was dedicated and lovely, always helping people." Sister Philomena sat on the edge of the couch with her hands folded in her lap. A faint but indeterminable accent flavored her speech. "I've thought of Bella every moment since it happened. Any help I needed here at the church, she came immediately."

"Tell me how she came to this country."

"It was always her dream, ever since she was a little girl. She loved Poland, but she loved America, too. The idea of it, I guess you'd say. But the idea was powerful for her. Even before coming here, she believed in America."

"What about her husband? I understand he died."

"Ralph, yes. He worked in the construction business. He was a good man and she was happy with him." Her eyes drifted on a memory. "His death was a terrible blow. But the Lord took Bella by the hand and she bounced back."

"The maid business."

"She worked fifteen hours a day. Her fingers were raw."

"You knew she worked for a wealthy man named Ash Sterling."

"Of course, she spoke of him often. She cleaned his house."

"She did more than that. They were romantic. You must've known they were involved."

Sister Philomena sipped her iced tea, put the glass on the coffee table, and smoothed the elaborate folds of her habit. "Let me just say, I live in this world, Mr. Stark. As we all must."

"I'm sure you're aware that he was killed, too."

She leaned forward, her voice becoming confidential. "I've thought a lot about that. Am I correct that what happened to Bella was connected?"

"It looks like she got caught up in Sterling's business."

"I only know of him what Bella told me. He was well off and treated her kindly. I don't know what else I can tell you."

"Did Bella ever mention Sterling's phone? I'm trying to find it. Whoever killed Bella wants to find it, too."

Her eyes sparked in surprise. "I don't know a thing about that."

"Did she talk about any troubles with Sterling, things going on in their relationship?"

"No, I'm sorry." It looked like Sister Philomena had more to say but stopped herself at the sound of a man's voice outside.

"Oh, my. What time is it?" She rushed to the front window, fingered the curtain back, and peered out. "I didn't realize it was so late. It's time for Father Bob's evening constitutional."

The pastor's summoning voice broke through the walls.

"Every night he wants us to walk with him, so we can talk about things. Scripture, parish work, the Wildcats football team. Mostly we listen to Father Bob talk."

"It must be fascinating."

"Goodness, no," she blurted, and caught herself and laughed.

I laughed, too. I was beginning to like Sister Joseph Philomena.

"I lost my fascination for Father Bob the day of our first meeting. But his fascination for himself goes on and on." She spied out the window. "I'm sorry, Mr. Stark, but you should leave. I don't like being so direct, but I can't have Father Bob find you here."

I wrote down my information and handed it to her. "Call if you think of anything. I need to find that phone."

"Certainly," she said, and resumed her sentry work. "Would you mind waiting? After I leave, you can let yourself out and please walk the other way."

"Only if you call me Whip."

"Of course. Whip." She pressed her nose into the crack in the curtain. "He's coming now."

I heard Father Bob's thumping heels and boot-camp voice. He knuckled on the door. "The time is nigh. Are you ready, Sister Phil?"

"One moment, Father." She glanced back at me with a dangerous grin. She was nervous and playful at the same time, having a grand adventure and enjoying it.

We heard Father Bob walk next door, knock, and make the same announcement. Sister Philomena wiggled her fingers at me in farewell, yanked the door open, and flew out on whirring feet, her habit billowing behind her.

I made a clean escape a few minutes later. As I walked away, I thought of all the situations I'd sneaked away from in my life, but never from a nun's apartment in the dark.

There are milestones, and then there are milestones.

CHAPTER TWENTY-TWO

On each of the next three days I returned to Bella's neighborhood looking for the kid and got nowhere.

Charlie's condition had improved enough that he could handle the chores I'd given him. He hadn't paid rent since his accident and agreed to erase his debt with handyman work.

One of those chores was to clean up the trash the smugglers left in the wash. But Charlie wouldn't go there unless Cash was with him.

"I ain't messing with the riffraff down there without an armed guard."

It was suppertime and Charlie had joined us in the Airstream to enjoy Opal's cooking.

He wore cargo shorts and a Tommy Bahama shirt. Charlie had his own Tommy Bahama guy. The fellow worked at the Goodwill store in town and called Charlie whenever a XXX Tommy Bahama came in.

Opal called her newest creation a Rez Wrap—steak strips cooked in a skillet with chili powder, olive oil, lime juice, and garlic, paired with ground mesquite beans, topped with salsa, and wrapped in a heated flour tortilla.

When she put a plate in front of Charlie, he splashed his coffee with gin from a skinny pocket flask he'd bought at Graceland, with Elvis's image embossed on it.

Before screwing the cap back on, he bent his face into the neck of it for a clandestine sip, as if the three of us sitting eighteen inches away wouldn't notice.

"I'm gonna finish every chore you give me, Mr. Mayor. I'm back in shape. And I have to say, I'm grateful for the work."

"He's grateful," Cash said and gave Charlie a cockeyed look. "You're like Ringo."

"You don't know this, Cashy, but I was in a band in high school. Yup, the Midnight Boys. But here's the thing: I had to be in bed by eleven." Charlie's face crinkled up, and he burst into his toothy, head-tilting laugh that invited you to join in.

Opal had been growing increasingly nervous as the night progressed, and when I asked why, she said the time had come to select the paintings she'd be shipping to New York.

"You promised to help, Mr. Whip," she said. "I can't do this myself. You have to come over right now." She scampered out the door and across the street.

I'd been offering to look at her work for days, but the prospect of having her paintings judged spooked her so badly she kept backing out. Now I had to do it in the next ten minutes.

When I got to her trailer, she'd locked the door.

"Opal, it's me, for crying out loud. You asked me to come over. Open up."

"I suck, Mr. Whip." The voice behind the door was miserable. "My paintings suck. Seriously, I can't do this."

I knocked and knocked until she finally threw the door open, after which she turned without a word and ran into the kitchen.

With six rooms, Opal's trailer was the largest at Double Wide, but she lived entirely in the living room. Her bed was a twin mattress dropped onto the ratty orange carpet in the middle of the floor. The only furniture was a couch with rolled-up sections of carpeting on top.

On a table in the middle of the room was a collection of odd store items, like razors, cosmetics, cell phones, and small tape recorders, packaged in the original plastic.

Beside them Opal had tossed some clothes with price tags still affixed.

"You promised me you'd quit shoplifting," I said.

Opal was still hiding in the kitchen. She pretended not to hear me.

She'd lined up seven of her paintings against the wall under the front window. One of them caught my eye. It showed a creature with features that weren't altogether human, but they didn't belong to any single animal either.

The head was square and scaly, the eyes diabolical. The left eye was a black hole and the right one was diamond-shaped. The nose resembled the beak of a large bird.

She drew the figure from the front, and it appeared to be walking forward in stealth. The wings on its back were shiny, black and finely layered, like a beautiful coat.

The creature had thin human legs going up to a normal torso. But the hands were not human hands. They were the oversized talons of an eagle, long, powerful, thick at the back and narrowing to sharp and curling points at the tips.

The right talon gripped something too vague to identify. It might've been a type of prey, an animal this strange creature had captured and was carrying off to eat.

The truth lay in the turbulent muck of Opal's imagination, and I had no idea how to access that dungeon.

"This is really something," I said. "How'd you come up with this beast?"

From the kitchen, she answered in a sparrow's voice. "I see him."

"You see this ... thing? Where do you see him?"

"Everywhere."

"Remind me never to go there."

In all seven paintings, the images were grim, violent, twisted, and blood soaked. Her characters had oversized eyes, sword teeth, crooked slash mouths, grossly misshapen heads, missing limbs, and expressions of imminent death, and the sooner the better.

To my mind she was brilliant. Her talent matched that in the best graphic comic books.

"You need to come out of that kitchen right now," I said.

Opal peered around the corner, said, "No, thank you," and drew her head back.

"These are fantastic. How many of these have the Gelmans seen?"

"The first three. The others are new. Wait, you like them?" The head turtled out again. All I could see was one ecstatic round eye and her long black hair hanging. "Is that what you just said to me?"

"You should be proud of what you've done."

She walked into the living room with her palms pressed against her face. "Are you being serious right now, Mr. Whip?"

"New York is going to love you."

She jumped against me for a hug. "I'm so happy. I thought you'd hate them. For real."

I pointed to the stolen items on the table. "You need to do something about this. If the Gelmans see this stuff, they'll drive away and you'll never see them again."

She was flying so high my words didn't register.

"Are you listening to me? You promised to quit."

"Those are from a long time ago. I haven't taken anything since I started at Waffle House. Some small stuff from the kitchen is all. Swear to God, Mr. Whip."

She bounced on her toes in excitement. "Do you really like my paintings? Promise me you're telling the truth?"

Opal's gruesome images had to be linked to her fleeing the reservation.

She'd never told me the story and I never asked. All I knew was that one night she shouldered a backpack stuffed with everything she owned and left her village, and nobody ever came looking for her.

CHAPTER TWENTY-THREE

The next day, I went back to the Eighth Street bridge, parked at the curb, and got out to check the drainage. Empty. I returned to the Bronco and sat behind the wheel and waited.

To show how much I hated cigars, I kept spares in the glove box. I grabbed one, rolled down my window, let the breeze carry the cellophane away, lit up, hung my left arm out the window, and sent the blue smoke flying.

It was a nice morning under a forgiving sun. A few cars passed. Moms hauling the kids to school, the UPS truck. I puffed my smoke and tried to parse out some things about the Champagne Cowboys that didn't make sense.

Overseas they were soldiers, brave men who killed the enemy with purpose and expertise. They did their job, their duty, and as Sergeant Major Burnside's writing made clear, they were widely admired for their skill.

They should've left all that behind when they came home.

But Sterling's comments to Roxy made it sound like they were present when the Mortons were murdered.

If so, what happened? What caused them to break pattern and slaughter two people?

They were thieves, not cold killers of innocents. The answer was likely on Sterling's missing phone—in a video, audio, or maybe an email or text message.

But the key word was "missing."

After two hours of waiting, I heard noises in the drainage, got out, and peered over the railing, and there was the blond kid with the red-wheeled bike.

He was riding the steep cement berms bordering the drainage. He'd ride down one berm to achieve the necessary speed, cross to the opposite side and up to the top of that berm, pull up and perform a midair turn, and splash-land in perfect balance in the narrow band of water trickling along the bottom.

I walked to the end of the bridge and down through the brush.

"Is that the matinee for today?" I said.

"I got skills, mister."

"I can tell. You ride down here a lot?"

"All the time. This place is dime."

He kept his arms straight out, gripping the high handlebars, feet spread for balance. He couldn't have weighed more than ninety pounds. He wore baggy black shorts and a white muscle shirt and had bangs below his eyebrows.

His straight blond hair fell to his shoulders and curled at the bottom.

The morning was drowning in sunlight, but only patches of it filtered through the trees lining the drainage.

"You were here the other day when that lady got killed, right?" I said.

He stared, wary.

"Friend of mine saw you," I said. "You're not in trouble, but I have some questions."

After a short wait he nodded and pointed. "Was up on the bridge."

I moved closer and stood beside him. "Name's Whip."

"Ozzie."

"Glad to know you, Ozzie. Can you tell me what you saw?"

"Two dudes booking down here, chasing each other. The shooting was so loud, man. Like, my ears were ringing."

"Can you describe these guys?"

"No way. I was looking down and they were coming straight at me and soon as the bang-bang started, I hit it hard." With his long hair and delicate features, Ozzie might've been mistaken for a girl, but for the alternating screech and growl of his teenage voice.

"Anything at all? Tall, short, black, white?"

He gave me a sly smile. "I could tell you what I saw on the street after." He pulled his pockets inside out to show me they were empty. "Ain't feeling it, dude."

He tried to put on a tough look, but his pink face doomed the effort. At the appearance of my twenty-dollar bill, his upturned grin reached the bottom of both ears. He looked like a happy second grader. The bill disappeared in his pocket.

"There was a pickup truck parked up there, like, a little down the street from the bridge. When I was riding out of there, I went past it and there was somebody behind the wheel."

"Man or woman?"

He shrugged. "I was going the same direction. All I seen was an arm sticking out the driver's window. When I got down the street, I looked back, and a guy was running out of the drainage and getting into the truck."

"Then what?"

"Truck took off." He tomahawked his hand to indicate speed. "Came up behind me on the street, like, inches."

"Chasing you? Like it was going to run you down?"

"Nice try. I peeled into an alley and got away. Like I say, I got skills."

"Can you describe the truck?"

"Didn't look at the truck. But the arm sticking out was tatted up. Looked like hearts. A funky face with two red hearts around it."

"You sure about that?"

"Rode right past it. Like, four feet."

I thought of Holly's tattoo. I only saw one red heart. The second one might've been hidden under the cuff of her shirt.

"It might be best if you stayed out of this area awhile," I said. "With that hair and those red wheels, you stand out."

"No way, this my hive."

"What's your last name, Ozzie?"

"Fish. Like the ocean, not the card game. Oswald Margo Fish."

We traded phone numbers. I told him to call if he saw the truck again. I handed him another twenty-dollar bill. He gave me the same giddy grin and my first twenty dollars got company in his pocket. He gripped the handlebars and reared back.

"Later, dude. Ozzie Fish gotta ride."

He stood up on the pedals, pumped his chicken legs, and was gone.

CHAPTER TWENTY-FOUR

I called Roxy and she agreed the red heart tattoo might be the break we needed. We had to find out if Holly's tattoo matched, and the trick was to do it without her knowing.

If Holly had already made a run at Ozzie, I didn't want to give her reason for another.

The pretext for a return visit to the sandstone duplex was to ask Jackie a second time about her last contact with Sterling.

She'd rattled the first time and maybe she would again.

I drove to Roxy's house downtown. She'd fixed her hair in a Veronica Lake side sweep, one ear exposed. She had on distressed jeans and pointy-toed black pumps.

Her sweater was black, with gold buttons up the sides and gold velour patches at the elbows and neck. She'd been eyeing it in her closet, awaiting the cooler weather, and this was its formal rollout.

Roxy paid close attention to fashion, and that made her stand out in a town where wearing pants was considered showing off.

"Wonderful, isn't it?" she said, spinning around for me.

"Yes, and the woman in front of me even more so."

She liked that a lot. Trap averted.

I wanted to get going to Holly's place, but Roxy wasn't done. She wanted to change shoes and had lined up three pairs for inspection. She put a fist on her hip and tapped her index finger against her lips and pointed to them one at a time.

"What do you think?" she said. "I've got Christian Louboutin, Prada, and Jimmy Choo."

I played ball with a Jimmy Belyeu, a center fielder whose glove saved several games for me. Belyeu sort of rhymed with Choo, so Jimmy Choo it was.

"You couldn't be more wrong," Roxy said. "It's Prada."

"Why'd you ask me?"

"I wanted your opinion."

"But you already knew which ones you were going to wear."

"What does that have to do with it?" She threw up her hands. "Men are hopeless."

We rode together in the Audi. Whenever there was a choice, Roxy insisted on the Audi over the Bronco, for purely stylish reasons, and she insisted that I drive.

"The man always drives," she said. "Everybody knows that."

In the car, she flipped on the overhead light and reached into her purse, launching a noisy and difficult exploration. She was in there forever.

Lewis and Clark had an easier time of it.

She eventually produced her compact and lipstick.

"In any kind of confrontation, lipstick and the right shoes are essential," she said.

We arrived at the sandstone duplex near University Hospital just before 7:00 p.m. Jackie's yellow Camaro was not in the driveway.

Holly opened the door. She was wearing pants.

"It's you two. Great." She had an oven mitt on her left hand. She used the right hand to brush the hair off her forehead. "Jackie isn't here and I'm cooking, so if you don't mind."

She kicked the door to close it and turned back to the kitchen, unaware I'd blocked the door with my foot. She was pulling a tray of cookies out of the oven when she realized we'd followed her.

"I don't remember inviting you in."

Holly seemed taller than I remembered, close to six feet. She had a hard face that didn't trust anybody. The jaw was long and her eyes a hard blue, and watchful. She wore beige pants, work boots, and a black T-shirt with *Handy Dandy Plumbing* written in white across the front.

The oven mitt obscured the tattoo on her left arm.

I told her I wanted to ask Jackie about the last time she'd seen Sterling. Holly wasn't in the room when I'd asked the same question on our previous visit.

"Tough luck, Jack's out for the evening. Anyways, didn't you already talk to her?"

"We wanted to make sure we heard her right. It's an important point."

"I don't know, not too long ago. Ask Jack."

"That's funny, she said it had been years."

"Okay, it was years. What're you asking me for?" Holly straightened up from the oven, and there was something in her eyes, a shadow of worry. She knew she'd made a mistake.

"You better hope Donny Jim doesn't come home. He's due any minute."

"Still mad about his tires?" I wanted to keep Holly talking until she pulled off that mitt.

"Donny looks out for Jack and so do I. Sometimes guys come by late at night drunk and wanting to start up. Jack's awful pretty in case you didn't notice."

"Speaking of Donny, was he ever in the military?"

"Sure was. Army. What of it?"

I asked what he did in the army, but Holly ignored the question. She had the tray of cookies on the counter and was using a spatula to move them onto a platter. Roxy caught my attention and nodded toward a calendar hanging on the kitchen wall.

Some of the squares were filled in with scribbled reminders of appointments. In one of the date squares were the words, "Whine and Women, Rocco's. 7:00 p.m."

Rocco's was a restaurant and lounge not far away on River Road.

Holly finished putting the cookies on the platter and dropped the tin into the sink.

Roxy tapped the calendar notation. "Whine and Women. That sounds interesting."

"It's Jackie's nurses' group. They meet Thursday nights for happy hour."

Roxy said, "That's tonight, isn't it? Thursday night at Rocco's."

"Canceled," Holly said, a little too quickly. "Tonight's been canceled."

"How come she didn't cross it out? She crossed out the others."

Holly hadn't exactly been loose before, but now her body went rigid. She pulled off the oven mitt and leaned her left arm on the counter, giving Roxy every bit of her intense eyes.

The sleeve tattoo, now plainly visible, was the queen of hearts playing card, with two large red hearts, at the upper left and lower right corners, close to what Ozzie had described.

Holly let the stare linger and threw in a nasty, up-and-down appraisal.

"It's the sweater, isn't it?" Roxy said, and motioned to me. "What'd I tell you? It's popping." To Holly, Roxy said, "Nordstrom. In case you're wondering."

"I haven't wondered since eighth grade." She stepped out of the kitchen holding her hands out in a sweeping motion to move us along. "I'm done talking with you two. Time to go."

I said we just had a few more questions, but Holly wasn't having it.

"Beat it. Right now."

"Before we go," Roxy said, "can you just tell me your last name?"

"Fuck off."

"Is that Russian?"

CHAPTER TWENTY-FIVE

I t was dark outside when we climbed into the Audi. I followed the side streets around the medical center out to Campbell Avenue and turned north toward the Foothills and Rocco's.

Our destination required no discussion. Holly had obviously lied about Whine and Women being canceled, and I was sure Jackie had lied about Sterling.

I wanted to squeeze her and see if anything popped out.

As I drove, a pair of headlights set on bright rolled up behind me, uncomfortably close.

Campbell Avenue is a two-lane north-south road with a turn lane in the middle.

Evening traffic was light. If the driver behind me wanted to pass, he had plenty of room. But I knew he had other plans when I sped up and he did the same, snuggling up to my bumper even closer than before.

His headlights blew up in my rear and side mirrors, blinding me.

"Come on, pal," I said. "What're you trying to do?"

"Slow down," Roxy said. "He'll go around."

"He could've gone around anytime. He likes where he is."

I was in the right lane. I'd started out going about forty miles an hour and slowed down from there. Twice he mashed his brakes to avoid hitting me, veered back and forth in the lane, fell back and hit the accelerator again to regain his place in my mirrors.

When the delivery truck in front of me slowed to turn into the parking lot of an Albertsons supermarket, my speed dropped below twenty.

My pursuer found that intolerable and blew his horn, hitting it repeatedly in long blasts.

After the truck completed its turn, I let the Bronco coast along at decreasing speed. The horn behind me became more frantic.

Roxy turned to look. "He's going to hit us. Really, Prospero."

Half a second later, he did. It was more a tap than a violent collision, but even a tap rearranges your insides.

With right-turning vehicles in front of me and my pursuer behind, I was stuck. The left lane gave me options, and I got there with a sudden swerve that set off more horns from unassuming drivers going shopping or heading home.

I goosed the accelerator and took off.

With several traffic lights ahead and figuring my pursuer would pull a similar maneuver and follow me, I knew my lead wouldn't last, and I was right. He jumped lanes, swung into the turn lane to my left, and came even with my window.

The truck was a black Dodge Ram and the driver was Donny Jim James.

He yelled for me to pull over through his rolled-down passenger window.

But there had to be a better option than getting into a wrestling match with a pissed-off behemoth in the middle of Campbell Avenue.

I sped ahead, jumping lanes as I went.

At River Road, which runs west to east along the Rillito River, I wheeled right without stopping at the red light, squealing my tires and causing two lanes of eastbound traffic to brake hard to avoid hitting me.

Donny Jim stayed with me.

A Tucson police car, lights flashing, filled my rear view.

I swung into a left-turn cutout in the median and bounced over to the westbound side and into the parking lot of Rocco's. Donny Jim didn't make the turn and the cop burned after him.

The parking lot served a row of storefronts that included a real estate office, a bridal store, and a bank. The sign in the bar's front window featured the word *Rocco's* in red neon script, with smaller signs touting its imported and craft beers.

I parked next to Jackie's yellow Camaro and we had already gotten out of the Bronco when Donny Jim's truck screeched to a stop in the middle of the lot.

He jumped out, leaving his headlights on and his door open, and marched over to me. As he neared, he dropped his right shoulder and drew his fist back, a windup that made it easy to sidestep his long, looping punch.

I had experience with large men charging me. As a pitcher, my job occasionally required plunking batters, and they sometimes reacted like a Pamplona bull.

Donny Jim's miss left him in a crooked stance. Figuring it was unwise to wait for him to rewind and try again, I hit him on the right side of the head, and he dropped to his knees.

The cop arrived. For something to do, he whooped his siren and jumped out of his car.

Donny Jim wanted to make another run at me, but the cop got to him first.

"You stay away from my girl!" he shouted.

"We were talking, Jimbo. Nothing more than that."

He pointed over the cop's shoulder. "You stay the hell away!"

Three more cruisers arrived, and the scene became a mess of uniforms and gawkers. The cops buzzed around enjoying the control they had over the scene and taking their time enjoying it. Their spinning roof lights and the false drama they created drew a crowd that delighted in being pulled away from their ordinary lives to watch spinning roof lights.

Having gotten a call from Holly saying Rocco's might be our destination, Jackie came out to see about the commotion.

She saw Jimbo handcuffed in the back of a cruiser and said, "Honestly, what's wrong with you?"

Jackie's hair was down, long, curled, dark, and she wore black yoga pants and a shiny green top, low-cut and probably silk. It was loose fitting and still managed to highlight her shape.

The cops noticed. That was evidence cops never missed.

We were standing beside Roxy's Audi. Her license plate said, *NEWSBABE.*

Jackie glanced down at it. "Shouldn't an investigative reporter go incognito? You need to know that plate tells everybody where you are. It's a billboard, darling."

Her voice had a distinct quality. It rolled out on a velvet runway, smooth, deep, full of conviction. There was confidence in it, a calm power that compelled your attention.

Jackie spread her hands in invitation. "Holly says you have more questions for me?"

"You told us the last time you saw Sterling was years ago," I said. "Holly just told us it was recent. Can you clear that up?"

Jackie didn't react. Her eyes were cool. Nothing bothered her.

"If my dear friend spoke out of turn, I apologize, but she'd have no way of knowing when I saw Ash Sterling. My goal the last time we talked was to be completely honest with you Mr. Stark, Miss Santa Cruz, and I was."

Jackie looked back and forth between us as she spoke. "If there were anything else I could tell you to help solve this horrible crime, I assure you I would."

A woman poked her head out of Rocco's.

"Jackie, darling, have you forsaken us?" She pronounced "darling" with a *K* at the end.

"I hope I've answered your questions," Jackie said. "If you have nothing else, Mr. Stark, Miss Santa Cruz, there's a mimosa waiting for me inside. I do love my Thursday mimosas."

CHAPTER TWENTY-SIX

With Donny Jim still handcuffed in the back of a police cruiser, Roxy and I climbed into the Audi and rolled back down Campbell Avenue. The night seemed to get more peaceful the farther we got from Rocco's.

"Well, we know one of them is lying," Roxy said.

"That comment about your license plate," I said. "What do you make of that?"

"Nothing. Why?"

"It's a weird thing to say."

"She's messing with me," Roxy said. "Pretty girls do that to each other the way you guys bash heads on the football field. Let's concentrate on the queen of hearts."

"Charming Holly."

"Can we be sure it was her arm Ozzie Fish saw sticking out the window?"

"I like the odds," I said, "but we need to find out more about her."

"All we know is she's a plumber and has lousy taste in men's clothes."

"If I had her last name, I could check her out."

"Why didn't you say so?"

I swung off Campbell at the medical center and rolled through the darkened residential streets to Jackie's sandstone duplex. I parked a few houses down, killed the headlights, told Roxy to sit tight, and walked down the sidewalk to Holly's sidewalk mailbox.

If she was preoccupied by the evening's excitement, she might not have picked up her mail. I pulled down the little door and there it was.

Grabbing the whole stack, I closed the door and walked back to the Audi. Roxy leaned over and used the flashlight on her cell phone to help me see.

I flipped through the stack until I found her electric bill.

"Here we go. Last name Winterset," I said, and tossed the stack into the backseat. "Go ahead and work your Google magic."

"Okay, Holly Winterset." Roxy tapped at her phone. "What nasty business have you stirred up?"

A moment later: "Listen to this," and Roxy read from a news account:

"'Holly Winterset, twenty-eight, originally from Katy, Texas, pleaded guilty to embezzling money from her employer, Jackrabbit Plumbing. The loss totaled less than two thousand dollars and the employer asked for mercy. Winterset got probation.'"

Roxy fingered more text onto the screen. The neighborhood was quiet. No traffic, no pedestrians. The beam from her phone brightened the dark cab of the Audi.

"After that," Roxy said, "Holly was arrested for firearms violations. She ran a gun shop in Three Points that sold to straw buyers. They'd turn around and run the weapons south across the Tohono O'odham Reservation to cartel people on the south side. She pleaded guilty."

Three Points was an unincorporated desert settlement west of the city.

"Dangerous business," I said.

Roxy read more. "She was having guys lie and sign the federal forms saying the guns were for them. If you wanted a semi-automatic .50-caliber rifle, Holly was your gal."

"Let me guess," I said. "She flipped and got a deal."

"Three years."

"Yet she still walks among us."

"Now we know why Jimbo's working so hard to keep us away from her. He doesn't want us finding out his sweetie's a badass with cartel connections."

"Do you think she could handle a four-hundred-yard rifle shot?"

"If she sold rifles, she probably knows how to use them."

I stared out at the starlit Catalina Mountains. Even in darkness they dominated the city, hovering, sheltering, solid and peaceful against the night sky.

"Try this out," Roxy said. "Holly does Sterling from the canyon and drives to Bella's house, and this time she's the getaway driver with the red heart tattoo and somebody else does Bella, that somebody being Donny Jim James."

"Bella used a knife on her killer," I said. "Jimbo showed no signs of being cut."

"Cash said the guy he was chasing was big, right?"

"Moving fast. Not like somebody who'd been stabbed."

"Okay, it was a small cut," Roxy said. "We know he's impulsive. Bella uses the knife on him and his temper blows."

"I don't know. Possible, I guess."

"Don't rule him out is all I'm saying."

We were long past suppertime, and at pauses in the conversation the only sound in the Audi was my stomach rumbling.

We drove to El Güero Canelo for a couple of Sonoran hotdogs, the height of fine dining in Tucson. A Sonoran dog is wrapped in bacon and grilled, and covered with beans, tomatoes, onions, and rocket-fuel salsa, the hotter the better.

The subsequent nuclear fallout in my stomach kept me awake at night, but I was powerless to resist.

CHAPTER TWENTY-SEVEN

When I got home, Cash was sitting on his front porch watching the mountain. If he saw headlights on the horse trail, he promised to fetch me, no matter the hour. I showered and fed Bundle and drank milk to counteract the Sonoran hotdog and had no regrets about ordering it.

Sleep was out of the question. The coyotes had gathered for their nightly sing.

No, sing was the wrong word. That was what town coyotes did.

At Double Wide, they screamed, a high, chasing, torture cry that sounded almost human and summoned every monster from my boy's imagination out from under the bed.

I flipped on the TV. The voices gave a counterpoint to the coyotes. The fridge was mostly empty. But I had leftover pizza. I popped a slice into the microwave and waited.

Donny Jim James, assassin.

The more I thought about it, and hearing Cash talk about the swift mind and cold heart of the sniper, the more I questioned whether Jimbo had what it took to lie out in the rocks to make the shot, then race to Bella's house to do another, far more difficult job.

Up close, eyeball to eyeball.

Stick a gun in a woman's belly and kill her because she knew too much.

Jimbo was made for muscle work, not that.

His army background didn't sway me. Rifle in his gun rack or not, he didn't have what it took to be a sniper. He was most likely a clerk, or a cook who tried not to poison anyone or cut off his own fingers as he put in his time before discharge.

The microwave beeped.

I dropped the slice on a plate, got a water bottle, and sat at the kitchen table.

Law and Order played on the overhead TV. The plot didn't matter. I'd seen them all before. The most notable thing was the double-bump sound, the perfect accompaniment to leftover pizza.

Holly was another story. She had a serious criminal background, was accustomed to doing business with rough men. In my mind, that made her capable of killing, and if the tattoo matched, we could place her behind the wheel of the getaway car at Bella Kowalik's murder.

But if Holly was involved, even with Jimbo helping, they weren't alone. They weren't planners and doers—they were followers. My visit to the sandstone duplex convinced me that Jackie was the leader of that odd group.

When she grabbed an agitated Jimbo by the shoulders, he sat down dutifully. When she told Holly to take Jimbo outside, Holly obeyed. Then Jackie told us how proud she was of Holly.

But Holly and Jimbo deferring to Jackie didn't implicate her in Sterling's murder, and I'd searched online superior court and federal court records for any reference to a Jackie Moreno and whiffed.

She was clean. No criminal background.

I finished eating, turned off the TV, and went back to my laptop and tried again, typing in Jackie's name and hunting around. I clicked on a series of photos taken at a nursing school function and found her.

She was on the left end in a line of five students laughing and goofing around with their arms around each other. I sent the image to my phone.

If you're so happy, why'd you lie about seeing Ash Sterling?

About eleven, I got into bed and caught up with Coffin Ed and the Grave Digger, and in the morning, I awoke to loud noises in the kitchen reminding me that today was Gelman day.

"That you, Opal?"

"Get up, Mr. Whip. They're coming soon. I don't know how you can sleep in there."

"I was thinking the same thing."

I showered and dressed, poured a cup of coffee, and sat at my kitchen table. Opal kept chattering as she made breakfast and peered repeatedly out the open door.

The Gelmans arrived shortly after 8:00 a.m., rolling down the mountainside in what I can confidently state was the first Mercedes van Double Wide had ever seen.

Lloyd Gelman was lean and erect in bearing. He had long salt-and-pepper hair tucked behind his ears and wore a black quilted vest over a long-sleeved blue-and-white-checked shirt.

He wore no socks and sporty canvas shoes, probably Burberry or Tommy Hilfiger.

He gazed around Double Wide, taking it all in.

At that hour of the morning, the slanting sun threw a forgiving light over the trailers surrounded by the wild emptiness of the desert, so distant from the money, manners, and expectations of Manhattan.

I doubt Lloyd was impressed. His expression fought to show no judgment, but in the difficulty of the effort he showed everything. He stood with one leg thrust forward, chin raised, his hands clasped behind his back.

Grace Gelman wore a pasted-on smile and a Navajo squash blossom necklace so big it could've broken the neck of a weaker woman. Her hair was cut short, highlighting all of her face and giving it the unmistakable air of reconstruction work incorrectly done.

It looked as if the surgeon had removed the features to work on them, and when he put them back, he missed their original locations by a smidge, leaving the whole arrangement off-kilter.

She was either joyous or about to scream, depending on the play of the sunlight.

She said, "Isn't the Sonoran Desert beguiling?"

The question drew a confounded silence.

"Tell me, Mr. Stark," Grace Gelman said, "do you summer here as well?"

Cash gave me a glance that said, "I'm out," and fled down the street to his trailer.

With Lloyd's help, Charlie O'Shea and I carried the paintings out to the van.

After the Gelmans drove away, I fired up the laptop to check my email, which consisted of pressing "delete" forty times until I got my saved emails below one hundred, and then my phone rang.

I didn't recognize the number and let it ring out, and a minute later listened to a message from someone named Tom Mohegan at Papa Joe's Pizza in Tempe.

Sounding young and scared, he said he had news about his boss, Elliott Duran, and to call back right away. Elliott had tacked my baseball card to a bulletin board at the store, with my number written on it in case Tom Sawyer came around.

"Is he there?" I said to Mohegan. "Is Tom Sawyer there now?"

"No, sir. But Mr. Duran's in the hospital."

"Hospital. What happened?"

Wanting to help find Sawyer, Mohegan said Duran had hiked into the wash with a backpack full of food. He found Sawyer and his shopping carts, but Sawyer didn't like the intrusion and got rough, and Duran was recovering in the hospital.

I told Mohegan I'd be there as soon as I could.

CHAPTER TWENTY-EIGHT

Cash had an appointment in town with his VA counselor, so I made the drive up I-10 alone. Duran was at St. Luke's Hospital in Tempe. I walked into his room and was shocked at what I saw.

His face looked like a honey-baked ham.

Tact prevented me from saying that. Instead, I exclaimed, "Jesus Christ!" and promptly fumbled around trying to explain that it really wasn't so bad.

Duran stopped me. "You don't have to, Whip. I got a whupping, no getting around it."

He was sitting up in bed with the TV on and the sound down. He had a white bandage around his forehead and bloody splits in his bottom lip.

The parts of his face that weren't red and puffy were purple and puffy.

"I was bringing food to him," Duran said. "Tom hadn't been to the store in so long I figured if he was really down there, he had to be hungry."

"He attacked you for trying to feed him?"

"Wasn't just him. There were four guys and they ganged up." Duran's voice crawled out on its belly. His teeth were clenched. "Sawyer hit me first and the others joined in. I thought I was going to die. I was trying to help you out."

He had a button-activated pump to deliver painkiller. He closed his eyes and thumbed it and was out of breath when he opened his eyes again.

"Tom Mohegan said you found Sawyer's shopping carts."

"Two of them. Nobody was around when I got to the camp, and I remembered you talking about a knife."

"You went through the carts?"

He drew a shallow breath and nodded shyly, as if he knew he'd made a bad mistake. "It made him super mad." He gave a pathetic half laugh.

"Did you find a knife?"

"I didn't get very far. He accused me of stealing his stuff. I wasn't stealing anything."

A curtain on a track divided the room. The guy in the other bed was watching an *I Love Lucy* rerun on TV. Fred Mertz was up to no good.

I asked Duran to describe what Sawyer was wearing.

"Clothes. Whatever, I don't know." He shrugged in frustration. "Junk clothes like they wear. I don't remember. Sorry, Whip."

"That's all right. I'll find him."

Duran described the location of the camp. It sounded close to where I'd met Raincoat and his friend, only farther east, judging by the cross street.

Before leaving, I ran out to the Bronco to retrieve a new baseball and autographed it for Duran. I thought it would cheer him up.

The gift got him so excited he screamed from a new surge of pain.

He was working the thumb pump hard when a nurse rushed in and said it might be better if I left. I thought about smoothing things over by giving her a ball, too, but it's best to ration the joy you spread.

By the time I got out to the parking lot, the sun had heated the interior of the Bronco to an intolerable level. That happens even in late October in Arizona. I started the engine, switched on the AC, stood outside the Bronco, and called Detective Wanda Dietz.

"Elliott Duran looks like he got in the ring with Conor McGregor."

"We're aware an assault occurred."

"Are you still claiming Tom Sawyer doesn't exist?"

"We've yet to identify a suspect, but Tempe PD is investigating."

I spoke with my phone arm draped over the open Bronco door and one foot on the runner. The parking lot was full and busy, as hospital parking lots always are.

"Is that supposed to inspire confidence?" I said.

"We'll find who did this. That's what we do."

"You've had years to find him. A pizza guy walks into the wash and there he is. You should be embarrassed."

Dietz's voice tightened with anger. "Is there a reason for this call, Stark?"

"I'm going into that wash to find Sawyer now. You can join me if you want."

"My advice is stay away. This is a police matter. I assure you, we will make an arrest."

"Sawyer's shopping carts are down there, and they might contain evidence in the Carlyle homicide."

Her voice rising, Dietz said, "I told you that case is closed."

"If I find anything, I'll be sure to hand it over to the chief of detectives first."

"Do you know how many 'opens' I've got on my desk?"

She was practically shouting by then, and that was that.

My touch confirmed that the AC had done little to cool the blazing seat. I did what Arizonans are trained to do and assumed the position.

Drivers get a certain facial expression under such circumstances.

Newcomers assume it's gastrointestinal, but desert veterans know better.

It lands somewhere between a grin and a grimace, has no name, and only occurs when your butt cheeks are being sautéed salmon pink.

I wore just such a look as I pulled out of the parking lot onto Mill Avenue.

CHAPTER TWENTY-NINE

Mill Avenue was packed with bicyclists headed for ASU, and the sidewalks were thick with students carrying backpacks. The men wore shorts and T-shirts. The women wore shorter shorts and better T-shirts.

Most of them had ear buds stuck in their ears and were grinning at the disembodied voices inside their heads. I saw only one student not carrying a cell phone.

He carried an actual book instead.

I rolled down my window and gave him a shout and a fist pump.

He looked like he might make a run for it.

At a convenience market, I bought a pint of Southern Comfort and followed the Mill Avenue curve onto Apache Boulevard to Cristy Carlyle's apartment complex. I parked in the lot and trotted across the street into the wash.

The racket of the city dimmed immediately. It was still there, but the sound moved far back in the order of considerations.

I walked west on the loose sand, past where Cash and I had been a few days before. Another half mile along, I came to a bridge with a cement abutment in the center and tunnels on either side measuring about eighty feet in length.

I heard distant voices and followed them into the tunnel. Cars and trucks passed above, the sound starting small and far-off, building to a loud hum, then a fast double thump on the bridge overhead, then a descending buzz.

The sound of my footsteps through the tunnel brought two men into view at the opposite end. They looked at me and, just as before, drifted away. By the time I emerged into the light on the other side, they'd made it into the brush beside the bridge.

"Hold up," I said. "I'm looking for a guy. I'm not a cop."

They didn't respond. They were scared, disheveled, and filthy. They peered back at me between the hanging branches like wounded animals. Only the suspicion on their faces marked them as human.

"This guy keeps his stuff in shopping carts," I said.

They gave me nothing. I reached into my back pocket for the Southern Comfort. Not sure what I was reaching for and unwilling to wait to find out, one of the men scrambled through the brush and was gone.

The second one started to follow but stopped when he saw the bottle. He had a slight build and sunken cheeks. He wore dark shorts, and his legs were so blackened by dirt that it was hard to see a distinction between flesh and fabric.

"You know who I mean," I said.

The skinny man eyed the bottle and stepped closer.

"His shopping carts. Where are they?"

Looking at the bottle and not me, he pointed to the opposite end of the bridge and beyond, where there was nothing but desert.

"His carts are there?"

He nodded. I gave him the bottle and he sat with his back against a tree to drink.

My hike lasted no more than two hundred yards over ocotillo hills connected by deep draws that were rarely seen or explored. The third draw held a camp consisting of several brush and cardboard huts, and outside one of them, two shopping carts.

Spying down, I saw no people and no movement.

After several minutes, believing that Tom Sawyer wasn't around, I scrambled down the hill and tipped over the carts and started picking apart what fell out.

The carts held random junk—blankets, shoes, tin cans, empty liquor bottles. There was some women's jewelry and men's watches. Other items looked to be what a homeowner would keep in the garage, like unopened cans of motor oil, a tennis racket, and workmen's tools.

The second time through I shook out a blanket and a knife fell out.

It had an eight-inch blade with a serrated edge and a brown wood-laminate handle with three fasteners. The description fit exactly the one in the private investigator's report of the knife missing from Cristy Carlyle's apartment.

The moment became isolated and unreal. I lost myself in it. Every sound the world could make had stopped. Am I holding the knife that killed Cristy Carlyle?

Yes, I am. That was what I believed. That was what I knew.

The blood surged through my veins like a swollen river. All this time. Sam in his cell.

The world thinking he was a killer. The state trying to kill him.

"I'm getting you out of that hole, Sam. I love you and you're coming home."

The air gusted out of my lungs and I pitched forward onto the ground. The pain took an instant to decide how bad it wanted to be, and it wanted to be very bad.

Waves of it started at the back of my neck and rushed out from there, anywhere pain could go, every pulse beat pushing it farther along the nerve trails.

The source of it was Tom Sawyer and the length of wood he was holding with two hands over his shoulder. He looked like a cleanup hitter who couldn't wait to hack at my four-seam fastball in the late innings, when it came in lazy and too high in the zone.

He posed for me that way, the parchment skin of his face stretched to battle tightness. He had a long beard of rainbow colors from a mixture of exposure to the sun and various items caught in its grubby tangles, like a Skittle or two.

His slit eyes gleamed with delight. His mistake was waiting. If he'd come at me immediately, when I was still on my knees and dazed, the outcome would've been preordained.

But he stalled to await reinforcement from Raincoat, who joined Sawyer at his side.

With his hands deep in the pockets of his long coat, Raincoat threw it wide open and grinned at me along a row of rotting teeth.

It was a way of saying, "Are you ready to do this?"

The fights I'd had were on baseball fields, and the only rule was stay on your feet. I thought of that as the adrenaline surged, and I spread my hands back at Raincoat.

"Yeah, I'm ready."

CHAPTER THIRTY

awyer charged. He was so wound up that he back-footed the swing, making it easy to duck underneath it. He let go of the wood with his top hand on the follow-through.

Some of baseball's best hitters released their top hand.

It was an effective technique for staying back on a pitch, but it didn't work in wash fighting.

I had an open shot at his ribs and took it. He groaned and bent sideways.

His long backswing brought the bat all the way around his body. I jerked it out of his hand and used it to whack him in the middle of the back.

It was no checked swing. I'd barreled him up good, and he collapsed.

Raincoat jumped in and wrapped his arms around me from behind, knocking the bat loose. He was stronger than he should've been on a diet of leaves and discarded apple cores.

Meth will do that.

He smelled like a bowling alley on raffle night.

We danced a little and it was an intimate business with his cheek pinned to mine, his hot spit running down my neck and his mouth producing sounds that alternated between grunting exertion and gleeful laughter.

I tried to shake him off, twisting violently back and forth and up and down. Raincoat had a lot of leg, two as I recall, and they came off the ground and helicoptered behind me.

But he held on, squealing like I was a ride at Disneyland.

A giant saguaro stood nearby. I swung his legs into the sharp spines. He squealed in pain. I twisted him away and did it again, and although he didn't let go, his resolve weakened enough that I was able to free my hands.

Reaching back to grip his coat at both shoulders, I bent forward and flipped him over my head. He landed with his butt flat on the ground, his legs split around the cactus, his body stuck with needles from chest to groin.

Seriously perforated, he emitted a guttural scream.

Sawyer had grabbed the knife and was running away. I left Raincoat to his misery and chased Sawyer up the hill behind the camp. I still had my pitcher's legs and was faster by a lot.

I leaped onto his back and forced him to the ground. The knife skipped away.

He was dazed. I got to the knife first and he bolted over the hill out of sight.

After searching for so long, I finally had the murder weapon in my hand.

I walked back to the camp, where Wanda Dietz and two patrol cops had just arrived. They had Raincoat in handcuffs. Between bouts of suppressed laughter, they were explaining that it wasn't their job to remove cactus needles from his private parts.

"I'm stuck! I'm stuck!" Raincoat squirmed in the dirt like a wounded toad.

One of the cops said, "I'm sure Mr. Johnson will be just fine."

I handed Dietz the knife.

"I found this in Sawyer's shopping cart. It's the knife that killed Cristy Carlyle."

Dietz smiled, if you could call it that. Her lips moved just enough to reveal a chipped front tooth, but the resemblance to a smile ended there.

"You're a psychic, Stark. Wish I had that power. The murder weapon, eh?"

"Do your duty and check this for blood. See that gunk in the grooves along the handle?"

"If Sawyer did this, don't you think he cleaned the knife?"

"People don't realize how hard it is to clean everything out of those grooves."

Dietz held it by two gloved fingers and drew the handle up to her eyes to inspect it. "Might be blood, might not. Could be dirt, rust, whatever."

"It'll be Carlyle's blood, and if we get lucky, Sawyer's, too. That attack was as violent as it gets and there was an unidentified blood type at the scene. I'm betting he cut himself and left his signature."

"I'm aware of what we found at the scene."

"You know I'm right, Dietz. Why else would you come down here?"

"I'm investigating the assault of Elliott Duran."

"Homicide doesn't do assaults. I'm glad you're finally on this. You need to test that knife for DNA and for prints as soon as you can."

"If we get a good set of Sawyer's prints and he's in the database, we'll get an ID quick. As for DNA, don't get your hopes up. But we'll do appropriate testing and live by the results."

"That's all I'm asking. Thanks."

"I don't want your thanks." Dietz's face turned to granite. "Let me make this clear, Stark. Don't tell me to do my duty. Don't ever say that to me again."

She sputtered in anger and said nothing more. She put the knife in an evidence bag, radioed for backup to help find Tom Sawyer, and ordered an ambulance for two injured men.

Turned out, what I'd thought was Raincoat's spit on my neck and shoulder was blood. Mine. He'd used a small knife to cut me, and the adrenaline was pumping so hard I didn't feel the pain at first.

CHAPTER THIRTY-ONE

The ER doc at St. Luke's said the wound wasn't as bad as the blood made it seem and should heal well. She was working the needle in and out of my skin when Roxy called for news on Sawyer.

I told her about finding the murder weapon, and she asked if I trusted Dietz to play it straight. "I don't have a choice. But she knows I'm watching."

"If you get Sam out of that place, you're going to hear me scream all over the great state of Arizona. Honest to God."

I said nothing about the cut and the stitches. If I'd told her about Raincoat's attack, she would've gotten excited and made it a thing, and I had enough "things" going on already.

The ER was making the usual ER noises.

"Sounds like you're at the bus station," Roxy said. "What's that beeping?"

"You know how noisy Phoenix is. Could be a truck backing up."

"I'll let you go. I don't want you to get run over."

Twenty-seven stitches. Wound shaped like Florida.

The doc gave me a blue scrub shirt to replace my bloody shirt. I wore it to Constant Lexus in Scottsdale. Jackie Moreno's stepmother, Valentine Constantine, wasn't available, and waiting in a luxury showroom wearing scrubs and bloodstained jeans only brought weird stares.

I jotted a note to My Pal Val, telling her it was urgent that we talk, and left it with the receptionist.

Next morning, I drove Opal to the airport for her predawn flight to New York. She'd never been on a plane and was flying first class. She wore sandals and no socks and a white pullover sweatshirt with a black peace sign on the front.

Her red velour sleep pants had a roaring grizzly bear on them.

Her hair was piled up in a messy bun held together with a pencil and a rubber band. She had earbuds in, and even then, I could hear the hypnotic, pounding music.

The voice belonged to the rapper 2 Chainz.

"Scared?" I asked across the front seat.

She pulled the left earbud out. "Only to death."

"The Gelmans will look after you. Follow their lead. Where are you staying?"

"At their house in West...ah, West. Some West place, I forget."

"Westchester?"

"That's it."

I tried to picture Opal Sanchez in a five-million-dollar stately white colonial with black shutters. So many rooms loaded with pocket-sized baubles.

All I could think of was all the things she could steal.

"Do yourself a favor and keep your hands to yourself."

"Told you, Mr. Whip, I don't do that anymore."

"The Tucson cops have warrants out for you. We need to take care of that."

She made a motorboat sound with her lips. "The fry-bread inspector. They don't know how to find us O'odhams. We're like spirits running through the bushes. Marco! Over here, paleface! Polo!" She giggled.

"It's not just TPD. The Rez cops are looking for you, too."

"Whatever."

"No whatever. It's important."

She flapped her lips again and put her earbuds back in.

When I pulled up to the terminal, the Gelmans were waiting on the sidewalk. They hugged her and took her bags. Before disappearing through the doors, Opal looked back at me and gave an uncertain wave.

After the automatic doors closed, I sat there staring at them, thinking she might change her mind and come running out. I watched until a cop gave me the thumb.

As I drove away, my phone buzzed with a text: "Love you, Mr. Whip!"

The cold darkness right before the morning sun always made me feel empty, and that didn't help. I'm a simple guy with no real ties to anything or anybody except Sam and Roxy.

That was the idea after Mexico. That was the point of the Airstream. Hook it up and go. Double Wide was a place to park. The scorpions were a bonus.

I didn't count on so many complications. Didn't count on an Indian runaway with a trailer loaded with stolen property.

Kino Boulevard was nearly empty under the breaking sky when I said to the windshield, "Keep making plans, Prospero. One of these days they'll work out the way you thought."

For the remainder of the day, Opal didn't send any more texts. I know because I kept checking. I helped Charlie with his chores and went inside and read more Chester Himes, and around 10:00 p.m., Sister Joseph Philomena called.

"I have a confession to make, Mr. Stark." Her voice trembled. "But first, I want you to know I don't normally behave in such a deplorable manner."

"I'm listening."

"I'm sorry I lied. About Bella. I can't keep her secret any longer. Can you come here?"

"I'll get in the car right now."

"My throat is sore, I've been praying about this so much. I can't tell you."

"Give me half an hour."

"Wait, I need to tell you something. I just had a phone call from a police detective asking about Bella. I didn't like him one bit. He's on his way here now."

I was already pulling my shoes on. "It's almost ten o'clock."

"Just so. I said this is impossible. I'm in my robe and can't receive a guest, but he insisted. He made me extremely uncomfortable."

I asked Sister Philomena to give me the detective's name and wait by the phone. I called Roxy and asked if John Weston was a legitimate TPD homicide detective. Without having to check, she knew the name was phony, and I called Sister Philomena back.

"Weston's not a cop," I said. "You need to get dressed and leave there."

"Leave? Where would I go?"

"There's a Starbucks around the corner."

"I don't drink caffeine. But I do treat myself to a decaf Starbucks three times a year."

"Make it four. You have to leave there." I stuck the Glock under my belt.

"Now you have me really frightened." Pause. "Okay, I'll get dressed. I could put my habit back on."

"It stands out too much."

"Of course. Well, I have my casual clothes. A parishioner donated a perfectly good pair of running shoes. They're teal."

"Sister Philomena, you have to get out of there."

"Please, call me Sister Phil. Everyone does."

"Are you listening to me? You need to go right now."

"I have to wear *something*. Should I go to Starbucks in my bloomers, Mr. Stark?"

"My friend is Roxanne Santa Cruz. I'll tell her to watch for somebody in teal shoes not wearing bloomers."

CHAPTER THIRTY-TWO

I drove like a madman over the mountain. On the sharp turns, my shoulder hugged the door, and on the downslopes my stomach did the roller-coaster swoon.

I wondered if I should've told Sister Phil that the man headed to her apartment might be Bella's killer. I stayed quiet to keep her from panicking, a judgment call, and maybe the wrong one. I had experience with those.

My plan was to go to Sister's apartment first to make sure she'd gotten out of there safely, and maybe lay eyes on the midnight caller posing as a homicide detective.

What I'd do then depended, on circumstance, and mostly luck.

On the way I called Roxy and told her to get to the Starbucks right away.

"You'll be meeting a nun," I said. "I'll be there as soon as I can."

"I'm not in the mood, Prospero. Is this some kind of joke? A nun?"

"Her name is Sister Joseph Philomena. She doesn't drink caffeine."

"They pulled on my ears at Catholic school. I think that's why they stick out."

"It's not their fault you blew on the trumpet too hard."

"Ha, ha. I've had revenge fantasies since fifth grade. I can't be responsible for what I might do."

"She'll be wearing teal running shoes. She's scared."

"So am I."

St. Anthony's front parking lot was empty and well lit. I parked under the lights close to Wilmot Road and trotted behind the church to the five casitas.

I came at them from the less traveled side, where the parking lot ended and the only thing connecting front to back was a patch of dirt that curled around. The only light came from widely spaced light poles and orange bulbs glowing over the apartment doors.

But I could see well enough.

The tall saguaros standing guard along the casita sidewalk had all their arms in the air, a demand of nature, not a skulking gunman. I saw no one and no sign of trouble until I noticed that four of the apartments had their overhead door lights on.

Only Sister Phil's light was off.

Coming closer, I saw her door ajar. Someone had kicked it in, leaving a sliver of busted wood jutting out from the jamb.

That brought to three my total of open doors in this case.

People gloom over what happens behind closed doors, but the open ones are much worse.

The apartment was dark. I toed the door all the way open, calling Sister Phil's name. Silence. I reached to my right and flipped on the overhead light.

What had been a perfectly kept apartment looked like the scene of a powerful explosion. The couch and chairs were tipped over, along with the cocktail table to my left. The kitchen floor beyond that was covered in assorted debris.

It smelled like the trash had been emptied.

I stepped inside and felt the crunch of glass underfoot from a shattered lamp.

"Sister?" I called. "Are you here?"

There was a noise behind me. The overhead light went out. Turning, I saw a figure in the doorway wearing black clothes and a gorilla mask. His hulking shadow filled the space. His arms looped wide off his shoulders and his hands were curled like claws.

That was all I could make out against the dim backlight.

Some big men can really move, and this one leaped like a cat to reach me before I could get to the Glock under my shirt. He bear-hugged me and turned me into a projectile. I seemed to be in the air a long time, as long as it took to reach the nearest wall, some ten feet away.

The wall had a quality I'd describe as hard, and likely to induce pain when the human noggin contacts it at high speed.

Plaster chips flew like snow, and lightning flashed inside my skull.

Somehow, I stayed upright, back to the wall and pain whipping through my body. The gorilla stalked closer and grabbed for my neck. I got my arms inside his hands, pushed them away, and kicked him in the groin with everything I had.

His body jackknifed, and he growled.

Bent over with his hands between his legs, he made a nice target. I wound up and hit him with a left uppercut that caught him squarely under the chin.

He lurched back and had enough steel to straighten right up again, seeming to decide whether he wanted more. Out on the casita walkway came the sound of voices, and without a word, he spun around and staggered out the door.

I listened to his heavy steps pounding away and stuck my head out. Down the walkway, two nuns were peering back over their shoulders, curious about the disturbance.

"Everything's fine, Sisters," I said. "A misunderstanding. Have a good night."

"Good evening to you as well," one of them said, and I shut the broken door as far as it would go.

My head throbbed off my shoulders, but I could still think.

I'd interrupted the gorilla as he tossed Sister Phil's apartment, likely hunting for Sterling's phone. The killers couldn't find it at Ash's house or at Bella's, learned of Bella's close relationship with Sister Phil, and now they were widening their search.

The living room and kitchen had already been tossed, so I walked down the short hall, which had a bathroom on one side and the bedroom on the other.

The bathroom was tiny. Nothing in the mirror cabinet or under the sink. I lifted the toilet tank lid, peered inside, and felt behind it, thinking of Michael Corleone finding the planted gun in *The Godfather*.

The bedroom was small and immaculate. It had a twin bed with waist-high bookshelves on either side, a dresser, a hard chair, and a closet. I looked under the bed and lifted the mattress and squeezed the pillows.

There was a large Bible on the nightstand. I fanned the pages and put it down.

In the closet I squeezed the clothes together, feeling for something hard, and fished through the dresser drawers. I caught a faint smell, maybe baby powder.

It felt entirely wrong to be going through Sister Phil's intimates.

The milestones kept falling.

I knelt in front of the bookcase left of the bed and pulled the books out one at a time, flipping through the pages and tossing them away. They were all hardbacks.

She liked Jane Austen and C. S. Lewis and anything by the Trappist monk Thomas Merton. She liked *The Confessions of St. Augustine*. I imagined her lying in bed at night plumbing the depths of the soul with Augustine.

Oh, oh. The next shelf held a full complement of steamy Danielle Steel novels.

From deep spiritual journey to edible underwear.

Another milestone down, and nobody could hang that one on me.

I cleared those four shelves and walked around to the bookcase on the other side and started again. The top three shelves yielded nothing. Halfway through the bottom shelf, I noticed that some of the volumes stood slightly higher on the shelf than others.

Feeling my breath quicken, I pulled those books out and there it was. Sister Philomena had placed Sterling's iPhone lengthwise on the shelf and lined books on top of it.

I pocketed it and drove around the corner to the Starbucks.

Through the window, I saw Sister Phil sitting at a table wearing a black cloche hat with a big red bow over the ear and a denim biker jacket with a marijuana leaf on the chest.

The words *Chemically Enhanced* curled in white script over the top and bottom of the leaf. I'd seen Roxy wearing both items at the Tucson Jazz Festival.

As I neared the table, the waitress brought two double espressos. Sister Phil was looking my way when Roxy snatched the one marked *D*, leaving the caffeinated one for Sister.

She peeled off the lid and closed her eyes to sniff the steam blast. "This puts me off schedule on my Starbucks trips. And it's almost midnight to boot." She hunched her shoulders. "I feel naughty."

In her best cocktail lounge voice, Roxy said, "You are naughty. Drink up."

I leaned close to Roxy and whispered, "You're a terrible person, you know that."

"No matter what happens for the rest of my life, I'll have something to smile about."

"Right now, we need a safe place to crack this thing open," I said, and pulled the phone slightly out of my pocket to let Roxy see it.

"Very cool. Very cool. My place is closer."

"Let's go."

Sister Phil used the backs of her legs to push her chair away from the table and bent down to sip her espresso. She made a loud slurping noise and wiggled in delight.

"Oooh, that tastes so good."

She pulled black sunglasses from her jacket pocket. They had bright white pearls circling the frame, and enormous lenses that looked like kibitzing black moons.

With the flapper hat, the dope jacket, and the movie star shades, she looked like the perfect Danielle Steel character.

CHAPTER THIRTY-THREE

She rode in the Bronco with me as we followed Roxy's tail-lights west on Broadway Boulevard toward downtown. There was a riot going on inside my head from my unticketed trip across Sister's living room.

Or maybe it was from Tom Sawyer's home-run swing.

I used to think pitching on three days' rest made for hard living.

"I have so much to tell you, Whip," Sister Phil said. "First, I have to say how sorry I am for lying to you."

"You already did. Start at the beginning."

She sat quietly for a moment as the Bronco rolled along.

"Bella called me in a panic the night before she was killed. She wanted me to come right over and I did. She looked terrible. Stricken, really. At first, I thought it was about money. Mr. Sterling promised to give Bella a significant piece of his fortune."

"She knew it was stolen money."

"Don't misunderstand, the money wasn't for Bella. She was planning to donate it to the church, to benefit our ministries. She fought her conscience over it for months before deciding to take it. It'd do so much good. But Bella wasn't upset about the money."

Sister Phil stopped as if unsure whether to continue. She dropped her voice. "It was something else."

"Ash told her his secret," I said.

"This is so difficult for me. I'm not in the habit of breaking promises."

"The murders of Paul and Donna Morton. Ash Sterling was there, right?"

"You knew?"

"Roxy's the reporter Ash was meeting with. He told her he was ready to talk."

"Bella was devastated, truly. What a terrible shock."

Nearing 1:00 a.m. and the traffic was intermittent. I checked my mirrors and looked around for a car driven by a gorilla.

Sister Phil said, "Bella knew for a long time he was meeting with a reporter and thought the story was about his life, his wartime experiences, how he made his money as a burglar. But that day he told her it was really about the two killings. Up in the Foothills."

Her voice cracked. She closed her eyes tight at the horror of it. "This whole thing."

Sister Phil composed herself and continued.

"You're right, Whip. Mr. Sterling's group, I guess they called themselves the Champagne Cowboys, were there when it happened. He promised Bella he didn't do it and neither did his men, and he wanted her to know that before she heard anything about it on the news. Mr. Sterling felt such guilt and wanted to clear his conscience before he died."

"Bella must've been shocked."

"She believed Ash that he and his men didn't do it, but just the same, think of it, the man she loved was at the scene of two … murders." The word barely escaped her lips. "It was simply too much. Bella left Mr. Sterling's house and called me immediately. She was never going to see him again and made me promise not to tell anyone they'd been involved."

"She was vulnerable legally," I said.

"She was aware of that, of course. That's why she didn't want police involved." Sister Phil exhaled in relief. "It feels so good to tell someone. Father Bob ordered us not to talk to anyone. He has his own concerns and they have nothing to do with the truth."

"Bad publicity hurts donations."

"And here I am going along. Isn't that what we do in the church now? Keep secrets?" She made a disgusted sound. "But if I spoke up and lost my position, what would happen to my children? Who would teach them?"

I drove through the glow of streetlights and caught the red light at Tucson Boulevard.

A white van rolled to a stop alongside. It had tinted windows, so I couldn't see the driver. I checked the rearview to see if anyone was behind me in case I had to back away and pull a getaway move. When the light flipped, I waited for the van to pull ahead before hitting the accelerator.

The downtown buildings loomed in the windshield.

Sterling's phone was in my pocket. Sister Phil hadn't mentioned it. She'd lied to me once, and I wanted to see if she would again.

"If you might lose your job," I said, "why're you're talking to me?"

"I needed to tell someone, and I trust you, Mr. Stark."

"Not enough to tell me everything."

She gave me a suspicious look. Her eyes were nervous in the half darkness. "No," she said in a tiny voice. "I haven't told you everything."

I waited. She waited. The sign for the Hotel Congress, a downtown landmark, stood against the sky just ahead. The Congress is Tucson's hipster palace. The chronically alienated gather there to compare piercings.

"I couldn't decide whether to give it to you or not," Sister Phil said. "I thought seriously of burning it." She stared out the window at the passing night. "No, I have to do this. If I can help resolve these awful crimes, I must do my part. Drive back to my apartment."

I pulled the phone out of my pocket and held it up. "Is this what you're talking about?"

"You found Mr. Sterling's phone?"

I told her of my encounter with the gorilla.

"There's a hole in my living room wall?"

"In the shape of my body," I said. "I can recommend a good drywall man."

"Goodness me, I hope you're all right."

"I could use some ice for the Titleist on my head."

Sister Phil moaned. "Am I doing the right thing?" She flopped her head back against the rest. "I've broken my promise to Bella, and now I'm handing over this phone. What if there are intimate things on it?"

Her voice dropped to a whisper. "Photographs of them … together. I'd hate to see Bella's reputation tarnished."

"We're dealing with multiple murders, including your dear friend. Things have changed." By that I meant that Bella was dead, but I didn't say it.

"I wasn't being dishonest again," she said. "I think I just … I needed time. I did plan to give the phone to you all along. You believe me, don't you?"

Sister Phil wore guilt like a winter coat. I let the question die.

"She gave you the phone the same night, right?"

"Oh, my word, she couldn't wait to hand it off. She wanted it out of her house. 'Take it, take it,' she kept saying. She didn't even want to touch it."

"I'm going to need Sterling's password."

"Bella had it, I'm sure." She held her palm up like a traffic cop. "But I didn't want to know it. Certain things I don't need to see."

"Whatever's on it's going to tell us the story."

"If I knew, I'd tell you. Mr. Sterling handed it to Bella and said, 'If anything happens to me.' That was it. Next morning, bless her heart, she was gone."

Sister Phil looked miserable in the seat beside me as I looped around the Hotel Congress and turned onto Fourth Avenue to Roxy's house.

CHAPTER THIRTY-FOUR

Roxy lived in a beautifully refurbished Sonoran adobe, white, boxy in shape, with a flat roof and an open porch along its entire length. The front door was sky blue. It had a peep window, and below that a knocker in the shape of a bull's head, complete with curling horns.

The grids in the small window to the left of the door were the same blue. To the right of the door was a large picture window set four inches into the thick adobe wall.

As soon as we stepped inside, Roxy fetched her shotgun from behind the front door. The living room was to the right and it had a dining area attached, the kitchen to the left of that.

The place was a mess. There were two empty wine bottles on the coffee table and clothes tossed over the backs of chairs.

Sister Phil frowned at the disarray and put her nose in the air. "What's that smell?"

"Weed. Why don't you take a seat." Roxy drew the blinds at the big window and laid the shotgun across the dining room table.

"May I ask what that is?" Sister Phil said.

"Gun."

"What I mean to say is, I hope it won't be necessary."

"If anybody followed us, you'll be glad I've got it."

"I've never seen one before. Well, television."

"It's a Beretta A400 shotgun," Roxy said. "My father gave it to me for my high school graduation. We go hunting together.

Rodrigo Santa Cruz is retired Pima County homicide. He was the best detective on the force."

"I'd be pleased to meet him." Sister Phil eyed the gun as if it might reach out and grab her. "Perhaps you could put it somewhere else."

Roxy ignored her. We were sitting around the dining room table. I held ice wrapped in a washcloth against the lump on my head.

"Let's talk passwords," Roxy said. "We've got six digits."

"Or a combination of numbers and letters." I had Sterling's iPhone in front of me. "After ten fails there's a data wipe."

"Passwords are always personal," Roxy said. "What do we know about him?"

My online research had told me a lot.

Sterling's hometown paper had called him a Christmas baby, and I counted back to 1974. The paper also gave me the date of his graduation from Cal Berkeley and, later, the dates of his enlistment and his commissioning.

"Start at the bottom," Roxy said. "Try his birthday."

"Too easy."

"A lot of smart people use really dumb passwords."

"Sterling was a marine and loved it. Let's start there."

His enlistment date was December 20, 1995. I punched in 122095. It didn't work. My second try was his commissioning, on April 30, 2002.

Another fail.

Sterling grew up wanting to be a marine, and becoming a captain had to be his pinnacle moment. Family and friends present, uniform pressed and perfect, his first salute as a captain. I stuck with it for a third try, adding two numbers.

I punched in marine captain 2002—MCAP02.

The same message popped up: *Try Again.*

Frustrated, I pushed the phone away and thought it over.

After coming home from the wars, Sterling kept his name off the Internet. That was smart. It meant he was thinking hard about security, and he'd apply that to his phone, too.

His home, and the headquarters for his burglary business, was his mansion. He had the place built, and it had to have cost a fortune. He put a lot of himself in the design, in the artwork, in the big safe behind the pantry, and in his front door doors.

Those big turquoise doors and the initials *AS* stuck in my mind.

They had to be specially carved. Vanity doors.

Maybe he used *AS* in his password, too.

I remembered that Sergeant Major Burnside, the blogger, had called him "Cap," not "Captain." I grabbed the phone and typed in MCAPAS—for Marine Captain Ash Sterling.

Try Again.

"This isn't working," I said.

"Wait, you might have the right idea," Roxy said. "Try his initials with his PO box. Forty-one-twenty-seven. I saw his mail stacked up on the kitchen counter."

Roxy got up and stood behind me with her hands on my shoulders. She was excited. "Go ahead, I bet we've got it. Punch it in. AS4127."

I did and got another fail.

Sister Phil had been observing quietly. "That's five tries. Only five to go."

Roxy gave her a nasty look.

"In case you weren't counting," Sister Phil said, and shrugged at me as if she wasn't sure what she'd done wrong. "If it's all right, may I clean up around here? For some reason I'm feeling itchy all over tonight. It must be my nerves."

Roxy waved over her shoulder in assent.

Sister Phil went around picking up wine bottles and food wrappers. Roxy walked to the front door and spied out the peep window and absently moved the curtain back to look out. She walked back to the dining room table and stared down at the phone with her hands on her hips.

"The answers we need are on there," she said. "What else you got?"

I had the photo of the Cowboys in my shirt pocket. I pulled it out. There were no numbers or letters on the Humvee. The uniforms on Sterling, Ortega, and Strong displayed no visible insignias that might work, no numbers of significance.

But there was the date on the back, July 21, 2013, and the words "last mission."

If the Cowboys' last go was important enough to document with a photo, the date might be important enough to be Sterling's password.

But 072113 failed, too.

"Four tries left," Roxy said. "It feels like we're throwing darts at a wall."

"Blindfolded. Let's hold off until we get more information."

"I could use a drink."

Sister Phil had found cleaning supplies under the sink and was busy scrubbing the countertops and sink. "What about tonight?" she said. "Where will I sleep?"

"The gorilla's not going to stop looking for that phone," I said. "You're not going back to your place."

"I can't be on the lam. I have to teach Bible class."

Those were words I never thought I'd hear.

"Do you have anyplace you can stay?" I said. "Do you have family here?"

"I grew up in the Philippines. All my family is there."

"You'll stay with me at Double Wide. It'll be safer there."

She held a bottle of Windex in one hand and paper towels in the other. Her face was tired, lined like a road map.

"Goodness me," she said, and went back to scrubbing.

Roxy grabbed a bottle of Scotch, banged through the dishwasher to find a clean drinking glass, and poured it three-quarters full. For her, that was a taste. For me, it'd be a night in a conga line with a bruiser named Ike and three cocktail waitresses.

She poured a glass of milk, handed it to me, and motioned me out the back door.

CHAPTER THIRTY-FIVE

The porch looked out over a patch of grass to some hedges backed by a row of anemic trees. After that came a twenty-foot easement leading to elevated ground holding the Southern Pacific railroad tracks.

Roxy set up a folding chair for me. She plopped into the cushiony chair next to it.

I filled her in on everything Sister Phil had said about Bella and Ash Sterling. Roxy wanted to know if I thought Sterling had told the truth that he didn't kill the Mortons and neither had the other Champagne Cowboys.

"Don't think a dying man would lie," I said.

"That means somebody else was there and that somebody was the shooter."

"A fourth Cowboy."

"If Sterling was killed for what he knew, Ortega and Strong might be next."

"Not if we find them first."

"Let me see if I've got this," Roxy said. "Right now, we're looking for Titus Ortega and Vincent Strong because they're potential victims. Only we're not totally sure about that. If Sterling lied, we could be looking for the perps, and maybe there's another Champagne Cowboy out there and that one could be even more dangerous than the ones we know about."

"Kind of funny, isn't it?"

"I'll try not to wet myself laughing."

Knocking and banging noises came from inside the house.

"She's going to clean the place until it's unrecognizable," Roxy said. "That mess in there was all mine. What if I don't want it clean?"

"You can go back inside and throw things around if you like."

"Don't think I won't." She gave a wry laugh. The Scotch had changed her voice, put some thunder and lightning in it.

"I had a guy over for dinner one time and he's eating and looking bothered all to hell and he tells me, 'How about we clean the place? We could make it a project, just the two of us.' He was out the door before the pie."

"She won't be here long. I'll put her up in Opal's trailer."

"Sister Phil will love that. With all that stolen stuff in there, it'll be like living in the evidence room at the cop shop."

A train was coming. The sound began as barely a whisper in the boondocks of my consciousness. In seconds, it grew to a distant drumming traveling the night wires.

"I have an idea," Roxy said. "Drop Sister at Double Wide and come back and stay with me. Cashmere Miller can watch over her."

"After she cleans this place, right?"

"I don't normally keep house that way."

"You forget how many times I've been here."

"That's right, you're an eyewitness." She chuckled and stretched out, crossing her legs at the ankles. They were wonderful legs. Tight jeans can make for pleasing carnal inspection by inviting the power of the imagination. "It's much easier to use my Kohl's Cash to buy a new outfit than do a wash. But if you were living here, I'd keep things neat."

"This again." The night was lovely, and after the phone difficulties I wanted to enjoy it.

"You never gave me an answer," Roxy said.

"Yeah, I did. You just didn't like it."

"You've got tons of money left over from baseball and you live at Double Wide. You could be here. You could buy a nice place in the Foothills."

"I don't like arugula."

"You don't even know what it is."

"Sure, I do. It's a vacation island in the Caribbean."

"Well, look at you."

"Come take our cruise to arugula."

"You surprise me every day, Prospero. A man to be reckoned with." Roxy sipped her drink. "Really, I have all you need. A beautiful home in a good neighborhood close to everything, two bedrooms. One for us and one for my shoes."

The thumping of the oncoming train grew louder. "I've even got trains to make sure you don't get too much sleep."

"You should be used to them by now."

"I don't accommodate myself to things. I just complain." Roxy held up the Scotch and said, "But I do it with style," and took a long drink. Her voice came back wet and throaty. "You complain about Double Wide all the time."

"It's mine, I'm allowed."

"I can't believe I'm with a guy from a trailer park. That's true love, honestly."

"Town's too civilized for me."

"We've got plenty of crime if that helps."

"Guys walking around wearing ties. I don't need to see that."

"What's wrong with ties?"

"General managers and owners wear ties. Fuck them. Fuck crosswalks."

"Better than drug trails," Roxy said. "Don't you want a real home? Home-field advantage and all? A place that doesn't rock in the wind?"

"I liked being on the road." I finished my milk and stood the empty glass on the grass between my feet. "When it was time to leave, I'd shut the hotel door behind me and go. There was nothing but the next town and the one after that."

We sat quietly in the pleasant darkness. October nights sometimes got stubborn and held on to the last stabs of summer. But the cool of this one felt like authentic autumn.

"That's what's going on here," Roxy said. "You want an escape hatch."

"You've never been traded, called into the GM and he says, 'Hey, we're moving you.' Like I'm a sofa."

"I promise I won't trade you, okay?" Roxy said. "Boy, baseball ruined you for real life, didn't it?"

"Ever since I quit, I don't know where to put my feet. Don't know where I belong."

"Come on, you belong everywhere. You're famous, you're a rock star. Whip Stark, sign my hand. Whip Stark, take a picture. People go nuts."

"Some days I don't want to be him."

"You think you're the only one, *mi cielo*? Some days I want to hide from myself, but I've got mirrors and I happen to know that chick looking back at me. She's a handful."

Drawers opened and closed in the kitchen. Cabinets were arranged. Roxy rolled her eyes and took another sip.

"If you had a regular childhood, I'd get it," I said. "But Rod married, what, four times?"

"Five. Officially. That's not counting suspicious toothbrushes. I lie awake nights trying to remember their names."

"When's he back from Montana?"

"Soon, couple days. I can't wait. He's packing prime elk meat."

"I'd feel better if he was watching this place. That comment Jackie made about your license plate, I can't get it out of my head."

"I've been careful to keep my address off all official documents," Roxy said. "It'd be hard for anybody to find me here. But just to ease your mind, I called two TPD uniforms, friends of mine. They'll drive by the house on their shifts."

She patted my arm in a comforting gesture, and a new thought occurred.

"Meant to tell you," she said, "the original investigator in the Foothills case might be ready to talk. Rod's going to hit him up again when he gets back to town."

Another police siren wailed out in the street, and Roxy said, "See, we've got trouble, too. Shootings, robberies. Don't think we can't keep up."

We listened to the siren. It started out as a shrieking elephant and in time became a kitten stuck in a drainpipe. Then someone stopped up the pipe.

Roxy turned to me with a mischievous expression. "You know what'd be wild? How about we go into the bedroom and bend one while Sister Phil cleans in the next room."

I threw my head back and laughed.

"I'm serious," Roxy said. "Make a lot of noise, knock over lamps. What do you say?"

"I can't believe you're still stuck in grade school."

"The older I get, the bigger the memories. We've got a unique moment here, historic. I can't believe you'd let it go."

The train arrived. The trees along the tracks split the engine's headlight beam into fractured pieces of light that made ghosts of us as they flickered past.

The stampeding sound ended further talk.

When it was quiet again, Sister Phil stuck her head out the door. "We just ran out of Febreze."

"Yeah, fine, fine. I'll pick some up," Roxy said.

When Sister Phil stepped back inside, Roxy raised the Scotch to her lips and snickered as she spoke into the glass. "You're going to have a ball with that one."

CHAPTER THIRTY-SIX

Figuring it too risky to drive back to Sister Phil's apartment to pack her things, I drove her to Target and bought her new clothes and personal items. We landed at Double Wide after 3:00 a.m. She saw the shoplifted goods in Opal's trailer.

"What's all this?"

"Oh. Opal's involved in, ah, retail."

"How nice. Sales?"

"Not usually, no."

I pulled out clean linens and blankets and got her settled.

"It's a tradition around Double Wide for everybody to come by my place for coffee in the morning," I said. "You're cordially invited."

"I believe I've acquired a taste. I'd be happy to. Right now, I must call Father Bob and explain why I won't be around. This qualifies as a personal emergency, don't you think?"

She said good night and gave me a straight-armed, single-pump handshake like we'd just closed a layaway loan on a three-piece sectional.

Before dawn, I got up and wobbled out to the kitchen, pressed the button on the coffee maker, opened the Airstream door, and breathed in the clean desert air.

Behind the Tucson Mountains, the night gasped and faded, going from black to gray to a fiery red that disappeared quickly, replaced by a white light that contoured the shipwreck peaks.

Sister Phil came strolling down Main Street in her Target clothes, a floral print shirt and baggy tan slacks with the teal runners, her black hair matted down from a shower.

"You have such wonderful views," she said. "Isn't nature a gift?"

"It's not a good idea to be out here alone."

"I've got so much on my mind."

"Come inside, I'll pour you a cup."

She ducked down and slid behind the kitchen table and onto the bench seat that curved around the rounded back of the Airstream. She took in the tight surroundings.

"This is an interesting way to live," she said. "I'll bet it helps set priorities."

"If you know your heart, you know what to keep."

"You know your heart, Whip?"

"Thought I did when I moved here. I'm not so sure anymore."

She turned her head in interest. "What changed?"

"I figured I'd be alone with my dogs and the horizon and that sounded perfect. But different people kept showing up and all of them were worse off than me. Nothing like it for feeling like a superstar again."

"You look after them?"

"It's like a job. Not sure I wanted it and not even sure what it is."

"It pulls you out of yourself, taking care of others."

"If it's not the other way around. Anyway, I'm talking too much."

Bundle snuggled in beside Sister Phil on the bench, his head resting on her thigh. "I love Mr. Bundle here." She scratched his ear. "How'd you come up with that name?"

I explained about the smuggling trail that ran through the wash behind the Airstream, and the dozens of others that spiderwebbed the desert. Bundle had an uncanny ability to sniff out drug loads and, without a command from me, lift his leg on them.

"So much criminal activity in such a pristine place," she said. "I had no idea."

"I didn't either until I got here. Day and night, every drug you can name."

"You tolerate that?"

"They tolerate me, Sister Phil. This is how a country dies. I've got corn muffins."

I put two on a plate and popped them into the microwave.

My front door was open. There was a concert going on outside.

A cactus wren had nested in a woodpecker boot in the saguaro near my door. Bertie and I had become good pals. But when she got going with her morning songs, she sounded like a duck with bad sinuses and a tickertape cough.

The microwave beeped. I put the corn muffins on the table with butter and sat down.

"You had something on your mind?" I said.

She put a hand over her mouth to cover her chewing. "All night I couldn't stop thinking about Bella, how she could get involved with a buzzard like Mr. Sterling."

"Just remember, he was a hero before he was thief."

"He was a thief just the same. All the Champagne Cowboys were. There's no getting around that."

I got up and refilled her coffee cup and mine. "I know some veterans. They're all reborn after combat, and what comes out the other side, you never know."

"She talked about Mr. Sterling like he was a saint."

"You said it yourself, she loved him."

"The human heart plots its own path. I try to understand." Sister Phil tamped her hands down in a self-calming gesture. "That's my struggle. I mustn't judge. Bella believed in forgiveness, as do I, and that goes for Mr. Sterling as well."

Cashmere Miller and Charlie O'Shea walked in. Cash poured a cup of coffee and sat with us at the table, unshaven, wordless, sipping. Charlie got out the frying pan and made eggs and heated more corn muffins as he cooked in his snazzy Tommy Bahama shirt, knee-length Bermuda shorts, sandals, and white socks.

Breakfast was good and the conversation, too.

When they left, Sister Phil gave me a grin of understanding.

"You should meet Opal," I said. "She sits on my steps listening to the morning concert. She says when her dead grandmother talks to her, she speaks through Bertie's songs."

Sister Phil smiled, brightening her whole face. "You have quite the crew here."

"A regular police lineup."

"That was something I wanted to ask. Why don't you turn this matter over to the authorities? Give them the phone and let them handle it."

I didn't answer. Sister Phil sipped her coffee and waited. We sat in the stillness of the desert morning listening to Bertie sing.

"You're taking such risks here," she said. "Roxanne as well."

"She never walked away from a story in her life."

"Have you tried talking her out of it?"

"You met her."

She made a silly mouth. "That I did."

"She could be in danger," I said. "And I want to know what happened as much as she does. More so, I need to know."

Sister Phil sat with her hands folded on the table. She tapped her thumbs together.

"Go ahead," I said.

"It's just that, well, I hesitate to say anything. But I woke up thinking of forgiveness."

"I woke up thinking about a cigar."

"If I can't practice it myself," she said, "I'm a hypocrite for even bringing it up. But shouldn't we forgive whoever killed the Mortons, too? Forgiveness is sometimes all we have."

"Pretty word you got there."

She pulled back, sheepish. "I'm sorry, I'm overstepping."

"Hang on a minute."

I went to the bedroom and retrieved a cigar box filled with old photos. Inside was a picture of me in my Thunder uniform and Paul Morton in his three-piece courtroom straitjacket. We were sitting together and grinning like clowns on the dugout bench at Hi Corbett Field. I walked back to the kitchen and handed it to Sister Phil.

"Is that you? Look at that hair. Those big smiles." She pointed. "I take it this young man is Paul Morton?"

"Happy and clueless. We thought life would always be that easy."

Sadness filled Sister Phil's face. "It's unimaginable."

Seeing the image again sent a scalding anger creeping up my spine. I made my voice as tight as I could to keep my emotions from running away.

"They lived in Sabino Canyon, real nice house. They found Paul by the front door and Donna in the garage. Detectives figure she ran and that was as far as she got. Killer came up behind her. She had a bullet in her back and a second one in her temple after she'd gone down, they figure, the kill shot."

Sister Phil gazed absently at the bright sunlight framing the open door. Hammering sounds echoed. Charlie whistled as he did his chores.

"Cops think the Mortons walked in on a burglary," I said. "But there were ways out of that that didn't require executing two people. They didn't have to die. All Paul and Donna did was come home at the wrong time. That was their only crime."

"I shouldn't have said anything. I didn't realize you were so close."

"They left two kids behind."

"Don't tell me that." Sister Phil winced and closed her eyes.

My stomach turned to iron. My voice was a low, strangled sound.

"I can't let that go for a pretty word."

CHAPTER THIRTY-SEVEN

When Sister Phil left to say her devotions, I finished a third cup of coffee and cut myself off. A fourth and I'd be singing along with Bertie and nobody needed to hear that.

At 10:00 a.m., my phone buzzed with a text from Opal in New York:

"There's people everywhere here and nobody looks at you. When I worked cattle at my village, at least the animals looked at me."

I'd only asked Opal about her past once, and she'd clammed up, refused to answer any questions. I didn't pursue the matter, figuring it better to let the truth dribble out in its own time.

That was the first I'd heard she'd lived on a ranch.

"Have you been on the subway yet?" I wrote back. "A thousand eyes all blind."

"No way I'm going down there. Reptiles live in burrows!"

I let that one hang in the digital ether and got a freezer bag from the kitchen drawer. Overnight, I'd left Sterling's phone on my desk right next to my Glock. But I needed a place to stash it when I was going to be away.

The Airstream was too obvious and too easy to break into.

Cash agreed that leaving it with him wouldn't work either. "If they come here and something happens to me, they'll find it," he said.

We decided to stash it in one of the junked cars stacked up every which way behind Opal's trailer. I put the phone in the freezer bag and stuck it in the glove compartment of a window-less Ford Fiesta, tucked away between two rusted-out pickups.

After that I drove over the mountain to pick up my mail.

The post office trip was a weekly one at best. Finding that much mail in my box was a big thrill, but not as big as the thrill five minutes later of throwing it all away.

I was driving home when Detective Wanda Dietz called. She'd gotten a hit on the fingerprints on Tom Sawyer's knife.

His real name was Earl "Bumpy" Topp, and he'd been previously arrested for vagrancy and disturbing the peace. They hadn't found him yet, but Tempe police had issued a be-on-the-lookout bulletin.

"We'll follow the forensics from here, Stark. The next step is a DNA analysis of the material on the handle of the knife. If you're right and it's blood, we'll go from there, but it'll take several weeks."

"Put a rush on it."

"I did put a rush on it," she snapped. "I promise we'll have Bumpy Topp in custody before long and we'll see where it leads."

The remainder of the day brought no call back from Valentine Constantine in Scottsdale.

But I found her on the Internet.

A TV reporter out of Phoenix did a piece on her with footage of her home in Paradise Valley, a gorgeous place with the fountains of Versailles outside and gleaming gold fixtures inside. Her second husband, Dimitri, owned a string of car dealerships.

Val grew up in the Mexican Sierra Madre, where her father ran a hunting lodge for international guests who wanted to see some of the continent's wildest land, ride horses, and tromp through the mountains with rifles.

A newspaper story said the family had lost the lodge after Val's father died.

No further details were given. The piece included a quote from Val: "Before I was 13, I knew how to shoot, skin a deer, and talk to rich Americans."

Her skills obviously didn't include returning phone calls.

I decided to do with her a variation of what I'd done with Father Rinerson.

In a bedroom closet in Opal's trailer, I rummaged through a box of things that had belonged to my former catcher, Rolando Molina. I found his cowboy boots, a Western shirt, Wranglers, a rodeo belt, and a hat.

Rolando stood only five foot eight. The boots were his prize possession. He paid nine hundred dollars for them, hoping for a boost in the dating department, and swore they worked like gold in the pan.

He'd only worn them a few times. Before disappearing inside the rehab center in Malibu, the last time I'd see him, he handed them to me for safekeeping.

Red ostrich skin covered the foot portion from instep to pointed toe. The twelve-inch shaft was bright white and patterned in black diamonds.

In addition to being visible from outer space, they had high slant heels that made a scene-stealing drum roll as you clogged along, as if scene stealing hadn't already been accomplished.

The boots squeezed my feet and put a shimmy in my step.

I could never fit into Rolando's Wranglers or his shirt, so I wore my own. The shirt was gold and black with a snap-up front and snap pockets on the chest.

Rolando's belt had a buckle decorated with intricate Mexican silverwork that included a furiously bucking bronc. His hat was a wide-brimmed Tom Mix–model silver belly with a turquoise and horsehair hatband.

The crown was high enough to make it rain.

Sister Phil watched the whole operation, trying very hard not to laugh.

"Call me Bucky Meadows," I said.

Cash gave me a snarky look. "You look like a rich dipshit."

Sister Phil let loose with a loud turkey gobble.

"That's exactly what I was shooting for," I said.

CHAPTER THIRTY-EIGHT

Next day I drove to Constant Lexus in Scottsdale in my regular clothes and changed into my cowboy clothes in the parking lot. The last time I'd walked into that showroom I was wearing hospital scrubs and bloodstained pants.

This time I looked like the line-dancing champion of Maricopa County.

Valentine Constantine came right out to shake my hand, and we were off on a test drive in an eighty-five-thousand-dollar car.

"Our customers are ecstatic about this particular model, Mr. Meadows."

I was tooling along Scottsdale Road.

"Please, you must call me Bucky."

"Only if you call me Val."

She had the iron face of a woman who'd been stunning in youth, but age had come for her and she wasn't inclined to let it win. The concealer was too thick, the eye liner too black, and her eyebrows had been plucked to paint streaks.

She wore a low-cut V-neck blouse that showed burgeoning wrinkles between her breasts. Her dirty blond hair added a brassy touch, as did the perpetually pouty lips that some Scottsdale hero with a white coat and a medical license had fussed over, then accepted American Express.

"I hate it when my brand-new shoes get smudged," Val said in a thick Spanish accent.

She leaned down and fingered dirt off her shoes. They were cream colored and had red platform soles, an open toe, and a six-inch stiletto heel.

"I love, love, love shopping the Polanco." The Polanco was a high-end shopping district in Mexico City, the equivalent of Rodeo Drive in Beverly Hills. I knew about it from my time with the Pirates. "Enrique's Boutique. They have the best shoes in the entire world. Aren't they lovely, Bucky?"

"I'm speechless."

She waved her hand across the dashboard like a showroom model. "May I say, we're having trouble keeping the GS F sedan on the lot. The ride is as smooth as any you'll find in the luxury space."

"I don't think this ride's going to be so smooth."

The smile stayed plastered on. "Pardon me, Bucky?"

"I'm Prospero Stark. I'm here about Ash Sterling."

"You're not a client," she said coldly. "You misrepresented yourself."

"You sell cars for a living."

She sputtered and fumed beside me. "I insist you turn around immediately."

"I just have a few questions."

"You've taken this vehicle out under false pretenses."

There was nothing to argue with there.

"I'd hate to have to call the police," Val said.

"To report what, an unhappy customer?"

She made another unsuccessful plea and cursed in perfect English. I gave her time to fully appreciate that she was trapped in a car with a determined and possibly deranged Tom Mix look-alike and wasn't getting out until she talked.

She fogged the passenger window with her indignation.

The Lexus was the quietest car I'd ever driven. It was like being in a silent picture. Everybody outside was moving and talking, and none of them made a peep.

Two red lights later, slowly and reluctantly, Val started talking.

"I didn't call you back because I vowed to never again think about Ash Sterling and the Champagne Cowboys. After we split, I wanted that part of my life to be over. It's too painful, especially now."

"I'm sorry about Ash."

"Thank you. What is it you need exactly?"

I showed her the photo I'd found in Sterling's kitchen. As she stared, a reluctant smile crossed her lips. "There he is, all dressed up and ready to fight. Ash loved being a soldier. His men called him the warrior." She pronounced the last word with particular derision.

"Was that a nickname?"

"Warrior King. That's what most of them called him. It sounds medieval or something, but soldiers are different."

I thought of Sterling's password. What if it combined "Ash Sterling" and "King"—ASKING? Six letters, easy to remember. Like asking a question.

"How about the other two guys? Do you know them?" I wanted to confirm Sergeant Major Burnside's information.

"Of course I know them. Titus Ortega and Vincent Strong."

"I need to find them."

"I've had no contact with anybody from that part of my life since the divorce. The last time I saw Jackie was five years ago, when Dimitri and I got married. I heard she's in nursing school down in Tucson now. Remarkable what she's overcome."

"You're referring to her life with Ash?"

"Well, it started before that when her mother died. Jackie was ten and had to deal with Ash alone until I came along. Even when he was home, he never made time for her and it was hurtful. She got to where she didn't want anything to do with him or the Sterling name."

"Did she know Ash was a thief?"

"I came out and told her," Val said. "One night, Ash, Vincent, and Titus were dancing and celebrating on the balcony after making their biggest score, a house on Burro Peak."

"Sure, up in the Catalinas," I said. "Most photographed spot in the range."

"That's the one. It lights up when the setting sun hits it. Well, I asked Ash what was going on and he said, 'Remember this night, because we're going to be rich.'"

The lines around her mouth deepened and her voice became harsh. "Ash didn't want Jackie to know what he did, but I didn't care. By that time, I was already talking to a lawyer. My only hesitation was Jackie, leaving her with him."

"You loved her."

Val breathed heavily and remembered.

"Like my own, and I did the best I could for her," she said. "To get her away, I'd take her to my father's old hunting lodge in El Salto, a village near the Sierra in Mexico. Jackie loved it, loved the outdoors."

The sidewalks along Scottsdale Road bustled with folks in their business finest. But no one looked as groovy as Bucky Meadows.

"She's a wonderful girl, she really is," Val said. "Life handed her hardships and she overcame all of them. I think the world of her." She motioned in a gesture of conclusion. "Is that all, Mr. Stark? I'm going through a divorce and need to get back to work."

"You're divorcing and Dimitri keeps you on?"

"I outsell everybody at that place. Dimitri's no fool. Is it alright if I go make some money now?

"I want to know about Ash, the kind of man he was."

She sighed audibly at my persistence. "Ash was Ash. I don't know what to say. He lived in a fantasy world. After the wars, he couldn't find a place in our world, so he invented one with its own rules and values, and Vincent and Titus went along. Ash was their captain over there and at home, too."

"Tell me about Titus," I said.

"A real good guy, a jokester, always clowning, at least before he went to those stupid wars. Vincent was darker, a brooder, and he had drug issues."

"After coming home?"

"Even before. One minute he was there, and everything was okay, and the next he'd get really angry. He could explode. And he was a big man, six foot four. Everybody joked about his feet. He had size sixteen feet."

Val reached for the dashboard and switched on the air conditioning. She had a white circle on her ring finger. It looked like she'd removed her wedding ring for work.

Smart. I'm sure it didn't help sell cars to male clients.

I said, "Have you ever heard the names Paul and Donna Morton?"

"No. Should I?"

"They were murdered in their home in the Catalina Foothills in Tucson a year ago."

"What does that have to do with Ash?"

"The Champagne Cowboys were there."

She wrinkled her eyebrows at me in disbelief. "That can't be. You must have bad information. They didn't make money killing people."

"There was someone else there," I said. "Ever hear of a fourth Champagne Cowboy?"

"Never. What does that have to do with Ash's murder?"

"He was going to talk to a reporter about what happened that night. Titus and Vincent obviously know what happened, too."

"That doesn't sound good. Are you saying they're next?"

"If I'm right, the shooter's doing cleanup."

Val sighed . "Let's hope you're wrong. As big a jerk as Ash was, his death hasn't been easy for me, and there's been enough killing."

I asked again if she knew where I could find Titus Ortega and Vincent Strong. She repeated that she knew nothing of their whereabouts, nothing of a fourth Cowboy, and nothing of the murders of Paul and Donna Morton.

After a few more questions, which yielded nothing new, she asked me to drive her back to Constant Lexus, and I did.

CHAPTER THIRTY-NINE

Late morning. I drove to the Denny's on McDowell Road in Scottsdale and sat in a booth by the window to watch the traffic and eat a Grand Slam breakfast.

I'd forgotten about the Bucky Meadows outfit until the boots got my feet aching, and I yanked them off. They took up so much room under the table I couldn't stretch out my ducks, so I stood them on the seat beside me.

The waitress gave them the screwy eye.

"I've seen worse in here. More coffee?"

My phone rang. My newest ringtone was the theme from the western *The Magnificent Seven* with Yul Brynner, Steve McQueen, and Charles Bronson. Best movie music ever.

Incoming said it was Val. I answered.

"It's me again, Mr. Stark. I hope I'm not bothering you."

"Not at all."

"I lied to you earlier." She sounded uncertain and contrite. "Do you have a minute?"

"Absolutely."

"It's about Titus. I have heard from him. I had no idea about those murders in Tucson, and with Titus maybe being in danger, I had to speak up."

I sat up and shifted the phone to my other ear and opened my notebook. "I'm listening."

She drew a deep breath and exhaled, and out came a secret.

"Titus and I were involved, Mr. Stark, way back in another life. We started up again after he came home from Afghanistan this last time."

"Okay, where is he now?"

"That's the thing, I don't know," Val said. "We were meeting regularly, and he just vanished. He's in bad shape and I wanted to be there for him. He took up painting as a way to heal and was even using a different name."

"What was the name?"

"Manuel. He created a new identity for himself, a before-the-war-and-after kind of thing. All these men struggled to adjust in their own way."

Denny's was emptying out after the lunch rush. The traffic and the horns never stopped out on McDowell.

"Maybe you could find him," Val said.

"I need a place to start looking," I said. "All I have is that combat picture."

"It doesn't capture him, his eyes. They're the saddest eyes I've seen." She grew silent, as if lost in a distant thought. "He did talk about finding a gallery to take his work. He told me a name. It had Abbott in it, or Abel, I don't remember."

"I'll poke around."

"He's in my heart every day and I do hope he's okay."

The waitress brought more coffee. She waved two fellow waitresses over to check out my boots. Only one of them one had a pencil behind her ear.

I sat by the window thinking about Val Constantine, the hottest TV personality in the valley, known to everyone, talked about, dreamed about, invited to all the best white wine and cleavage parties to blink her laser eyes at men in open-neck shirts and gorgeous winter tans.

Was she telling the truth? I put it at no better than fifty-fifty.

She'd lived the role so long, pampered, shallow, obsessed with her sales numbers, that lying had to be part of the job description.

But judging by our phone chat, she was definitely in love with Titus Ortega.

Sitting in my booth at Denny's, I looked up local art galleries with Abbott or Abel in the name. The lady at Abbott's Fine Prints knew nothing, and neither did Tyson Abbott's Creations.

I looked for galleries that might be owned by individuals named Abbott or Abel.

That got me to the former New York portrait painter Marcy Abel, who used her Radcliffe voice to inform me that she'd never heard of Titus Ortega, and down went the phone.

Like she knew I was calling from Denny's.

The clock ticked into the afternoon. I stayed put at the table. Office hours. I made nine more calls, crossing out each fail in my notebook, and expanding the possibilities to Babbitt, Gable, and whatever else might be remotely close.

Opal texted me: "New York has bigger canyons than we do. Ate a scone. Yuck!"

I told her I'd just finished a Grand Slam and she responded, "So jealous!"

As I was getting ready to quit, I found the number for a gallery called Kokopelli Station, run by Abigail Whitcomb, who went by Abbey.

She was pleasant and not put out by having to pick up the phone and say hello, especially to a former baseball star. She recognized my name. Her husband had season tickets to the Arizona Diamondbacks, and that started a conversation about what I was doing now, did I enjoy post-baseball life, all the usual questions.

With that done, Whitcomb said, yes, she handled Titus's work under the name Manuel, and said I was the second person to contact her about him.

She didn't get the name of the first caller and could only tell me it was a man.

"It doesn't surprise me he's generating interest," she said. "Manuel sells very well. He's got pieces ready to be picked up and I've been meaning to drive up to the Apache Reservation to get them, but I've been so busy."

"Did you tell that to this man who called?"

"He said he was an old soldier friend and I thought Titus could use one." She hesitated. "Did I do something wrong?"

"Forget it. Titus lives on Apache?"

"With an Apache wife, yes, and he never leaves. We have an arrangement where I drive up there to pick up his work and he says thank you for coming."

"Give me directions and I'll pick them up for you."

"Oh, I couldn't ask you to do that, Whip. It's such a long drive."

Without explaining why, I said it was important that I talk to Titus.

"To be honest, I am desperate," she said. "Are you familiar with a place called Cibecue?"

It was a village deep in Apache country. I asked if Titus had a phone.

"He won't give out his number. You need to call his wife's family. I've found it easier to drive there than to go through the rigmarole of leaving a message with his in-laws and they send a runner to his house. It's a very tribal form of communication. But I suppose it's worth a try."

"You say he's got some pieces ready. Do you know how many?"

"I imagine quite a number by now. He works quickly on simple representations of bears, coyotes, pasture scenes of cows staring at nothing, that sort of thing."

"You don't sound thrilled."

"With his work? Gosh, no." She gave a high-pitched laugh. "But he's so bad he's become quite popular."

"Art versus commerce."

"The eternal conundrum in my line," Abigail Whitcomb said. "People enjoy Manuel personally, and I do as well. He's a sweet man, and I hate to say this, it sounds so patronizing, but all the sweeter for his suffering. I trust you'll tread lightly. He survives hour by hour."

She texted me directions and the phone number for Titus's in-laws. I called and the woman who answered wouldn't give her name and was all mumbles and half words in that clipped dialect Rez Indians use when they know they're talking to an outsider.

Even though it was probably pointless, I left a message.

It was coming up on 2:00 p.m.

From where I sat, the drive was three hours, which left enough time to get there before dark. I went out to the Bronco, changed into my regular clothes, and started out.

CHAPTER FORTY

It took ninety minutes to get clear of the rumble and smoke of Phoenix and onto State Highway 60 to the old copper-mining town of Globe. I gassed up, bought pink lemonade and a Subway foot-long, and jumped onto Highway 77 into the mountains of east-central Arizona.

Soon, the road crossed the boundary of the San Carlos Apache Reservation and onto the contiguous White Mountain Apache Reservation.

Except for lone houses on distant hills, the trip was empty of anything resembling development. Mainly it was twisting highway and the whir of the occasional passing car as the Bronco groaned and climbed.

The air became chilly and the wind whistled as I climbed deeper onto the Rez and blew right past the turnoff. I had to pull a U-turn on the highway, and when I straightened out, a tribal cop was behind me.

He was so close I could see his face in the rearview.

I turned onto the Cibecue road expecting him to follow. But he parked sideways across the lanes to give me a keen looking over before driving away.

I'd never been to Cibecue, but I'd seen enough reservation towns to know what I'd find.

There'd be lots of dust and blowing trash and hound dogs with too many ribs and American flags flying and bicycles lying on their sides and basketball hoops with no nets.

In all of Arizona's reservation land, there wasn't a single basketball hoop with the net still in place. It was federal law.

There would be no business to speak of, except for an overpriced market and gas station, and a commercial center that opened with high hopes and was now mostly shuttered. The houses would be small wood-frame units with pitched roofs and smoke trailing from the roof pipes.

The school would look fine and cared for in sterile government white, and that bustle of activity just ahead is the health clinic, busy as always, so take a seat and the third replacement doctor we've had this year—all younger than thirty and idealistic on the first day, broken on the last—will see you when he's ready.

Cibecue had all that, and watching over the town towered a massive red cliff, the inner sanctum of which held a secret waterfall that seemed impossible on such a brittle land.

But higher up beyond the ridge stood the piñon and juniper trees, and back of these, higher still beyond the massive Mogollon Rim, the reservation turned green under tall mountaintop pines.

Whitcomb said Titus Ortega lived on a dirt trail north of Cibecue's main road, right underneath the ridge. The house had a 1962 Ford pickup beside it. I had no knowledge of Ford pickups, but the one I spotted looked old enough to qualify.

I could hear the TV blaring inside as I approached the house. My knock drew no response, and I turned the knob and pushed the door open.

The living room was a mess and smelled of food left out. Against the wall to my left, right inside the door, were a dozen or so paintings partly covered in brown paper. Beyond these on the same wall was a big TV that sent out flickering images and yammering voices.

"Titus Ortega."

No answer. I called his name again.

"Abigail told me how to find you. Titus, are you home?"

I heard nothing in response and waited. The wind blew hard and the TV blared, but there were no other signs of life. I looked around to see if there was a neighbor to ask about Titus's whereabouts, but the nearest house was too far away.

On my cell, I called his in-laws and got the same machine message.

I explained that Abigail Whitcomb wanted me to pick up some of Titus's paintings and that I was standing outside the house. I talked for a long time, hoping someone would pick up.

After five minutes of waiting, I decided there was no point driving all that way for nothing and I might as well take the paintings. I backed the Bronco up to the open door, dropped the tailgate, and had them loaded onto a blanket in back when I heard a man's voice behind me.

"Abigail Whitcomb?"

I turned and saw Titus standing in the doorway. His face bore no readable expression, but the pistol in his right hand said a lot.

CHAPTER FORTY-ONE

Titus was short and square with a powerful build, a hawk nose, and an unshaven face. He had black hair cut in a high-and-tight that he'd let go, leaving the sides looking like a donkey's back in summer and the top a plate of spinach.

He wore a black T-shirt and stood in a tense, forward-leaning stance. The same sword tattoo from the photo took up most of his right arm.

"Yes, Abigail at Kokopelli. She needs more of your work. I told her I'd pick up what you have. Hope you don't mind."

"Abigail comes herself. Nobody comes to my house. Only Abigail comes to my house." His voice sounded robotic, like a recording.

"She was busy." I swung my arm wide. "You're living way off the track up here."

"Rainbow trout."

"Sorry?" I smiled, hoping to coax an explanation, but he only stared. I banged the tailgate shut and stepped toward the door. "Can I come inside? I need to talk to you about something."

"Stay where you are. I can hear you."

"I want to talk about Captain Ash Sterling."

"No better marine."

Ortega's voice didn't change. His eyes didn't change. He hadn't heard.

"Sorry to tell you, but the captain's gone," I said. "A sniper took him out from the canyon behind his house."

Titus's jaw rose slightly, but that was his only reaction. Otherwise, he stood perfectly still, his blank face barely registering a click above a dead man's. I explained about Sterling's phone and asked if he had any idea what his password might be.

He said nothing.

"Warrior King," I said. "Ever hear that nickname before?"

He stared, unblinking. Val was right about Titus's eyes. They were two faded stars in a lonely sky. I pulled out the picture of the Cowboys and showed it to him.

He studied it and turned it over and looked at the back.

"Your last mission," I said.

He nodded and formed his lips to show pride. "Abdul Khogyani Ali, KIA."

"Who's that?"

"Taliban bomb maker. Killed a lot of marines. Cap wanted him bad and got him."

"Tell me about the Champagne Cowboys."

His face became granite again. He held the gun tight against his right leg.

"Look, I know what happened to Paul and Donna Morton last year in Tucson," I said. "I know the Cowboys were there."

His gun arm stiffened.

"I understand you've got every reason not to talk," I said. "But whoever killed the Mortons is behind the captain's murder. I know it wasn't one of you three Cowboys."

"Better hurry," Titus said. "Gloria's coming back. She watches out for me."

I assumed Gloria was his Apache wife.

"All I need is a name and I'm gone," I said. "Who else was there?"

His finger moved inside the trigger guard.

"No way this blows back on you," I said. "I know you didn't do it, Titus." Val Constantine and Abigail Whitcomb had both described Titus favorably, and I believed them. I was counting on that as protection against him shooting me.

He brought the gun up slowly until it was pointed at my heart.

Of course, I could've been wrong.

If he fired, nobody would hear it for the wind howling off the ridge. He'd deposit my body in a deep crevice up there, and a hundred years from now some bone-worshipping archaeologist in a bush vest would find my femur and wonder what a white man was doing in that unforgiving country.

So was I for that matter.

I had to come up with something. The barrel of his gun was inches from my right eye.

"Val sends her love, Titus. I just talked to her."

Something came into his face, a light, a softening. But he kept me in the front sight of his Colt revolver, his arm straight and steady.

"The captain's killer might be coming for you, too. You need to know that."

I heard footsteps to my left and half turned and saw an Apache woman striding purposefully toward me. She wore white painter's pants and a men's red bush shirt, untucked and the top two buttons undone.

She was bowlegged and top-heavy, her breasts bouncing around under the shirt as she moved. She held a big revolver with a long barrel. She pressed it against my temple and cocked the hammer back.

It was so heavy she needed two hands to hold it.

Titus said, "Meet Gloria."

The wind tossed her long black hair every which way, obscuring her face.

"Hello, Gloria."

"Hey, there."

"You wanna put that gun down?"

"No, thank you."

Titus smiled and put his gun under his belt.

Gloria said, "Better say something." Her voice lacked tone of any kind. She might as well have been folding laundry.

"It's hard to talk with that gun to my head."

"I know." She started a deliberate count, putting a two-second space between the numbers. "One … two … three."

"Like I told Titus, somebody might be coming here to kill him. I'm not the enemy here."

Gloria said, "That true, Titus?"

"Yup."

Gloria said, "Titus belongs to one of the great warrior societies of all time. I shoot good, too. Killed my first elk on Baldy when I was fourteen. Gave the liver to my grandma for Christmas."

The pink shadows of twilight settled against the ridge. The roaring wind made Gloria's hair look like blood spatter on a wall.

She said, "Titus, you ready for supper?"

"I'm real hungry, Gloria."

"Should I shoot him, or should we eat?"

A tribal police car rolled to a stop on the street behind us. The cop stepped out and hugged the roof with his outstretched arms. It was the same cop who'd been eyeballing me at the turnoff. He had a big smile on his face.

"You should've stayed lost, friend."

Gloria said, "Hey there, Wendell."

The cop said, "Evening, Gloria."

Titus said, "We all set for fishing tomorrow, Wendell?"

"There's big rainbows waiting for us. Got a spot picked out on the Black."

"Excellent."

"Truck's all packed," Wendell said. "Pick you up at five?"

"Five's good." Titus turned his attention to me. "That's why I live here. Rainbow trout. Apache's got the best trout fishing in the world."

"It's good to get away."

A wicked minute hobbled by on a wounded pony with Gloria double-gripping the revolver, my head yowling like the bullet had already made its hole, the Apache wind moaning through it, the cop smiling, and Titus smiling now, too, happy about his fishing trip.

I broke the silence. "All day I've been thinking I left the oven on in my trailer."

The cop said, "You should go home and turn it off."

"Believe I will."

"Okay with you, Gloria?" the cop said. "He goes home and turns off his oven?"

After another long wait, she lowered the gun and leaned her mouth against my ear and whispered, "Come back anytime," and disappeared inside the house.

I walked to the Bronco and drove off.

CHAPTER FORTY-TWO

wanted to push the Bronco to a hundred miles an hour to get away from Cibecue. But the smiling cop tailed me all the way to the reservation boundary. One click over the speed limit and he'd turn my life inside out, and my pockets.

Happy to be alive, heart pounding, I crawled along and didn't reach Globe until after dark.

At the highway junction, I went into the men's room at the QuikTrip and splashed water on my face, waited around until deciding I wasn't going to throw up, and got back on the road thinking even damn fools can accomplish something now and then.

I'd earned a mattress pass to sleep at night by warning Titus about the canyon sniper.

And the name Abdul Khogyani Ali had given me another possibility for Sterling's password—ALIKIA.

My regular visit to Sam was the next day, so instead of driving back to Tucson, I drove south to Florence and took a room at the Blue Mist Motel. I couldn't wait to tell Sam I'd found a knife matching the one that had killed Cristy Carlyle, and the real killer was Earl "Bumpy" Topp.

I was confident that Carlyle's blood would be on that knife and, with a little luck, Bumpy Topp's, too, given the violence of the attack.

A 5:00 a.m. call from the prison jarred me awake.

The voice on the line stumbled through several beginnings until I told him to hurry up and talk before I fell back asleep. He wanted to know how soon I could get to Florence.

I said I was in Florence already, right down the street at the Blue Mist, and could come over as soon as I had a shower and got some coffee in me.

"Why? What's going on?"

That was when he told me that Sam Houston Stark had died overnight.

The warden and some of the staff were waiting when I got there. They were white-faced and jittery and said the body had been discovered during a bed check. They offered me juice and aspirin and whatever else I might need.

All I wanted was to see him.

The warden, heavyset, with a silver mustache and black eyebrows, said the coroner was sending his wagon to pick Sam up. We stood around his office, six of us shuffling our feet.

Nobody wanted to sit.

Roxy called while we were waiting.

"I'm so sorry, Prospero. What a terrible shock. I am so, so sorry."

"How'd you find out? I just found out twenty minutes ago."

"My number's on the contact list. They said his heart just stopped."

"I was going to call you, but I didn't...they woke me up...I...I just got here."

"I'm coming to Florence."

"There's nothing you can do here. I'm fine."

"No, you're not. Don't tell me you're fine. I can hear your voice."

I felt a great weight on my chest. My arms were lead. "I can't believe he's gone. He wasn't what they said he was."

"He was a good man."

"But nobody's going to know that now. His name, his reputation, it can't be taken back."

"You know the kind of man he was. He's in your heart and will be forever."

"He did everything for me. Never missed a game, never missed a birthday."

There was a long pause.

"Tig Watson wants a story," Roxy said. "Sam Houston Stark cheats the chair, his exact words. He wants a standup in front of the razor wire. I went off on him. Said he'd get his standup, only it'd be about how Sam got railroaded. He said that was okay, too. I told Tig he'd get his story and then I told him to go fuck himself just to keep in shape."

I didn't say anything to that.

When Roxy spoke again, her voice cracked. "I want you to know I'm coming there for you and for Sam. I love you and I'm on my way."

The warden led me down official corridors and through massive metal doors that banged and echoed when they opened and closed. They rolled the gurney out a back door.

It bumped down a step and Sam's arm fell out from under the blanket.

I took the hand in mine and for a moment studied its familiar shapes and lines, remembering different things, different times those hands helped me or held me.

The two gurney men stopped to give me time. I put the hand back under the blanket and peeled it all the way back and looked at Sam's face, and he was smiling faintly.

My heart beat so loud I could hear only its bloody roar.

I've always been glad I looked, because his expression, his smile of satisfaction, told me he knew that he'd finally made it out of there.

Out from behind those bars and free, and in the place he was going, there'd be no needles or pain or need, and nobody would tell him he couldn't read Shakespeare whenever he wanted, any time of day or night, by electric light, by candlelight, by flashlight, or naked and sipping tequila in his captain's chair with the big shining moon for a hat.

CHAPTER FORTY-THREE

The remainder of the day was a blur. I didn't so much hear voices as their echoes. I had the feeling I was moving through time slowed down, with every moment a separate episode, and later I'd remember perfectly all the words and details of the day.

Not that I wanted to, but some life events are outsized, and like it or not, they'll stick in your brain for all time.

I rode with the coroner in his wagon to the Pinal County building. He was a gracious and polite Mr. Everly. Roxy came, and Mr. Everly let us sit with Sam for several hours, and then, not wanting to leave but needing to be close, we sat in a nearby office for the remainder of the day, talking in hushed voices.

After dark, we went back to the Blue Mist.

When the door closed behind us, Roxy came into my arms and cried a little and so did I. I held her with my back to the wall for several minutes.

"I have something to show you," she said. "Let me take a shower first."

She showered, came out of the bathroom with nothing on and her eyes red and wet. She'd been crying again.

With her fingertips, she wiped the tears from beneath one eye and then the other, and with her back to me stared into the mirror above the bureau in front of the bed.

She tore the plastic off a motel cup, pulled a pint bottle of Scotch out of her purse, poured an inch, and had a drink, staring into the mirror.

In the half-light from the bathroom, I could see her eyes and her full breasts and black nipples, the smooth, perfect flesh and the big round belly button.

For her there was nothing awkward or self-conscious about being naked. She was that way the first time.

"Is this something new?" There was a tattoo at the small of her back.

"Almost forgot. That's what I wanted to show you." She twisted her upper body, threw her chin over her shoulder, and looked down at her butt. "They're my ass antlers. What do you think? There's a new artist down on Congress Street and he's amazing."

"Is that a deer?"

"Can't you tell? It's a ten-point white-tail buck. I shot him in Arivaca last fall and Rod mounted the head in his living room. The guy did this from a photo. Can you believe it?" She wiggled. "Want to try it out?"

"I'm not sure I want to feel good yet."

"Don't say that. I need you tonight."

"Rox, I never felt this way. I feel lost. I'm falling."

"I know, baby. But let me pick you up. Let's be done crying for the night. I can't anymore, or I'll fall apart and never come back. Honestly."

"Sam died before I could prove him innocent. That's the worst part."

"When we get the DNA results and find Bumpy Topp, I'll do another story."

"Dietz might bury it. She's sounded better lately, but I don't trust her."

"I won't let her." Roxy stared at herself in the mirror and pushed her hair around to get it lying right. "I'll make her regret ever hearing the name Sam Houston Stark."

"Isn't that a violation of journalistic ethics?"

"That's an interesting idea," Roxy said. "Somebody should write an op-ed on it and come down on the side of truth and informing the people because it's their right to know. Somebody should do it, but it won't be me."

She walked to the bed and, still standing, leaned down and kissed me on the lips. She put her glass of Scotch down on the night table next to the lamp and sat on the edge of the bed.

I reached over and traced the deer tattoo with my finger.

"That's fine work, really intricate."

She shivered. "Quit it. That tickles."

"I like the way you kiss."

"I was born knowing how to do that."

"Practice doesn't help?"

"It's not like throwing a baseball. There's no spring training for smooching." She was barely able to finish the sentence for her laughter, and I laughed, too. Burning emotions made the laughter hard to control.

"You should go down to Congress and get one, too," Roxy said. "I'll go with."

"What would I have painted on my body?"

"He does a cool Doc Holliday face. You're Doc Holliday kind of guy. Except, I don't know."

"Except what?"

"He was one ugly motherfucker."

She laughed hard again and fell straight back with her feet on the floor and her head on my stomach. The whole front of her, the up and down of her shape, the lines of her thighs, her face in profile, was all laid out before me.

"I'm sure they've got other stuff," I said, and dragged the back of my fingernails down her neck and between her breasts.

"Oh, lots and lots." Her stomach moved up and down. Faster and faster. "Flags, eagles, a skull wearing a sombrero. Nah, do the Doc Holliday one."

My hand moved lower. She closed her eyes. "There's whole sentences if you like ... they can write all kinds of ... You can use whole ... Oh, God ... Oh, yes."

At that her concentration flagged, and her voice became low and breathy.

"Right there." She covered my hand with hers. "I'm your huckleberry."

She rolled over and lay next to me and put her arm across my chest and her lips against my neck. I kissed her and tasted the Scotch. Her mouth opened, and I tasted more of it, and she climbed on top of me with her palms on my chest.

No more tears fell as I put my hands on the tattoo and pulled her to me, and she moved in a way that doesn't have to be learned, and that's how it went until all the stars fell from the sky.

CHAPTER FORTY-FOUR

The funeral service wasn't morbid or weepy, just long. I counted twelve media people roaching around with their skinny notebooks, coupon haircuts, and ingratiating grins. There were twelve mourners, so few the church echoed.

Nobody wanted to be photographed sending off a convicted murderer.

Afterward I spent three days at my mother's house in Tempe.

She had lived most of her life in Sam's formidable shadow, and that was partially by design. She'd happily accepted that part of her life and found expression for her own energy as archivist for the Arizona Collection at the ASU Library.

The two worlds blended, if not seamlessly, then well enough.

But when Sam's life exploded in scandal, the archives became her dark attic, a self-contained hiding place that she could entirely control, while letting the rest of the world pass by like a parade outside the window.

I worried that Sam's death would deepen her withdrawal and arranged for two of his former students to check up on her after I left.

As I was driving back to Tucson, I called Detective Dietz to ask if she'd found Bumpy Topp.

"Didn't you just bury your father a few days ago, Stark?"

"It's been a week. I want Topp found and charged with Carlyle's murder."

"I'm sorry for your loss. It might help you to take time off from all this."

"That means you haven't found him."

"Soon. I have some news. In Topp's shopping carts we found a rag doll that belonged to Miss Carlyle. Acquaintances tell us it was on the bed in her apartment."

"That places Topp there, right? Now we know he was inside the apartment."

"If we find Topp's DNA on the knife, we can bring that and the doll to the county attorney and I think we'll have something."

"Call me when you hear anything at all."

"You have to let me do my job, Stark. I promise I'll find this man and we'll follow the evidence from there."

I arrived at Double Wide late morning and fetched Sterling's phone out of its glove box hiding place. Removing it from the freezer bag, I sat down at my kitchen table.

The two new password ideas had been bouncing around in my head.

ASKING, based on Sterling's Warrior King nickname.

Val had said his men loved him, and the name would've meant a lot to him.

ALIKIA, based on the last Taliban enemy he'd killed, a man he wanted so badly he'd delayed his departure from Afghanistan until the job was done.

I tried both and neither worked.

Two tries remained before the phone locked up for good.

At 4:00 p.m. that day, Roxy's father, Rod Santa Cruz, called and said the first homicide investigator on the Foothills case had agreed to talk and a meeting was set.

I'd met Rod a few times. He'd been retired two years and was still all cop from heel to molar. He didn't ask if I was busy, didn't apologize for the late notice, and didn't ask if I could get there in time.

"Six tonight. Meet me at the entrance to Wagon Wheel Ranch." The ranch was a retirement community in the satellite town of Oro Valley, northwest of Tucson.

"Can you tell me who this guy is?"

"Lonesome Eddie Palmer. He worked the case before he got sick and they made him retire. He printed out the whole case file before walking away."

I asked about the nickname and Rod didn't answer. All he said was, "Six o'clock," and hung up.

Cash stayed behind at Double Wide with Sister Phil, and I drove to the Waffle House in town for an early supper. I dropped a big tip on one of Opal's waitress friends and tried to explain to the manager why she hadn't told him she'd be in New York for a few days.

The conversation didn't start well, but he calmed down after a while and said he'd think about not firing her.

I got back in the Bronco and headed to Oro Valley.

CHAPTER FORTY-FIVE

Thirty minutes of driving on Oracle Road took me above the city into the Catalina Foothills. The Wagon Wheel Ranch was just past where Oracle curled around the range's western edge. The road was elevated, so my first glimpse of the ranch was from above, thousands of rooftops spreading across the desert.

The place had its own traffic light. After waiting for the green arrow, I swung into the wide circular driveway that narrowed at the back to a single-lane entrance road beneath a massive stone arch worthy of an Aztec empire.

Rod was leaning on his elbow against an older-model red Lincoln Continental parked beside the guardhouse.

His black hair was slicked down with something shiny and he had an equally black skinny Zorro mustache, both clearly dyed. He wore a wide-lapelled bright red shirt with the top two buttons undone, a gold cross dangling in the wide V.

He bounced upright when he spotted the Bronco. Rod was long-legged and rangy. He leaned an elbow on the driver's door and started talking without a hello or buildup of any kind.

"Eddie ain't doing too good. We'll see how this goes." Rod started to move away.

"Hold on," I said. "You didn't tell me why the nickname, Lonesome."

Rod leaned back in the window, bringing with him a blast of cologne. I'd caught the scent the first time but assumed it was the death secretion of a wayward animal or a chemical spill.

"How can I put this? Eddie don't do human relations too good. Has a way of, ah, pissing off the population, okay? I worked him hard to get this meet, so don't make him mad. You do and he'll shut down."

Rod straightened up, rolled his shoulders, and nodded toward the guard booth, and the gate swung open. He knocked twice on the roof of the Bronco.

"Follow me."

The red Lincoln smoked along on roads that had ridiculously long Spanish names and all looked the same. The houses did, too. Off-white stucco walls, arched windows, red tile roofs, cactus-and-rock lawns, and kingly front doors.

The ranch was a paradise of order and worry-free living. No trash, no potholes, no kids, no loud music. Everything was perfect, and perfectly bloodless.

It had the feel of the last stop, the place where the ball game ended.

Rod pulled into the driveway and got out carrying a plastic supermarket bag. I parked the Bronco at the curb.

Pointing to the house, I said, "Is this what you get when you parachute?"

"Eddie's lady wanted to live here. She passed, and he figured what the hell."

Palmer met us at the door. He had one eye that was three-quarters closed and all white. He gave me everything he had with the good one and nodded us into a high-ceilinged foyer that echoed with our voices.

In the kitchen, he took a plate of cut limes out of the refrigerator, grabbed a file off the counter, and led us out the sliding glass door to the patio beside the swimming pool. Rod took a six-pack of Coronas out of the plastic bag, some chips, salsa, and several prescription bags.

Palmer paid no attention to the medicine.

He cracked open a Corona and tossed the cap onto the table and sipped.

Rod gave him a frustrated look, shook a pill out of one of the bottles, held it in front of Palmer's face to make a point, and put it on the table in front of him.

Palmer squeezed a lime over the neck of his bottle, held the pill up to Rod to make a point of his own, popped it into his mouth, and washed it down with the beer.

Rod shook his head. "Ain't going to be any fun without you, Eddie."

"You get caught having fun around here and they call an emergency fucking meeting."

Palmer had a pinched face with small features and mostly gray hair cut short. He stood about five foot ten. His arms were thin beneath a white guayabera shirt. His last shave might've been a week ago, giving him a pool-hall beard. His good eye was a striking blue.

"I understand you and Rod worked together," I said.

Palmer ignored me. He was busy with the chips and salsa.

Rod said, "Partners out of the academy, street cops. Long time ago, eh, Eddie?"

He chewed and kept quiet. At the back of the property stood a wrought iron fence, and beyond that, a stretch of open desert running all the way to the mountains.

"I haven't talked about this case since I left the department," Palmer said. "But Rod called and so did Roxanne. I hear you two go around together."

"That's right."

"You take care of her, understand? I bounced that girl on my knee."

Rod said, "She's on TV all the time, Eddie. Doing real good."

Palmer gave me the blue eye to make sure I got the point. When somebody uses two eyes, he's just looking at you. But with one, he's drilling a hole.

"Case went dry on me," Palmer said. "Tried everything. I thought Morton's lawyer work might've got him killed. Pissed-off client, guy he prosecuted, gang business. Spent a lot of time looking into his cases."

"Couldn't find an angle?"

"Dead end." He tapped the file with his finger. "It's all in here."

"I'll need that file," I said.

The statement came out like a demand. Rod gave me a look that said, "What'd I just tell you?"

Palmer's face curled in contempt. "Just like that, eh? You want everything I got? Walk in here in your fucking cowboy boots."

"I'm just telling you, Eddie, I can't leave without it."

"Well, screw you, then." He tapped an angry finger against his beer bottle. "Eight months. I don't sleep trying to close this, can't eat, and you think you can do it?"

"No disrespect."

"Me," he said and flattened his palm against his chest and his voice shook: "It was my job. Mine. My last case and I didn't get it done."

Rod knew that handing over the file had to be Palmer's call, done his way and in his time. He held a hand up to me, indicating that I should keep quiet, and spoke calmly to Palmer.

"He's got a personal interest here, Eddie. He's tied in real tight."

He explained my connection to the Mortons.

The whole time he talked, Palmer glared across the table at me. Rod read the situation perfectly and kept talking, moving the topic to old times, until Palmer's color returned to normal and he said he was hungry.

The two of them went inside and returned with leftovers they'd heated in the microwave.

Rod took a pill from each of the prescription bottles and lined them up on the table in front of Palmer. Because Rod didn't insist that he take them, and in fact pretended he wasn't paying attention, Palmer readily swallowed the pills and got busy eating.

Done with the food, he cracked open another Corona and sipped. "Tell me what you know, Stark."

I did. He hadn't heard the name Champagne Cowboys.

"I put together a list of jobs I figured this bunch for." He shrugged. "They were pros. In and out fast, no good forensics. You said three Cowboys usually, but four on the Morton job? Gang like that don't pick up hitchhikers."

"Someone else was there and that's your shooter."

He sat up, interested, and tilted his jaw at me. "Male or female?"

"You look like you know something," I said.

"Shooter's identity, can't tell you," Palmer said. "But it was a female, that much I know."

"What're you basing that on?"

His mouth turned stubborn again. "Based on thirty-seven fucking years. That long enough for you?"

I said nothing. Palmer sunk a chip into the dip like he was digging a grave. He didn't start again until he finished chewing and wiped the salt off his hands.

"The Mortons were celebrating Donna's birthday," he said. "Out with another couple, restaurant, drinks. Took pictures, the whole bit. Paul Morton was killed by the front door, the wife in the garage. Same footprints around both bodies, same gun. Donna's wearing diamond earrings in the pictures, but when we find the body, the earrings are gone. Killer ripped them off, left her ears tore up."

"That's it? Earrings?"

"Man wouldn't do that."

"They're diamond earrings," I said. "A man might grab them for his girl or his wife."

Palmer said, "You know an awful shit lot for a guy threw baseballs for a living."

Rod stepped in. "Eddie's got a point, Whip. Men and diamonds? Maybe. But women? Two of my exes wore diamond earrings and it's like, Jesus Christ, don't even bring it up."

Holding his free hand under it to catch any falloff, Palmer slid the chip between his lips. With his mouth full, he said, "You wanted my opinion, Stark, there it is. I don't know it like in court, raising my right hand. But I know it."

I looked at Rod. "You on board with a female killer?"

"Put it this way," he said. "You doubt Eddie Palmer, you usually come down on the dope side of the truth. Best I ever seen, this man. That's why they think he's an asshole downtown."

Palmer grinned proudly, like he'd just been knighted by the queen.

Sounding conciliatory, Rod said, "You understand what I'm saying, Eddie. You showed 'em up."

Palmer nodded and waved, a grant of absolution.

I pointed to the file. "There's only one way this can go, Eddie."

"Yeah, how's that?"

"Either I get that file, or you get a roommate, because I ain't leaving without it."

"People in my house? Not a good situation." He smirked. "For them."

"We both want the same thing here, Eddie," I said. "You've done good work getting as far as you did and I'm going to finish the job you started."

His face twisted up like he might blow again. But the tension leaked out of it, replaced with a look of resignation. When that faded, he grinned in admiration.

"Gotta give it to you, Stark, you got a pair. Reminds me of this guy back when we worked the cocktail shift together." He pointed to Rod.

Palmer looked at the mountains and drank his beer. A breeze rippled the green water of the pool. The air smelled faintly of chlorine.

"What I want more than anything is to see this case closed before my time's up," he said. "No way I'll work with the rodents pushed me out, but I wouldn't mind seeing Roxanne talking about it on TV. Keep it in the family."

Rod placed his hand on the file. "Whip's squared away, Eddie. He'll do what he says."

Palmer studied me across the table with appraising eyes. He motioned absently toward the file and turned back toward the mountains.

"All I ask, Stark, is I'm the first call you make when you get her."

CHAPTER FORTY-SIX

Nine p.m. A sickle moon hung over Double Wide when I pulled up in front of the Airstream. Bundle was out, and that meant at any moment there could be a loud encounter between a crazy black Lab and wild coyotes.

I dropped the six-inch-thick file on the kitchen table and leafed through it, not sure what I was looking for. Anything, a random note, a name that clicked.

A few pages in I saw the crime scene photos. Driving back from Palmer's, I'd debated whether to look at them and decided that I would and should.

But they rocked me. My throat tightened, and my mouth went dry.

I got up and went to the fridge. There was a single bottle of Coors Light inside. I don't care much for beer, but I twisted off the cap and had a sip anyway, to change things up, to move my mind somewhere else, anywhere that wasn't on those pictures.

I sat down again.

Lonesome Eddie had done a thorough job.

On a cover page, he listed the jobs he suspected the burglary ring of doing by address and a rundown of what was taken, with an estimated dollar amount. On additional pages, he'd listed Paul's cases, those in Pima County Superior Court and federal court.

I started with superior court. The file numbers were on the left side, below the defendant's name, and on the right side the outcome, either guilty, a plea deal, or an acquittal. I skipped the acquittals.

There should be nothing to complain about in an acquittal.

For those who'd pled out or been found guilty, I flipped inside to a corresponding page with a few paragraphs of information on each case, and nothing jumped out.

Palmer's second cover page listed Paul's federal cases, which included a kidnapping, two aggravated assaults, and an attempted murder.

He'd also defended a client for running guns on the Tohono O'odham Reservation.

Her name was Angela Rios.

Holly Winterset had owned a gun shop in Three Points and got busted for gunrunning on the Rez. Its eastern boundary directly abuts Three Points.

That didn't prove a connection. The Rez is huge, the size of Connecticut, and lots of people make money running guns south to the cartels. But if the cases occurred at the same time, and in the same area, I'd have something.

I looked up Angela Rios on PACER, the online database of federal court cases, and the first thing I saw gave me a kick of excitement.

Angela Rios was from Three Points, too.

In her presentencing statement, she admitted loading her truck with guns and ammunition, driving to the San Miguel Gate on the Mexican line, and handing everything over to an unnamed man on the south side.

She claimed she'd made only one run and didn't know the name of her contact with the smuggling gang. She said she was messed up on cocaine at the time, but the person was a woman and that was all she remembered.

In her statement, Rios said, "She threatened my daughter, telling me, 'We know where your kid gets the school bus in the morning. Can you help us out?' I did it to protect my daughter. If I refused and she disappeared, how could I live with that?"

She was a first-time offender, and Paul Morton convinced the judge that drugs had so scrambled her mind that she was telling the truth about not remembering her handler's name.

She pleaded guilty, got time served, and was put into a residential treatment program.

Reading that made me grin. I'd bet anything that Angela Rios remembered her handler. Anybody who admits to making one run has usually made many more.

She kept the name in her pocket to stay alive.

"You had a helluva lawyer, girl," I said.

There were noises outside. Either a truck full of hysterical chickens had crashed or Bundle had met his enemies and they were waltzing in the desert.

Opening the door, I whistled Bundle inside and fed him, and after three minutes of ferocious tail wagging, he was asleep on the floor under the table.

Next, I looked up Holly's case. She'd been arrested five months after Angela.

Close, but not close enough to prove they'd worked together.

Reading on, I found a solid connection. The indictment said Holly had used the same pass-through, the San Miguel Gate.

Border smuggling routes are all owned. Angela Rios wouldn't have used the San Miguel Gate while Holly was still operating there unless she was working for Holly. One iron rule in the smuggling racket is that anybody who uses a bought-and-paid-for trail without permission gets their head put on a pike.

I needed to find Angela Rios.

She wasn't on Spokeo, but that wasn't a surprise. A lot of people living around Three Points didn't want to be found. It was a lost settlement twenty miles away, a smugglers' paradise named for three highways that came together there and led nowhere, a specialty of Arizona's backcountry.

A Google search brought me to the website for the Trail's End Lounge.

A singer named Angela Rios was appearing there.

The chance of it being a different Angela Rios was small. I called. The bartender wouldn't give me her number but said she ran the landscaping crew at the Ray Turner Institute, a nonprofit dedicated to studying desert plants.

I called Roxy. "Let's take a drive and say howdy to Angela Rios."

"Oh, goody. Three Points. I'll bring sunscreen and my .380."

"If I'm right about Holly, I'll bet Jackie Moreno was out there, too."

"I'm editing a piece tomorrow, but I'll be done, say, late afternoon. Ish."

As much as she didn't like the Bronco, we needed it for off-road driving. I was going to be running errands in town anyway, so I told her I'd pick her up at her house.

CHAPTER FORTY-SEVEN

We drove west on Ajo Way out of Tucson proper, past the last houses and stores and into the nothingness of creosote, saguaros, and dust devils.

The most obvious sign of civilization was an airport so small we might've missed it but for the buzzing black dots floating down through the sunlight to become small planes bound for the landing strip.

At the highway junction, we drove south three miles and turned west into open desert that might as well have been the back side of Mars. Another seven miles of bumpy dirt road brought us to a tin-roofed, drab-yellow office building with three trailers beside it, headquarters of the Turner Institute.

Fenced-off research plots and glass houses dotted the desert behind the office.

The road past the entry gate led to a cluster of Quonset huts around a gravel clearing. I stopped at the security booth and waited for the wizened guard to notice me.

When I hit the horn, he wrestled the window open and leaned out just enough to give his overwatered walrus mustache some air. The thing needed serious gardening, and more with a weed whacker than trimming scissors.

"Looking for Angela Rios," I said.

"Third building on the right." He aimed a sausage finger in that direction. "You have to check in at the office. There's a sign."

"Must've missed it."

"I can't let in anybody that don't register." His name tag said Joe Nelson.

"It's almost six and everybody's gone," I said. "You the only one works a full shift?"

"Ten hours a day in this lousy shack." His mustache danced a rumba as he talked.

"I won't be long."

He hesitated, glancing at the office and back at the gate, a metal bar swinging loose on its hinge. "They want me to be J. Edgar Hoover around here and Joe Handyman on top of that."

"Five minutes."

"After that I come get you." He pointed again. "That's her yonder, the white truck."

I pulled up to the third Quonset hut and stopped.

Angela sat on the open tailgate of a pickup underneath an awning that served as carport and shelter. Next to her stood a white-haired man in green work clothes. They looked to be having a pleasant after-hours conversation.

As we stepped out of the Bronco, Angela must've sensed something in our manner and said to her companion, "That's all for today, Walt," and he went inside.

"I'm Whip Stark and this is Roxanne Santa Cruz," I said.

Angela Rios nodded, unsure, waiting.

"We're looking into the murder of someone you knew. Name was Paul Morton."

Her eyes widened with surprise. "Mr. Morton's dead?"

"He got you out of a big hole a while back."

"No fooling. Geez, I'm sorry to hear that. Mr. Morton. Boy, I sure liked him."

Angela stood up. She was about five foot five and thickly built but carried it well. She had a wide mouth and pothole cheeks under prominent cheekbones. She was probably early thirties, but the skin around her eyes had begun to spider, the work of a relentless sun.

Her long black ponytail hung beneath a broad-brimmed straw sun hat. She pulled off the hat and turned it in her hands along the brim.

"But why do you want to talk to me?" she said. "It's been four years."

"You kept a name off the boards back then, the woman you worked for."

"I couldn't remember anything. My mind wasn't right."

"Cocaine."

The bend of her mouth told me she didn't like that word. But she stayed polite. She had an attitude of reserve, a dignity that came from facing the storm and beating it.

"Near killed me," she said and looked away at nothing. "Long time ago."

"We were hoping your memory might've come back."

Angela nodded toward Roxy. "Is this for TV?"

"Just between us," Roxy said.

"They don't like us talking to people, all the smugglers we get messing with our stuff." Angela stretched her neck toward the guard booth. "Joe let you guys in?"

"Paul and Donna Morton were close friends of mine," I said. "She's gone, too."

"Donna was his wife?"

"Yes."

"Somebody killed both of them?"

"Yes."

"God, why?"

I told her what I knew. Angela sat down hard on the tailgate. There was a lot of summer left in that vast desert, and even the shadows remembered. She used her forearm to clear the sweat from her forehead.

"I'm sad, really I am," she said. "But I can't do them any favors now."

"They had two young kids."

"I have one myself, a little girl. I need this job." Angela pointed at the mountains to the south. "You know what they call this place? Cocaine alley. Everybody goes around armed. Everybody keeps their animals corralled and their mouths shut. Gets to be a habit."

"Four people have been murdered in town."

"Four people." Angela shut her eyes and shook her head.

"The woman you protected back then, she's involved. It was Holly Winterset, right?"

Angela gave me a surprised look.

"Whatever you tell us stays locked up," I said.

The gravel path to the office crunched under marching footsteps. "Excuse me," a voice called out. "Turner security here. Could we get a minute?"

Angela looked at the sky and exhaled. "I had a feeling today was going to suck."

There were two of them, dressed as twins. They had on gray pants with black stripes up the leg and blue shirts with badge-shaped emblems on the chest.

The talker was smiling and had an acne-scarred face and thick glasses. His partner was short and had stout legs that could've held up the CEO's conference table. He had a fat nose and his black hair lay flat and looked wet, an oil spill.

He stayed a few steps behind Talker, whose smile had no welcome in it at all. Joe Nelson walked behind them, bent over and struggling along on balky knees.

"You know you're not supposed to invite anyone onto the grounds," Talker said.

"Sir, I didn't invite them," Angela said.

"You know the regulations. All visitors cleared through the office. You think the rules don't apply to you?"

Angela tried to speak, but Talker held up his hand to stop her. He looked over his shoulder and said, "Joe."

Pointing to me and Roxy, Joe Nelson said, "These two drove right past me before I could stop 'em, and it sure looked like she was waiting for them."

"That's crap," I said. "She had no idea we were coming."

When Talker turned back to me, Joe gave me an apology shrug.

"It won't happen again, sir." Angela's chin fell onto her chest.

"Miss Rios, you know the situation we have here," Talker said. "The rules are for everyone's safety. Gather your things."

I broke in to defend Angela and Talker interrupted. "This is private property, sir. I'm going to need you two to come to the office. We'll need to see some identification."

When I began to argue, Roxy put a hand on my shoulder and said to Talker, "Of course." As we walked toward the office, she whispered, "I'll handle this knob."

The office was a drab setup with a gray metal desk, a smaller one in the corner, and several filing cabinets. On the wall was a poster showing a mature multiarmed saguaro against a pretty sky, and above it the words: *Did you know I might be 200 years old?*

Using as much time and pointed mannerisms as he could, Talker got himself seated behind the main desk. He was temporary king of the world.

The attitude vanished when Roxy handed him her KPIN business card.

"Oh, I think I've seen you on TV." Talker squeezed his chin with the tips of his fingers as he stared at the card. "Doesn't your station cover our Cactus Christmas fund-raiser every December?"

"Have for years," Roxy said. "I did the story myself when I started out. The girl who does it now is a good friend of mine."

Talker tugged on his ear. Evidently not achieving the desired result, he did it several more times, only harder. He was trying to ring the cathedral bell. "Boss says that darn thing makes his annual budget."

"Be a shame if the station somehow missed it."

He looked at Roxy over his black glasses. "Mighty big, yes, ma'am."

"Even bigger shame if Angela Rios lost her job."

Pug had been close by listening, but now he read the scoreboard and retreated to his corner desk topped by papers that needed urgent moving around and got busy doing it.

"Well," Talker said, "seeing as how she's been here two whole years."

He told Pug to reinstate Angela. Pug left, and nothing more needed to be said, but Talker didn't see it that way. He pulled his phony smile out of storage and went on about all the great work the institute's scientists were doing and suggested a few stories the station could cover.

Roxy showed her interest by studying her nails.

Back at the Bronco, I found a note from Angela on the front seat.

"Trail's End. I go on at nine."

CHAPTER FORTY-EIGHT

The lounge sat at the southwest corner where the three highways met and looked like a renovated convenience store. The walls on two sides and in back had been partially knocked out and a saguaro-rib fence built around them.

Burning torches surrounded the outdoor seating areas.

A tall sign over the parking lot read, *Angie and the Outlaws*, in big black letters.

Another sign, this one on the front door, said, *Sorry, We're Open*.

"I like it so far," Roxy said.

The music boomed out the door when we walked in. Angela was on stage singing. Her hair was down and curled, her jeans tucked into her cowboy boots.

The place was packed. It was a standard beer and corn dog bar with a jukebox, sawdust floors, and the mixed aromas of range stock and too many slow dances on summer nights.

The men were sunburned backhoe cowboys who'd traded their John Deere caps for knockoff George Strait Stetsons. The women had long curled hair and tight Wranglers and walked in hippy strides that said they knew they were being watched.

Roxy and I stood with our backs against the bar and listened.

"A good country fiddler can make me cry," Roxy said.

"Bad shortstops did it for me."

"The man can stroke it. I'm getting misty here."

"Try to hold it together."

When Angela's set ended, she gave us a discreet nod, and we shouldered through the crowd to the open-air courtyard behind the building, all the way to the back fence.

She stood in a dark patch, a shadow between two flaming torches. She pulled out a pack of smokes and stuck one in her lips. A man rushed up and stuck his fist under her nose, and, using his own lighter, lit her cigarette.

The back of his shirt hung over his belt.

"You knocked 'em dead again, Angie," he said. "Buy you a shot of Beam?"

"Thanks, not tonight," she said.

He pressed. She kept saying no, and when I spoke up, he turned to stare at me, wobbling on his boot heels. "Sure got ugly around here."

"Easy does it, Hercules," I said.

"What'd you say?"

"He's a ballplayer I used to know. Hit five-hundred-foot homers. Hungover."

He squared his shoulders at me. "Yeah? And just who the hell are you?"

There was only one way that could go, until Roxy jumped in front of him and stuck her face close to his. He tumbled for the distraction. She took him by the arm and led him away, talking close to his ear as they walked.

Angela motioned toward Roxy. "She going to be okay?"

I smiled. Roxanne Santa Cruz in torchlight wasn't a fair fight for any man.

"Got your note," I said.

"You guys saved my job." Angela puffed her cigarette, the red glow arcing up to her mouth and down again. "I try to keep it simple. Work at the institute, sing my songs to heal the people's hurts, and go home to my daughter."

Jukebox music thumped and banged inside.

"The idea of that woman still hurting people, somebody's got to stop her," she said. "You had it right. It was Holly Winterset."

"You ran guns for her?"

She nodded. "Holly's the one I usually dealt with, but she wasn't the leader."

"Let me guess. Jackie Moreno."

"That's right. But she was Jackie Garcia for most of her time here."

"You know where Garcia came from?"

"Sorry, no idea."

I remembered Val Constantine telling me Jackie wanted nothing to do with the Sterling name. My guess was she'd changed it from Sterling to Garcia when she turned eighteen.

To be sure we were talking about the same person, on my phone I called up the photo I'd found of Jackie at a nursing school party.

Angela angled her head to catch some light and looked at it.

"That's her," she said. "My heart's racing just seeing that face."

"How'd she become Moreno?"

"Just before leaving Three Points, she married Ardis Moreno, a contractor."

"I need to talk to him."

"Good luck," Jackie said and made a sarcastic sound. "She disappeared him quick. Did the same to a boyfriend before that. Fellow from Three Points named Guy Villanueva. Long-distance trucker."

When I heard Three Points and trucker, I knew he wasn't hauling hay.

"Jackie and Holly, they ran everything around here," Angela said. "Nobody crossed them and stayed alive."

The courtyard crowd hooted and barked around us. They threw down shots and banged on their tables. Couples danced, straight-arming each other, pulling back and falling into awkward twirls and dips, laughing all the while.

"How'd you get mixed up with those two?" I asked.

"Jackie was my supplier." Angela puffed, turned her face up, and blew toward a sky emptied of stars by the glow of the torches. "I came around every day to get my candy and she fed me. All I had to do was whatever Holly said."

"Are Moreno and Villanueva still missing?"

"Moreno, yeah."

"Villanueva?"

"They found his bones in the desert."

"Two in the hat?"

"Mercy's like water around here, Whip. You have to look hard to find it."

"How?"

"She staked him out in the sun and left him for the ants and whatever else got hungry."

"Jesus." My mind skipped out for a moment as I processed that. "You're sure Jackie did this?"

"I'd bet my truck." She puffed and blew. "Dashboard Jesus included."

"Was she ever arrested?"

"They got her for some small stuff, I don't remember. The girl's smart and deadly, a real stick of dynamite. Cross her and look out."

Roxy returned, stepping back into our dark patch by the fence. "That was fun."

Angela grinned. "Thanks for that. What'd you say to him?"

"I explained the origin of the universe."

We laughed.

"He's okay," Roxy said. "The old boy needed some attention, that's all. We good here?"

I turned to Angela. "Anything else I need to know?"

She shrugged and smoked. "Jackie had a cabin in the mountains. Up in the Galiuros, I think. She liked spending time there, if that helps."

She dropped her cigarette and killed it with the toe of her boot.

"I gotta get back in there. My name stays out of this, right?"

"We never talked," I said.

CHAPTER FORTY-NINE

We landed back at Roxy's house around eleven and got on the computer. I was right about Jackie Moreno. Online records showed that six months after turning eighteen, she legally changed her name from Sterling to Garcia.

She'd been arrested twice under the Garcia name, once for drug possession and again for aggravated assault that got pled down to simple assault.

She got probation on both, no time in the hole.

We had no way of proving that Jackie had murdered Villanueva and Moreno. A news site reported that Villanueva's bones had been lying in the sun so long they were white by the time a hiker found them, outlined by four stakes driven into the ground.

No arrests had been made, and the case remained open.

Ardis Moreno was officially a missing person.

By then it was creeping toward midnight and we hadn't eaten supper. Roxy heated a leftover pasta dish in the microwave and threw together a salad, and we sat at her dining room table eating and talking.

"When Holly gets tagged on the gun scheme," Roxy said, "their operation in Three Points collapses and Jackie needs a place go."

"She skates on a couple of busts and moves into town. New name, new life."

"Holly does her time, starts a plumbing business, and moves in next to Jackie."

"Under the Moreno name, nothing bad shows up on her record and the nursing school lets her in. Things are looking good."

"Couple of gals digging the redemption," Roxy said. "It's a Hallmark movie except for all the dead people."

We ate in silence as a train rumbled by behind the house. The vibration shook the pictures on the walls.

"We still have nothing solid connecting Jackie to Sterling's murder," Roxy said.

"But there's plenty of motive. After Three Points she needed to get money somewhere, and there's Ash with his big old safe."

"Remember when Jackie told us she wasn't interested in his fortune?"

"You were right to be skeptical."

"When people talk about money, listen carefully," Roxy said. "They're telling you everything you need to know." She finished her food and took her plate to the sink. "This is pretty good, don't you think? I'm getting to be quite a cook."

Roxy had taken up cooking as a serious hobby and it wasn't working. The pasta dish was awful. I'd choked down as much as I could and said, "If I could only describe it."

"I've got other recipes I want to try."

"Can't wait."

The new information on Jackie had me nervous. Before leaving, I told Roxy she should pack a bag and move with me to Double Wide.

"I like it where I am," she said. "But I'll sleep with the Beretta by my bed. How's that?"

"You've got a stubborn streak as wide as the Colorado River."

She smiled beautifully. "What's your point?"

We kissed by her front door, and as I was going down the steps my phone played *The Magnificent Seven* theme. It was Ozzie Fish, the bike-riding teenager.

"They tried to kill me again," he said.

"Who tried to kill you?" I said.

Roxy heard me and stood at the open front door to listen.

"Beats me," Ozzie said. "A truck went up on the sidewalk and almost run me down. It was a big red pickup going, like, superfast."

"Are you all right?"

"Whaddaya think? Dude, I'm standing here right now, ain't I? Having, like, a conversation?" Ozzie talked fast, his words tripping over themselves getting out.

I heard voices and thumping music in the background and asked where he was.

"The Blue Note. It's a bar on Ninth Street and Fourth Avenue."

"I know what it is," I said. "Billy and I go back."

The Tucson Thunder's players used to drink at the Blue Note. Last time I saw Billy Hamm, the owner, he'd offered to stock milk if I came in more often.

He'd lost the sports crowd and thought my being there would help. I never went back, and all Billy got out of it was sour milk.

"What're you doing in a bar, Ozzie?"

"Hiding out. You gave your number, remember?"

"I'm five minutes away. Do not step outside that bar, understand?" I ended the call and said to Roxy, "Looks like things are heating up. Want to come?"

"I go where you go."

We rode to the Blue Note in the Audi.

CHAPTER FIFTY

ourth Avenue is lined with bars and restaurants. It's a street of dreams for the student crowd, if your dreams include brooding in Che Guevara cafés and choking down too many tequila shots and trying not to fall down walking home.

But on a Tuesday night only a handful of dedicated drinkers tripped along the sidewalks.

The Blue Note anchored the downtown end of Fourth Avenue. I pulled to the curb at Ninth Street, across from the bar's front door, and texted Ozzie to say we were outside.

He came out leading his bicycle and walked across to the Audi.

"Nobody can outrun Ozzie Fish. I know the alleys, man." His face was drawn and sweaty, his long blond hair hanging in clumps.

"Where'd this happen?"

"Near my house." He pointed toward the university's tall buildings, the window lights brightening the sky to the east. "I rode all the way here. My mom tends bar for Billy sometimes."

"Is your mom in there now?"

"She's in Phoenix with her alkie boyfriend."

"What about your dad?"

He frowned like it was a crazy question.

It wasn't safe for the kid to be home alone, and I had room at Double Wide.

"You're staying with me a few days," I said. "Tell your mom."

"Okay, sure. Totally. I'll text her." A phone appeared in Ozzie's hand. His thumbs blazed over the glass for a dizzying moment, and like a gunfighter holstering his pistol, he flicked his wrist and the phone was gone again, back in the thigh pocket of his shorts.

After removing the front wheel, Ozzie jammed his bike into the backseat, and he squeezed in beside it.

"Let's drive by Ozzie's apartment and look around," I said.

"A red pickup isn't much to go on."

"They're not going to quit. They've tried twice and they'll try again."

Roxy turned to Ozzie. "Would you recognize the truck if you saw it?"

"Didn't see it good, dude. Happened too fast. Hey, do you think we could grab, like, my Xbox? Like, while we're there?"

I drove slowly up Ninth Street into a neighborhood of tired brick and adobe houses and a few wood-frame jobs. Most needed paint and a few could've benefited from the wrecking ball, unless I was mistaken, and it'd already arrived. The cement hulk of the university's football stadium loomed just north of us, on Sixth Street.

"Up there," Ozzie said. "On the right."

The Bear Down Apartments came into view. The building looked like it had been thrown up for cheap student living in the 1960s.

It was white with gray trim, had two stories with six apartments on the first floor and six more on top. An open metal staircase climbed the side of the building, and individual air conditioners stuck out of the exterior walls of each unit.

"Mine's on the first floor," Ozzie said. "Last one down. Number six."

A bumper-to-bumper line of parked cars filled the curb on both sides of Ninth Street approaching the apartments. I drove between them, and as I cleared the cars, Ozzie thrust his head over the seat and pointed across the intersection.

"That's it, right there. That's the truck."

"I thought you didn't see it," Roxy said.

"I remember the roof lights."

A red pickup with five lights atop the cab had rolled to a stop on the cross street in front of the apartment building. After a brief pause, it inched ahead, stopped again, didn't move for a moment, then backed to the curb in the shadow of some over-hanging trees and killed its lights.

I tooled straight through the intersection, peeled around the block, and pulled up behind the line of parked cars.

"What do we do?" Roxy asked.

"Sit and wait. I want to know who's in that truck."

The night was all shadow and darkness. The neighborhood had no streetlamps. Nearby houses threw out squares of lazy light, their windows like watching eyes.

"Is this a stakeout?" Ozzie said. "Do I get, like, popcorn? Butter would be a necessary, like, condiment. I'd really like to get my Xbox."

The truck stayed there fifteen minutes, until the passenger door opened and a woman stepped out. She spied around the neighborhood, looking over one shoulder and the other.

"Holly Winterset," Roxy said.

"Yup."

She wore a black T-shirt, black pants, and a ball cap set low over her forehead. It obscured her face, but her body type was unique. She had long legs and walked with a pigeon-toed stride. A man got out from behind the wheel. He was well over six feet and wore a cap, too.

I didn't recognize him and neither did Roxy.

Together, they crossed the street to Ozzie's place. There was a light over the apartment door, and in its glow, I saw that Holly was carrying a tire iron.

As the two of them peered through the front window, a car approached.

They both jerked upright and turned to watch the car pass, and when it was out of sight, they walked around the corner and disappeared into the darkness between the end of the building and a chain-link fence along the edge of the property.

"What's on the other side, Ozzie?" I asked.

"A window to my bedroom. Wait a minute, are they gonna steal my stuff?"

After a moment of silence, we heard the unmistakable sound of glass breaking.

"I'd say that's a yes," Roxy said. "But that's instead of killing you, so it's a push."

"My room is, like, a crime scene? This is ragin', dudes. I can't believe this is happening. There's somebody in my room, man. Like, a killer in my room. I'm ragin' back here!'"

Staring toward the apartments, Roxy said, "Ozzie?"

"Yeah?"

"Shut up."

"Whoa. You're acting all perplexed, which can cause a stroke. Proven fact."

A screeching sound muffled by the distance made it out the apartment window and across the street. It sounded like a thousand ticked-off cicadas all screaming at once.

"That's Artemus, my mother's bird. I hope they steal it." Another round of screeching and Ozzie said, "It speaks four languages and I don't know any of them."

Roxy looked over the seat at him. "That makes no sense whatsoever. How do you know there are four if you don't understand them?"

"Because I listen. Think it through." Ozzie used his hand to push his hair back off his face. "If she takes my Xbox, I can still play *Fortnite* on my phone. It's better with the Xbox, but I can still, like, do it. But I'll trade the Xbox for Artemus, straight up."

"That's enough talking," Roxy said. "Really."

"I'm worried about your perplexion. Stroke? Hello? I've seen it happen. Blah-bitty-blah-bitty-blah. Drooling. Don't even."

"I'm begging you, Ozzie."

"Like, take the stupid bird. Please."

I opened the Audi door and stepped out. I told Roxy to slide behind the wheel and stay ready in case we had to buzz out of there in a hurry.

"I need to ID that guy," I said. "I'm going to check the registration on the truck."

"Better work quick. That's not a big apartment."

I ran along the sidewalk on the north side of the street, using the parked cars for cover. Reaching the end of the line, I angled across the intersection and ran straight for the red pickup and opened the driver's door.

Sliding in on my belly, I popped open the glove box, grabbed everything inside, crawled out, and ran back to the Audi. Roxy slid over and I got in behind the wheel.

A few minutes later Holly and the unknown man reappeared at the opposite end of the building, having walked all the way around it. She carried a small item under her arm.

"Know what, Ozzie? That might be your Xbox after all," Roxy said with obvious satisfaction.

"What a rip," he said.

I flipped through the truck driver's papers and found the name on the registration.

"Well, I sure didn't expect this," I said.

"Who is it?"

"Vincent Strong."

"Holly's working with one of the Champagne Cowboys?"

There was a moment of silence as we considered that news.

"Well, well," Roxy said.

"Now I know who jumped me at Sister Phil's."

The address listed on the registration matched that of Holly's business. Without headlights, I backed up along Ninth Street all the way to the next intersection, and when we were well clear of the red pickup, I sped away toward Handy Dandy Plumbing.

CHAPTER FIFTY-ONE

The drive was less than three miles on a dark night, past 2:00 a.m. Handy Dandy sat along a strip of shabby midtown businesses lining the south side of Prince Road. To the left of it was a used-furniture store and to the right a vacuum cleaner repair store that also sold fish tacos while you waited, a dollar a pop.

Nobody was making big money on Prince Road.

After the sidewalk there was a pavement strip for angle parking. I pulled sideways in front of Handy Dandy. Roxy got out of the passenger seat, cupped her hand against the glass to peer inside, and got back in the car.

"Looks like a normal office," she said. "But there's a second room attached. I'll bet there's a back door that opens onto the alley."

"Let's have a look," I said, and drove around and entered the alley at the west end.

It was a narrow unpaved strip with big trash bins lining the rear of the businesses and a tall cinder-block wall bordering the far side. I counted seven businesses down and stopped.

Ozzie stayed in the car. Roxy and I got out. I tried the knob on the rickety back door. Locked. Lowering my shoulder, I busted it open with a single thrust.

The room was small and the smell pungent, of something dead or wishing it was.

Most of the linoleum floor was covered with debris, empty cans of Monster Energy, discarded Big Mac boxes, and a ratty mattress with bedding piled on top. Next to it stood a portable closet with wheels on two bottom slats and clothes hanging from a rod.

Under the clothes were two pairs of hiking boots and a backpack.

Empty prescription bottles littered the floor. They were for the pain meds oxycodone and hydrocodone. Some of them had no markings identifying the doctor or the patient and looked as if they'd come straight from a pharmacist's shop.

Scattered among them were several used needles.

Roxy wrinkled her nose. "I can't believe Strong lives here. It's gross."

She leaned over and used the tips of her fingers to pick through a packed trash bin. She found a prescription bottle with Vincent Strong's name on it.

She held the bottle up to me to see the name.

"Holly sold guns and Vincent was a marine," I said. "That must've been their connection."

Roxy dropped the bottle into the bin and wiped her hands together. "Strong had a dangerous hobby."

"Val Constantine said he had a drug problem," I said.

A rifle stood against the wall in one corner. To my untrained eye, it looked like a marksman's rifle. I stepped over to it for a closer look.

It had a Leupold scope and no lens cover. I'd bet anything the cover I'd found in Sterling's canyon would fit that scope. The barrel was thick and round, measured maybe two feet in length, and had a forward grip, then the magazine, and behind that, the trigger housing.

I snapped a picture of it with my phone and sent it to Cash.

From the Audi, Ozzie called to us through the open back door.

"Get out here quick, you guys," he said. "We got company. That truck's back there."

We hurried outside and saw the same red truck parked sideways across the alley. The driver's window was open, but it was too far away to see who was behind the wheel, though Vincent Strong was a fair guess.

As soon as he saw us, the truck backed up, swung into the alley, and surged forward. I tossed Roxy the keys and she jumped behind the wheel of the Audi while I ran back ten feet or so, grabbed a big trash bin, and pulled it over.

The red truck kept coming, fishtailing on the dirt surface. I ran to catch up to the Audi, now moving toward the opposite end of the alley.

Roxy hung her head out the window. "Let's go! Hurry!"

I tipped over two more trash bins, ran around to the slow-moving Audi's passenger door, and wrestled it open as I sprinted alongside and dived inside.

Looking back, I saw the truck hit the first bin and hurl it airborne. The bin landed with a crash, and the truck hit the other two, pinning them against the wall and blocking its passage.

The truck backed up and rammed them again.

Ozzie bounced around in the backseat. "Dude! What's happening! Oh, man! Oh, man!"

The last I saw before Roxy gunned it out of there, the truck had to stop, back up, and roar forward again, trying to bull the bins out of the way.

CHAPTER FIFTY-TWO

Roxy tore through a web of side streets, blowing stop signs and going as fast as she could go. After clearing the neighborhood, she got onto Speedway Boulevard and wheeled into a twenty-four-hour McDonald's near the university.

She parked in a darkened spot behind the building.

"I need to catch my breath," she said. Her face had lost some color. "That was ridiculous."

From the backseat Ozzie piped up, "Preach, lady." He leaned on his chin, arms crossed on the seat back. "Could I get some fries?"

My phone chirped with a return text from Cash. He recognized Vincent's rifle. It was a Stoner 25, a sniper favorite. Navy SEALs used the Stoner extensively in Iraq and Afghanistan and the marines, too, though less so.

"Now we know for sure who the canyon sniper is," I said.

"Vincent survives two wars with the guy, comes home, and murders him that way. Man, that's cold."

"Drugs," I said. "They made him a monster."

"Jackie was his supplier."

"She'd have access through the medical center."

"She did the same with Angela, fed her drugs to control her," Roxy said.

"Jackie gets him to handle Ash and Bella Kowalik, and Holly the queen of hearts is the getaway driver."

"And Jackie was the one in her father's house when Vincent took him out?"

"Can't be any other way," I said.

It was coming up on 3:00 a.m. The parking lot was dead quiet. Beside it loomed a university dorm, and there were few signs of life there either.

The air held a heavy smell of burgers and hot grease.

Ozzie kept chirping for French fries. Roxy got three singles out of her purse and gave them to him. He flattened them out in his palm and cleared his throat.

"Maybe a beverage, too," he said.

She fished out a few more bills and handed them over, and Ozzie jumped out and ran to the McDonald's. Roxy watched him go. "So, Prospero, how many kids you want to have?"

When I didn't answer, she said, "Okay, seven it is," and looked for some reaction in my stone face. "What's on your mind?"

"Paul and Donna Morton."

"Vincent did them, too, right? He was junked up and panicked." She paused and thought a minute. "But that would mean Sterling lied when he said none of the Champagne Cowboys pulled the trigger up there."

"Sterling was dying. He told the truth."

A truck pulled up to the drive-through window. Roxy and I stared at it, even though it wasn't red and wasn't driven by Vincent Strong. The voice of the girl taking the order was an electronic growl in the quiet night.

I said, "Remember Jackie's comment about your license plate being a billboard?"

"You still grinding on that?"

"What if Jackie saw you at Sterling's house?"

"Thing is, I never saw her there."

"But she could've driven up while you were inside, spotted the *NEWSBABE* plate, and turned around and left," I said. "She knows Ash's secret and puts it together why you're there. He's going to whistle about the murders."

"Okay, but how would she know his secret?" As soon as the question came out, Roxy knew the answer. Her face came alive. "Unless she was in the Foothills when it happened."

"Exactly. Lonesome Eddie stakes his name on a female shooter."

"Vincent had been in much tighter spots overseas than the Mortons' house," Roxy said. "He didn't panic up there, Jackie did."

"She was the fourth Champagne Cowboy."

"All we have to do is prove it," Roxy said. "If you've got any more ideas about opening that phone, now is the time."

Ozzie came back with a drink and a bag of food. He slurped from the straw and belched. "With one regular order of fries and a medium Coke, I can burp whole entire songs. It's a skill very few people have."

He rummaged the bag for the last few elusive French fries.

"First things first," I said to Roxy. "You're staying with me at Double Wide. No argument."

"Agreed, but let's bring in the police. These people, they're too dangerous."

"Can't do that, Rox, not without conditions."

There were too many things I needed to keep quiet.

I'd been at the scene of two homicides and hadn't called the police. They get cranky about that. And I couldn't talk about Bella Kowalik's murder without mentioning Cash's gunfight in the drainage, and that would land him in jail for possessing a firearm.

Roxy suggested meeting with Pima County homicide detective Benny Diaz. He'd been working with the Sterling case team, and she knew him well. I knew him, too.

We'd had trouble at Double Wide the year before and he handled it.

"I'll tell him we have information, but there are questions we can't answer," Roxy said.

"He won't like leaving facts on the table."

"But he's ambitious, I can use that."

"Be nice to have extra leverage."

"I know exactly what you're thinking."

Roxy said she'd call Diaz to set up the meet and call her father. Rod Santa Cruz was the extra leverage. His name was royalty in the Pima County Sheriff's Department, and having him on our side of the table would give us definite clout.

We drove to Roxy's house to pick up some of her things.

Ozzie and I switched to the Bronco, putting his bike in back. As we waited with the motor running, I hit redial on Sergeant Major Burnside's phone number and got his message.

"I know it's late, but I need help cracking Sterling's phone," I said. "Call me back."

Roxy came out wheeling two suitcases. The bigger of the two was for clothes. The second one, only slightly smaller, held her makeup. There was no such thing as a choice between the two bags. She never went anywhere without both.

She tossed them into the trunk of the Audi, gave me a wait-a-minute finger, ran back inside, and came out with the Beretta shotgun.

She put it on her front seat, used the light from the open door for a spot hair check in the rearview, pulled her leg inside, shut the door, and eased away from the curb.

I fell in behind her in the Bronco and we caravanned to Double Wide.

CHAPTER FIFTY-THREE

The wind was up, and it found a rip in the Bronco's ragtop that drum-rolled all the way across the sleeping city. As we neared the mountains, I called Cash to tell him we were on our way in, and to get Sister Phil and Charlie out of bed and meet us in the Airstream.

Cash waited out on the county road, the AR-15 slung over his shoulder, and walked us the remainder of the way in.

When Ozzie stepped from the Bronco, he gazed around like he was on a distant planet.

"Is this for real? People live way out here?"

"Not people," Cash said. "Just us."

I brought the kid inside and introduced him around.

Sister Phil said, "Hello there, Ozzie Fish."

"Oswald Margo Fish," he said. "Like the ocean, not the card game."

Sister Phil gave him a quizzical grin. She extended her hand to Roxy, who shook it. But she would've gripped a dead carp with more enthusiasm.

I explained what had happened and that everyone needed to be extra vigilant. We talked about where to put Ozzie for the night.

The best option was with Cash, which didn't please him.

Ozzie saw his reaction and grinned. "Dude's strokin'."

Cash yanked off his cap and gave his cabbage a hard scratching, like he was trying to kill whatever might be living there. "Why do I get the food court twerp?"

"Seriously?" Ozzie swept his hair back off his face. He used hair flips like exclamation marks. "I'm standing right here."

Cash fitted the cap back on snugly, one hand on the bill and the other in back. He snapped his chin at Ozzie and walked out the door. Ozzie made a crazy face and, with mocking swings of his arms and legs, followed Cash out, Sister Phil and Charlie close behind.

"Guess we're living together now," Roxy said, and looked around the Airstream. "Not what I had in mind."

"It oozes romance, doesn't it?"

"It oozes something. Anything to drink?"

She searched my cabinets and found a bottle of Gran Patrón tequila. She poured three fingers and went to take a shower, and while she was gone, I retrieved Sterling's phone from the junked Ford Fiesta.

Roxy reemerged wearing only a Green Bay Packers T-shirt and black panties. She was drying her hair with a towel and looked sexy as hell.

"Burnside call back?"

"I'll keep trying."

Sterling's last mission stuck with me. I'd already tried 072113 and ALIKIA, but the mission meant a lot to him and there could be more to it. I needed to ask Burnside.

Roxy sat sideways on the kitchen bench in a pose that was a little bit Renaissance art and a little bit West Hollywood pole dancer. She was barefoot, toes painted flaming red, and she had one arm bent behind her head, the raised T-shirt showing her belly.

Her legs were stretched out along the length of the bench, their smooth skin cut by lines of muscle and bone that were never straight for long and curved in just the right places and at just the right times.

She sipped the tequila and looked at the glass.

"Tequila doesn't do it for me. I should get my Chivas out of the car. When I shower at night, I never feel like putting my shoes back on. Are you like that?"

I shrugged. She looked at me with careful eyes. "You look wiped out. I know I am."

"Holly and that tire iron. If she'd found Ozzie, she would've busted his head open."

"Like dropping a watermelon out a fifth-floor window."

"Ever think about what people do to each other?" I said.

She sipped. "Used to. Until I was sixteen."

"You know the exact year. What happened at sixteen?"

"Rod started showing me his files, police reports, crime scene photos, all of it."

"He wanted you to know the world."

She bent her head sideways and ran her fingers up through her wet hair several times to air it out. "He wanted me to know him. My stepmom had died, and it hit him hard. He was afraid of losing me, too."

"I'm guessing you didn't spend a lot of time at home at sixteen."

"Not much."

"Rod tried to keep you close with images of dead bodies?"

"What'd Sam use? Shakespeare?"

"What else?"

She sipped the tequila again. She held the glass with the little finger on her right hand concealed behind it. A childhood accident had severed the finger at the first knuckle, and keeping it hidden had become an unbreakable habit.

She saw me looking at the way she held the glass and frowned, as if she'd been caught.

"You don't have to do that with me," I said.

"Habit."

"On TV the other day somebody said showing your imper-fections lets other people in."

She cranked her eyebrows off the ceiling. "Did you just say that to me? We're breaking up right now. No way you came up with that on your own."

"Dr. Phil."

"I knew it. The man's a menace to society. And bald, I might add."

"I was playing with the remote waiting for *Bonanza*."

"Don't know who's worse, you or me." She sipped and relaxed and her eyes drifted off in thought. "Rod's photos never bothered me. He was reaching out the only way he knew how. For a while, I thought of going to the academy myself."

"I get why you didn't, daughter of a legend and all that."

"Nah, drug tests." She gave a high trill of a laugh and gathered herself off the bench. "I'm going to grab my Chivas. What'd I do with my shoes?"

She couldn't find them and slipped her feet into mine. She looked funny with the Packers T-shirt barely below her waist and her lovely legs making the long trip down the devil's highway to my ratty Adidas runners.

Near the door, she stopped and adopted a listening posture.

"I keep hearing a knocking out there."

"Hoist chains on the flagpoles," I said. "The wind comes off the mountains pretty hard."

"Hmm." She paused again, and her face darkened. "We were lucky in that alley."

"It was close."

"They know we're here. I mean, right now."

"Yeah, they know."

I flipped on the outside lights as Roxy started down the steps, clumsily in my shoes. I held the door open against the wind. She reached into the Audi to retrieve her pint bottle of Chivas Regal from the glove box.

The clouds had made the night darker than normal. No stars, no moon, and the desert and the mountains were hiding beyond the perimeter of my lights.

Roxy came back and poured herself a drink, no ice.

I closed and locked the door and we went back to the bedroom.

The shotgun stood in the corner. I could smell the gunpowder. You can always smell gunpowder, and it carries a certain energy, a power. Roxy smelled fine from the shampoo, and there's a different kind of power in that.

Mix them together and it can do things to you.

"Tell me what Sam did," she said. "Quote Shakespeare to you and your brothers?"

"At supper every night. Went around the table. Like a college seminar."

"How'd I know that?"

I took hold of her T-shirt from the bottom and pulled it up over her head and tossed it. She wiggled out of the black panties, leaving her naked but for my shoes. She held the Scotch glass with such care that even with her arms stretched over her head she didn't spill a drop.

She wrapped her arms around my neck, including the glass.

"He'd recite a passage and we'd have to give the next line," I said. *But, soft! what light through yonder window breaks?*

Roxy finished the quote: *It is the east, and Juliet is the sun.*

I gave her a big smile, partly from surprise and partly approval.

"You didn't think I knew that, did you?" Roxy said. "I read it again because I knew it was your fave."

"I believe they call that romantic."

"My jam, baby." She took a sip of Scotch, said, "That's more like it," and put the glass on the desk next to my laptop.

She turned to face me in the dark, pressing tight against me. We kissed and it was good, and we kissed again, and it was better.

With her lips and body against mine, I managed to get my clothes off, hurriedly and with commendable skill. She never removed the Adidas shoes. There just wasn't time.

The bed was narrow, not built for two, but we made it work.

CHAPTER FIFTY-FOUR

The only ride we could use that Jackie, Vincent and Holly hadn't seen was Cash's blue Malibu, so the next day Roxy and I drove it to one of those leaky-faucet trucker motels along the freeway. There was a restaurant attached. Lunchtime at Johnny's was bright and loud with the rolling energy of voices all going at once and sprinting waitresses.

On the way inside I said to Roxy, "Follow my lead on this."

"Yeah, sure."

We waved off the smiling hostess and found Rod Santa Cruz and Benny Diaz sitting at a corner table. They stood when they saw Roxy approaching.

Diaz had perfectly trimmed black hair and looked earnest in his bland discount warehouse suit jacket. Rod wore a black silk shirt and a black sequined blazer with a red floral design below the side pockets.

As I talked, he sipped iced tea and stared out the window, except when the waitress came, and then he stared at her. He acted oblivious to what I was saying.

But his eyes told me he wasn't missing a word.

Diaz listened intently and jotted in a notebook.

I told him the story, leaving out what I didn't want him to know. He sniffed out the gaps, and when he asked a question that compromised me, Rod steered him away.

Diaz let it happen because of what I was giving him.

If you hand a detective solid leads on two high-profile homicides, as I was doing with the Sterling and Kowalik murders, with the promise of prime news coverage from Roxanne Santa Cruz, he'll take the ride every time.

"I'll find Holly Winterset and Vincent Strong," Diaz said. "I want to emphasize, Whip, these people are killers. Let us handle it."

Roxy said she'd do a piece on a possible break in the murders with Winterset and Strong as persons of interest.

"Can I get you on camera, Benny?" she said. "That pretty face?"

He angled his jaw in a preening way. "Absolutely."

Diaz left. Rod watched out the restaurant window as he got into his car.

"That freakin' jacket, man. These young guys don't know how to dress." He shook his head. "A cop's gotta project."

Before leaving, Rod threw out his arms and said, "Baby girl," and gave his daughter a hug and kiss. He said to me, "You need anything at all, Whip, call me. ¿Entiendes?"

Back in the Malibu, Roxy said, "You didn't mention Jackie Moreno."

"Must've forgot."

"You didn't forget. You're keeping her for yourself."

I pulled onto the frontage until I reached Speedway and turned east to go across town to the TV station. Roxy wanted to get started on her piece and I planned to pick her up later.

"Diaz will get to her soon enough," I said.

"But you want to be first."

"I'm going to stay on her until I get something. Long as it takes. That okay with you?"

"You're making this too personal."

"Is that what I'm doing? When did I start doing that? Was it when Paul and Donna got shot down in their own home? For nothing? Is that when I started making it too personal?"

Roxy let the conversation drop and we rolled along amid one of those long silences that follow heated words. I pulled into the

KPIN lot and she swiped her ID in the wall pad by the side door and disappeared inside.

Midafternoon, I turned back west and drove to the sandstone duplex, not sure what I was going to do when I got there except watch, and if Jackie moved, follow her.

The Camaro wasn't in the driveway, so I drove to the only other place I thought she might be, the University Medical Center. I made the three-block hop into the surface parking lot, drove up and down the aisles of parked cars, and found the Camaro.

A few minutes later, as I was cruising the lot waiting for a space to open, Jackie came out of the building walking quickly and carrying a cardboard box.

She loaded it into the Camaro and drove away, and I swung in behind her as she headed north up Oracle Road, passing five traffic lights before turning into a Target store. I followed her into the busy lot, found a space two lanes away, parked facing the Camaro, and waited.

Fifteen minutes later, she came out carrying a small plastic bag, got behind the wheel, and sat for several minutes with her head down as if fidgeting with something in her lap.

Her right hand came up holding a phone. She draped her left arm over the steering wheel. As she talked, she gestured and poked angrily at the air as if arguing.

I noticed something. The phone was small and white.

The one she'd used at her house was an iPhone, dark colored and bigger than a back pocket. Jackie had just bought a prepaid burner phone for calls she didn't want anyone to know about. I needed to get my hands on it.

After five minutes of animated talk, she backed out of the space and drove to the edge of the Target lot. As she waited for northbound traffic to clear, she draped both arms over the steering wheel, holding the phone with two hands and using her thumbs to punch in another call.

LEO W. BANKS

When a space opened, she turned north onto Oracle talking on the phone.

The traffic was solid. I stayed three cars back, a luxury I could easily afford. A bright yellow Camaro was hard to lose.

Everybody tickled bumpers, and nobody was having any fun.

Horns blared. Hands were thrust out open windows to deliver angry messages. You knew the offense was serious when both driver and passenger rolled down their windows to deliver double freedom rockets.

The coolest guy around was sound asleep under a bus bench, hands folded neatly on his stomach and using a spare tire for a pillow.

We inched past Bo Hung's Fitness, a cancer treatment center, the Black Hat Lounge, and a Taco Bell. After that came a CBD store that promised to cure everything that went wrong at the previous four stops.

At the traffic light opposite the Tucson Mall, Jackie crawled to a stop in the left lane, the phone still pressed to her right ear. I came up behind her in the right lane, one car back and with a partial view through her passenger window.

The light flipped to green.

As the Camaro inched forward, Jackie leaned to her right, looking down, and when her right hand returned to the steering wheel, the phone wasn't in it.

She'd dropped it into the console.

Three traffic lights later, she turned into the parking lot of an outdoor gear store called Peak Mountain. I drove past the entrance and made a U-turn, and by the time I got back to the store she was inside. I found a space for more waiting.

Jackie was inside twenty-five minutes and came out carrying a camouflage backpack, heavy, judging by the way it bent her shoulder. I remembered what Angela had said about Jackie having a cabin in the mountains.

It looked like she might be getting ready to run.

She drove back down into the main part of the city.

I stayed with her until she turned into her neighborhood, clearly headed home. I backed off and went to an Ace Hardware and bought a three-dollar razor-blade paint scraper that could put a handy tear in the Camaro's canvas top.

Shortly before 5:00 p.m., I drove back to the duplex.

The Camaro was in the driveway.

Three houses down the street, I turned around and parked facing Jackie Moreno's apartment, waiting for darkness.

CHAPTER FIFTY-FIVE

Night fell slowly over the Catalinas, and even when the sun had finished its work, the darkness wasn't complete. Light from the medical center towers bathed the neighborhood in a strange yellow glow.

Lights shone through Jackie's front window.

Initially I wanted to wait until her lights went out to make my move.

But if she was going to run, she could step out of the house at any moment and drive off. If I lost her in night traffic, I might never get my hands on that burner. Even though the lights in her window still shone, now was my best chance to grab it.

As I was about to step out of the car, my phone chirped with a text from Roxy.

"We're dealing with a crooked cop," she wrote. "She just solved all her problems."

The text included a link to a story the *Arizona Republic* had posted saying Bumpy Topp was dead. Detective Wanda Dietz had encountered him in the wash earlier that day, and when he charged her with a hunk of rebar, she shot him.

Details were sparse.

Sitting outside Jackie Moreno's apartment, I called Dietz's cell and had barely finished leaving a message when she texted me: "This changes nothing. Waiting for DNA and will proceed on results."

The impact of Topp's death ping-ponged through my head.

He could never be questioned. He could never be squeezed for a confession.

Dietz would never have to explain why she couldn't find him before the trial but a guy from Papa Joe's Pizza could, and why her so-called evidence had convicted the wrong man.

That's why she killed him.

To avoid answering questions. To keep her reputation intact.

I fought that conclusion. That might've been naïve, but I didn't want to believe it.

I pushed those thoughts aside and walked down to the Camaro and used the paint scraper to slice a hole in the roof. Reaching inside, I popped the lock and opened the door.

The interior smelled of stale perfume. The cardboard box and the camo backpack were still in the car, more indications she planned to take off. There was no reason to haul them into the house only to carry them back out again.

The Target bag was on the floor in front of the passenger seat, along with the torn plastic and cardboard packaging for the burner.

I lifted the console lid and the white phone was there. I slipped it into my pocket.

A car door slammed, and an engine roared to life over my shoulder. I straightened out of the Camaro and looked. The noisy car was backed into a carport directly across the street.

When its headlights flashed on, they turned me into a birthday cake, all lit up next to the Camaro. The driver obviously saw me and, wanting to see more, hit his high beams, which sent light all the way up the driveway to Jackie's apartment.

I was as inconspicuous as a guy wearing a raccoon mask walking out of a bank carrying a tommy gun and a sack of cash.

The driver sat unmoving, revving the engine before rolling out from under his carport.

The curtain in Jackie's front window moved. Or it could've been a shadow made by the headlights as the neighbor's car turned at the bottom of the driveway.

The driver, old and very bald, gave me a long look as he passed beside me.

I walked back to the Malibu and worked the buttons on Jackie's phone, hoping she hadn't yet set up password protection, and she hadn't.

The log of outgoing calls listed three numbers.

The one she'd made from Target was to a number I knew well, in the 480 area code. It belonged to Jackie's stepmom, Valentine Constantine. Val had told me she'd had no contact with Jackie in years, but now, a week after Ash Sterling's death, they were talking.

That could've been innocent enough. They'd reconnected following his murder.

But if that were true, why did Jackie appear angry during the call?

The second call was to Mexico. I did a number search and found that it was for a branch of the Bancomer Bank in Mexico City, in the Polanco.

Hiding Sterling's million in cash wouldn't be easy. You couldn't stuff it under a mattress, and banks in the States ask too many questions.

But a safety-deposit box in Mexico City would work just fine.

Sitting in the Malibu, I remembered my meeting with Val in Scottsdale, when I'd trapped her in the Lexus. Before I'd identified myself, she pointed out her shoes and told me she'd recently bought them at Enrique's in the Polanco.

Maybe she and Jackie had gone there together. Maybe they were in on Ash Sterling's murder together.

Feeling excited, I called Roxy at the station.

"I think I know where Sterling's cash is," I said, and explained what I'd learned.

"If Val went to Mexico City, she must've been in for a cut."

"My guess."

"If you're right that their call was heated, that's another word for money."

I said, "Can you get someone to drive you back to Double Wide?"

"You plan to sit out there all night?"

"Jackie's going to bounce, I'm sure of it. I want to keep eyes on her."

"Danny can drive me," Roxy said, referring to her cameraman. "He never goes home except to turn his underwear inside out and eat a Pop-Tart."

After hanging up, I clicked through Jackie's burner to the third call she'd made. It was a local number. I hit redial, a machine kicked on, and a voice I recognized said, "If you owe me money, go. Otherwise, ain't here, ain't home, ain't talkin'."

It was Donny Jim James.

I hung up and sat staring down the street at Jackie's apartment. Another hour passed. The neighborhood was night quiet and very dark, until police lights flashed in my rearview.

Seeing them, I suspected that either Jackie or the onion-headed geezer vigilante had called 911 about the suspicious man in the blue Chevy Malibu.

My conversation with the cop went as those conversations do. Howdy. Fine, you? What brings you to this quiet neighborhood at night? I told him I'd stopped to make some calls and didn't want to do so while driving.

The cop told me to sit tight while he ran my information.

When he came back, he said, "Kind of a junker car for an ex–big leaguer."

"Borrowed it."

"Who from?"

"Cashmere Miller."

The cop had obviously run Cash's name and was testing me. "You might think about getting a better class of friends."

"I lie awake nights hoping for a better class of friends. Some days I think I should take out a personal. Desperately seeking normal."

The cop leaned in the window and his eyes roamed over the backseat and up to the front again. He handed my paperwork back.

"Best move it along, Whip Stark. It's getting late."

With the black-and-white still parked behind me, I drove out of the neighborhood to the same all-night McDonald's near the university, bought coffee from the drive-through and had a few sips while I waited for the cop to get busy with other calls, and returned to the sandstone duplex.

The Camaro was gone, and that told me Jackie had seen me and called the cops.

I trotted up the sidewalk and into her backyard. The sliding glass door by the dining room was unlocked, another sign she didn't plan on coming back. Walking through the rooms confirmed that. They looked to have been swept in a hurry, with items dropped on the floor and clothes left hanging in the closet.

I called Roxy back.

"I can't believe this, but I just got played. Jackie's gone."

CHAPTER FIFTY-SIX

Roxy called off Danny the cameraman and I picked her up at the station. We passed a quiet night at Double Wide and next morning I drove her back to work. After watching her into KPIN's side door, I returned to the sandstone duplex figuring Jackie wouldn't be there.

But I wanted to be certain.

She wasn't, and it looked as if Holly had cleared out of her side overnight. Boxes and random household items had been tossed into the dirt beside her driveway.

The story was the same at Handy Dandy Plumbing. The front office and Vincent Strong's back room had been gone over and emptied of valuables.

The four of them were on the run, and the only lead I had was Angela's remark that Jackie had a cabin in the mountains. But I had no idea where the cabin might be.

With a couple of hours to kill, I stopped at a coffee shop and called Sergeant Major Burnside. He didn't pick up and I left another message.

Jackie's burner was in my pocket. I pulled it out and hit redial on Donny Jim's number.

After the beep, I said: "Congratulations! You're a grand prize winner in the Publishers Clearing House Sweepstakes. This is life-changing money, Mr. James. Without delay, call me back, Howard Q. Farquar, and I'll provide instructions on how to pick up your massive check. Thank you for entering and being such a giant douche nugget."

I hadn't planned to say that. It just found its way out and I laughed out loud.

The laptop ranger at the next table glanced over his screen at me.

"Sometimes I crack myself up," I said.

He pretended not to hear me and went back to his work.

Over the next hour, I hit redial again and again on Jimbo's number. I was an overcaffeinated stalker. When he didn't pick up, I switched to my own phone and did the same, and on the ninth try, he answered.

"Who the hell's this, keeps calling me?"

"How come you don't answer the phone for your gal pal?"

"What are you talking about?"

"I know about Jackie Moreno and the murders, Jimbo."

He sounded like I'd woken him up. There were rustling noises on his end. "That you, Baseball? How'd you get my number?"

"It's all falling apart and I'm right behind you."

"I ain't part of them no more. Don't hang their shit on me."

"If you weren't involved, I can help you. I know people." That was a line. I didn't know anybody well enough to make that claim. But he didn't know that.

"They wanna kill you. Walk away, bro. They're crazy, all three of 'em."

"Jackie has a cabin the mountains, right?"

He didn't say anything, but that didn't mean he was quiet. He coughed, snorted, and sniffed, and every breath came with a loud blowing sound.

"Jackie, Vincent, and Holly, tell me how to find them, Jimbo."

I waited. Nothing.

He'd hung up.

After lunch, I picked up Roxy and we drove back to Double Wide. The wind had picked up, and we could feel it banging against the Bronco as we rolled down the mountain.

Cash was on his front porch with binoculars ranging the mountain horse trail.

"Looks clear," he said. "I'll drive up in a bit and lock around."

Later in the afternoon, Roxy announced that she wanted to make dinner using a recipe she'd found for Margarita Chicken Quesadillas.

Please, no, I thought. "You really don't have to go to the trouble."

"I don't mind," she said. "I've been meaning to try this out."

"I've got a pizza in the freezer out back. One of those giant ones from Costco."

"Gross. Costco?"

"No, they taste good. They're huge. They're like manhole covers."

For some reason, that didn't dissuade her, so Margarita Quesadillas it was.

With an hour of daylight remaining and my hoist chains rattling, Cash called. I looked out the door. His Malibu was a blue dot on the mountain trail.

"Don't expect a shooter today," he said. "Not in this wind."

I invited him down for supper. "Might as well get Ozzie, too. I haven't had enough aggravation today."

"All riiight, pizza," he said.

"I tried, Cashy. But it's a no-go."

"You mean Roxanne's cooking again? God. I'll just boil some dogs at my place."

"Don't leave me alone."

Cash huffed and stalled and finally relented. "The things I do for you."

"My man."

"I know, I'll get Charlie. He'll clean everybody's plate."

In a little while Ozzie and Cash came in and sat at my table and Charlie walked in a few minutes after that. He slid onto the bench and bumped his butt against Cash and said, "Scooch,

scooch," and the two of them scooched as Charlie rubbed his hands together with glee.

He said to Roxy, "I hear we're having a big feast."

Cash gave me a conspiratorial nod.

The overhead TV was on. While Roxy committed serious crimes in the kitchen, the three of us watched a CNN story about a guy in Nebraska who played checkers with his potbellied pig.

At 5:15 p.m., Burnside called back.

Seeing his number, I sprang to my feet. "Sergeant Major. Finally. I've been trying to get you."

"Would've called sooner but I got nothing for you. You don't give up, do you?"

"Five minutes."

"Go," he said in that cannon-shot voice.

"On Captain Sterling's last mission, he killed this Taliban guy, Ali. Okay? Right? I need to know everything you can tell me about that mission."

He let out a long breath. "Nothing to tell, Stark. Cap was a soldier and did his job, killed what had to be killed."

"He wouldn't rotate out until he got Ali, correct?"

"Affirmative. After his target went tango down, Cap was ready to go home and make money. He liked money. He was grade three and that wasn't near enough for Cap."

"Grade three?"

"A marine captain is a commissioned officer, grade three on the DOD pay scale."

That sounded like a good password possibility. "Hang on a minute." I knew I was taking a big chance, but I had a good feeling. I grabbed the phone and typed in CAP3AS.

No luck. That was the ninth try.

Only one remained before the phone permanently locked. "Shit!"

"There's always that," Burnside said, and hung up.

"Sorry, babe," Roxy said. She was chopping onions on the kitchen counter. "But I'm liking Sterling's birthday more and more."

A sudden weariness came over me. I poured a glass of milk and stepped outside for some air. The low sun shared the sky with the western mountains. Darkness wouldn't be long coming.

As my foot touched the bottom step, a bullet slammed into the Airstream right beside me. A puff of air tickled my ear as it passed.

That's a breeze you never want to feel.

CHAPTER FIFTY-SEVEN

I dived to the ground, got a mouthful of dirt, and rolled under the Airstream. About twenty seconds later Cash leaped out the door.

While still in the air, he tossed the Glock onto the ground in front of the Airstream. I leaned out and grabbed it and scrambled back. Cash ran around the trailer and down into the wash. A bullet thumped into the ground near his feet as he ran.

Sister Phil popped her head out of Opal's trailer.

"Stay inside!" I shouted.

She made a panicked face and slammed the door.

Through the sliver of light between the ground and the underside of the Airstream, I saw Cash emerge from the wash at a point opposite his trailer. He darted across Main Street, jumped the railing on the west end of his porch, and ran to the opposite side.

He peered around the corner at the horse trail winding around the mountain. The wind had raised a dust devil that moved in a perfect spiral across the desert.

Cash poked his head out and back three times quickly and called to me.

"Can't see nothing up there."

The next shot arrived in the form of a distant sound, a dull thump, like someone had banged a drum in a broom closet. The bullet hit a second later, smashing into the porch pole nearest Cash.

The wood made a loud crack, and the pole went crooked at the point of impact.

Cash flattened the length of his body against his trailer like he was part of it.

"Stoner 25," he called across the street.

"Vincent Strong," I said.

"I shoulda been up there, Mayor. I must've just missed him."

I hollered to Roxy. "You all right in there?"

She shouted back, "Fine, we're good, we're good."

I told her and Charlie to stay put and crawled to the protection of the Airstream's back side. From there, I stood and stuck my head out and saw the faint image of a black truck trailing dust as it sped along the mountain trail.

"Strong's on the run," I called to Cash. "He's moving."

"I'm on my way."

"Be quick. I'll take care of things down here."

Cash gripped the porch railing with two hands, swung his legs over, and ran to the Malibu. He got behind the wheel and stuck his head out the window.

"Might be more than one," he said. "Watch your six."

He screamed out of Double Wide on spinning wheels.

I watched as Strong's dust cloud moved out of sight, around to the back side of the mountain. I ran to the front of the Airstream and got on my haunches behind the Bronco.

Next thing I knew Roxy was at my side.

She was barefoot, wore gym shorts, the Packers T-shirt, and an American flag ball cap turned backward. She crouched there with the Beretta tucked against her shoulder, scanning the wash behind me.

It was a beautiful sunset, and cool with a blood sky. Everything looked clear. Main Street was empty. No sounds that couldn't be explained and no sign of another attacker.

But when a bullet buzzes that close, there's no such thing as all clear. In your mind, there's always another one coming.

"My hands are shaking," I said.

"Me, too."

"You shouldn't be out here, Rox."

"Tell me about it. My dinner's going to be ruined."

That made it two close calls in one night.

CHAPTER FIFTY-EIGHT

Strong got away easily. On the back side of the mountain, the dirt road turned to pavement, and from there it was a fast run down into the city. Cash had no doubt the rifle was a Stoner 25. He knew from his time in Iraq and Afghanistan.

"Hear that sound all night long," he said.

There was a mouse hole in the side of the Airstream, and Cash found the spent 7.62-millimeter bullet on the floor inside.

Before I could tell her not to, Sister Phil had called 911. I preferred keeping the cops away, but they streamed over the mountain with flashing lights and wailing sirens, swarming Double Wide for the remainder of that night and into the next day.

Benny Diaz wanted to know where to look for Vincent Strong. I told him I had no clue, but he didn't believe me.

"I don't recommend holding anything back, Whip. He's hunting you and he isn't alone. Anything else you want to tell me?"

"Can't help you, Benny."

"You understand there's nothing we can do for you. All the way out here."

I didn't say anything. He stared, giving me time to change my mind.

When I didn't, he said, "Roxanne says she'll have her story ready in a day or two. If somebody recognizes him, we might get lucky."

The only play I had left was Val Constantine.

The day after the shooting, I drove to Constant Lexus in Scottsdale. Figuring she wouldn't take my call anyway, I didn't let her know beforehand that I was coming and had no plan other than putting her in a corner and seeing what shook loose.

But it was a waste of time. Val was away on a trip, and I turned around and jumped onto I-10 for the drive back to Tucson. Between the monotony of the highway and the giant eighteen-wheelers trying to kill me, I had plenty of time to think.

Burnside's remarks about Sterling kept running through my mind. He liked money and, after killing Ali, wanted to go home to get some.

That convinced me to change the way I'd been thinking about his password.

I started out trying combinations related to his early life, his home life. Then I went to his time in the marines and his last mission.

But what if the password had nothing to do with either of those? What if it was about his life after returning stateside, his life as a Champagne Cowboy?

That's where the money was.

I exited the freeway on Speedway Boulevard and started driving west for home.

The air held the renegade smell of rain as I came over Gates Pass and saw Paradise Mountain on the horizon. Storm clouds canopied the sky in black and gray, but for one spot where the sun elbowed through and turned the peak into a burning candle.

The sight made me think of Burro Peak.

Val had described the night the Cowboys were on Ash's balcony, jumping around in celebration. They'd just made a big score on Burro Peak.

"We're going to be rich," Sterling said to Val.

In his file, Lonesome Eddie Palmer listed the jobs he suspected the Champagne Cowboys had done, and Burro Peak was among them.

The address was 500 Sleeping Burro Lane, but I couldn't remember the amount stolen.

The first thing I did after pulling into Double Wide was grab Sterling's phone out of the Ford Fiesta. I sat at the kitchen table and leafed through Lonesome Eddie's file, dragging my finger down to 500 Sleeping Burro Lane and Palmer's estimate of the amount stolen.

Two hundred and ten thousand in cash and diamonds.

Roxy was sitting with me. "That's not couch change. Was that their biggest job?"

I checked the others listed, and nothing came close.

"You've got one try left," she said. "You sure you want to use it on Burro Peak?"

"Ash Sterling was dancing on the balcony, Rox."

I got up and paced around the kitchen. My muscles felt tight from a combination of hope and desperation. The phone sat on the table. I looked at it as if it might start talking and tell me the answer.

As I was thinking it over, my own phone chirped with a text from Gloria in Cibecue, on the Apache Reservation.

Titus Ortega had been killed by a sniper firing from the ridge behind their house.

Gloria wrote, "I tracked him. Big feet, white man's feet. Tribal cops will never find him Can you help?"

"Damn," I said, and put the phone down. My body sagged.

"What is it?" Roxy said.

I told her. "I warned Titus," I said. "He was a thief, but he didn't deserve this."

"You did the best you could."

"I drove up there and warned him."

"Just going there put your life in danger. There was nothing more you could've done."

The news made my stomach flip over, and it took a minute to calm down. When I turned my attention back to Sterling's phone, I knew I had to try.

"I'm going to do this," I said.

I leaned over the table and typed in 500SBL, and the phone opened.

Roxy jumped into my arms. I grabbed her in a bear hug and spun her around and took her face in my hands and kissed her.

Sitting down again with Roxy leaning over my shoulder, I looked through Sterling's texts and emails and found nothing. I hit photos and then albums and there were no videos. I hit tools and voice memos and found a nine-minute audio recording.

It was made the day before his murder.

I hit play, and the first few seconds consisted of voices too far off to be intelligible, but the tone was angry. Then came footsteps on tile and the voices got louder and louder until they sounded like they were in the Airstream with us.

I'd never heard Ash talk and said to Roxy, "That him?"

"Definitely. And Jackie."

There was the scrape of a chair being moved on the hard floor, the click of glass on a countertop, a liquid being poured. I assumed they'd walked from the front door to the kitchen.

The first words came from Ash: "I'd offer you juice, but you won't be here long."

"I need to know," Jackie Moreno said.

"What do you think? Of course. Yes, yes."

"The reporter, Newsbabe? You've been talking to her?"

"I like her company," Ash said in matter-of-fact tone, but with a definite dig in it.

"That fly with the extensions, the one that does crime stories?"

Roxy got a shocked look. "What bullshit. Since when do I work for Fox? I've never worn extensions in my life. Bitch." She leaned closer over my shoulder.

"Does she know?" Jackie said.

"So unnecessary," Ash said. "I brought you in to help you make money and you go and lose your mind." There was a pause. I heard him breathing. He spoke more softly this time. "Guilt's a waste of time. I had to learn that one the hard way."

"No good deed," Jackie said. Her words had a smile in them.

"Two people dead for no reason. That's hard to live with."

"The good news is the doctor says you don't have to worry about it for long." Jackie laughed, a cruel cackle. "Witnesses complicate things, don't they? If I didn't do it, all you heroes, you Champagne Cowboys, would be behind bars right now. I did you a favor."

Rage ran through me all over again. I'd suspected for some time that she'd killed Paul and Donna Morton, but hearing her say the words made it more real, and visceral.

After a long silence Jackie said, "Well?"

Sterling didn't respond. I heard a sipping sound.

"Does the reporter know?" Jackie pressed. "I'm asking you directly."

"No. She doesn't."

"You know what's good for you. That's smart." Confident, satisfied.

"Not yet. I haven't decided."

"Are you threatening me?" Jackie's anger jumped out of the phone. There was a long pause, and with a strained calm in her voice, she said, "You could make this easy and promise to cut it off with her, no more interviews."

"If I don't?"

"I could kill you now. Daddy." The last word came out in a low growl. "Give you a head start on your life in hell."

"I wouldn't recommend it," he said. "You talk too much."

"What does that mean?"

" You just handed me an insurance policy."

Jackie made a choking sound and the breath whistled out of her. "Tell … me … what … that … means." Her voice got louder on each word, and then came a crashing sound, as if she'd tossed something against a wall and it rattled around on the floor.

The footsteps going away were fast and angry, and a door slammed.

A silence fell hard. Then Ash in a pained whisper: "My little girl."

Roxy wanted to know what I planned to do with the recording.

"It's hard to think right now," I said.

"Give it to Benny, Prospero. Please. We've got everything we need. This can be over."

"You're probably right."

We talked for an hour, and when Roxy went to bed, I stayed at the kitchen table and listened to the recording again. The sound of Jackie's voice admitting what she'd done cut through me like a sword.

I turned the TV on at the same time. It let me hear other voices, connected me to something human. No one should die the way the Mortons died.

There was evil in Jackie's voice, and an ugly pride.

If I turned the tape over to Benny Diaz, the law would put her on trial and treat her like any other human being, and at the end she'd still be breathing the same air as the rest of us.

She didn't deserve that.

About 2:00 a.m., I went back to the bedroom and threw a blanket over Roxy.

Heading back to the kitchen, I heard engine noises outside. I opened the door and through the spitting rain saw a truck turn off the county road, with Cash's Malibu hard on its bumper.

CHAPTER FIFTY-NINE

The truck was Donny Jim James's black Dodge Ram. He pulled up sideways outside the Airstream, killed the engine, and sat. Multiple holes spaced a few inches apart dotted the side of the truck. Bullet holes.

It looked like somebody had blasted the Big Dipper into the side panels.

Cash angled the Malibu in behind him, jumped out, rested the AR on the open driver's door, and took aim directly at Jimbo's truck.

"Slow and easy," Cash said.

The driver's door opened and Jimbo pulled himself out in stages. He put one foot on the ground, shifted his body weight to ensure balance, and, gripping the side of the truck, let the other foot down as he slid on his butt off the seat.

His elaborate choreography ended with a grunt of pain.

"Intercepted him coming over the mountain, Mayor," Cash said. "Had a .38-caliber revolver in his pocket. In the truck a Remington pump-action shotgun, a Springfield 9 mm handgun, and a Colt Python .357 magnum."

"Some arsenal, Jimbo," I said.

"Gimme a break. I left in a hurry."

"You mean there's more?"

He shrugged. "Cold dead hands, bro."

"Says he's got something for us," Cash said. "Keep your hands up where we can see them, plunger boy."

"You already searched me," he snarled over his shoulder.

"Just do it, shithead."

Bent feebly at his back, Jimbo hung his meaty hands over the open door.

"I didn't come here for trouble," he said. "You said you could help me. I wanna talk."

I gave Cash a signal to relax and he slowly lowered the rifle.

Jimbo stepped around the door into the open. His left arm was wrapped in a bloodstained white bandage. He wore a loose-fitting gray T-shirt, bloodstained, and his jeans were spattered with blood as well.

Raindrops had beaded on his face, creating a sparkle effect in my lights, but behind the twinkle he looked beaten down and exhausted.

The noise of the vehicles and the voices had drawn Sister Phil out of Opal's trailer. She gasped when she saw Jimbo's condition.

"He needs help," she said and started toward him.

I held my hand out to stop her and said to Jimbo, "You came to talk, talk."

"I got nothing left, Baseball. No house, no job, no girl. When I found out they was going after some kid, that tore it for me, and I split."

He motioned to the holes in his truck. "They caught up with me last night. I was in town driving along, and the shooting started. Don't know how I got out of there alive, but you're next, you and your bony-ass friend."

"Leave my ass out of this," Cash said. "It's been through a lot."

"I'll tell you what I know," Jimbo said. "But you gotta help me with the law."

"Already told you I would."

"I could use a beer or two. They gimme me Percs in the hospital and I need something to wash 'em down."

"Didn't know I was running a saloon."

"Don't hard-ass me, bro. I got no smoke with you. Never did except for my tires. You shouldn'ta done that."

"You tried to run me down on Campbell Avenue."

He waved like it was nothing. "When my temper goes, it goes. I was protecting Holly. But stuff's changed, okay?"

"What's changed?"

"Me and Holly, that's what." Anguish seized his face and made a mess of it. "She dumped me and went over to Jackie. They're like snuggle bunnies every night now. Two years Holly and me worked on the plumbing business, talking about all the stuff we had going on. It was gonna be great."

"Match.com. Too bad she's a murderer."

"She ain't my girl no more, so that's that." Jimbo kept one hand on the fender of his truck to stay upright.

I told Cash to get a few beers from his trailer. He came back with a six-pack of Pabst Blue Ribbon bottles in a plastic supermarket bag. Jimbo grabbed one, swooshed off the cap, and practically broke his neck getting it down.

He stood the empty on the side panel of his truck.

"Jackie killed Ash Sterling and that maid lady," he said.

"Go on," I said.

"Well, she had Vincent do it anyways, and he's going down next, soon as she's done with you. She gets people doing her dirty work and walks away. She held a gun to her father's head to open the safe and led him out to the living room so Vincent could shoot him. Her own father. I'm telling you, bro, the lady's dark. Like midnight."

"Where's the money?" I had a pretty good idea where it was, but I wanted to know if Jimbo was playing it straight.

"Three days after Sterling, Jackie flew to Mexico City and stashed it in a safety-deposit box." Jimbo closed his eyes from the pain and breathed through his teeth. "She wasn't alone. That big-shot Val lady from Scottsdale that's on the TV all the time, she went with."

He was doing well. Two for two.

"I need to find Jackie Moreno."

Cash handed him another beer and Jimbo drained it and stood the empty beside the first. He started to speak, suppressed a burp with his fist against his mouth, pulled out a hanky, and shook it open like he was signaling surrender.

When he blew his nose it sounded like a disturbance in the exotic bird exhibit.

"Jackie has a cabin up in the Galiuro Mountains." Jimbo waved the hanky back and forth under his nose to finish up. "But on account of last night, it looks like they're back in town. She won't be around long."

"Mexico."

"Some property her family owned when she was a kid. Jackie and Holly, they're gonna buy it back and set up housekeeping down there. But she wants you bad, Baseball, and ain't going south until she finishes business."

"Give me her phone number."

"Jackie's? Which one? She changes out phones like underwears."

"All right, Holly's then."

He pulled out his phone, found the number, and handed me the phone. The bloodstain on Jimbo's arm bandage had spread.

"I need a place to stay for the night, bro. Okay I rack up here? Back of my truck?"

"This man needs attention, Whip," Sister Phil said. "I'll change that dressing."

Cash pulled the Dodge Ram down Main Street and parked in front of Charlie O'Shea's trailer. Drawn by the noise, Charlie stepped onto his porch.

"What's up, gents?" he said.

His eyes were glassy. He was munching from a bag of Cheetos, not a good sign if I needed his help. Charlie's road to bender town was always paved with Cheetos. The Graceland flask had to be close by, probably in his back pocket.

He flipped on his porch lights to help Sister Phil see.

Jimbo sat on the tailgate while she worked on him.

"I have a feeling you worked up a plan," Cash said. "Wanna fill me in?"

I took out my phone and called Holly. After listening to her message, I said: "Tell Jackie I've got Ash Sterling's insurance policy and need a new truck. Time for a deal."

A few lonesome raindrops fell. But they didn't amount to much, barely made a sound, like mice whispering. The fading storm had left behind a wet night that felt colder than it was.

I stood outside the Airstream with Cash, waiting.

CHAPTER SIXTY

ess than a minute later, my phone rang. I hit the talk button and said nothing.

"Insurance policy," Jackie said.

"Witnesses complicate things, you did the Champagne Cowboys a favor, all that."

A grim silence hung between us.

"Just for my own satisfaction," I said, "I need to know what you did with your father's fingers."

"Get to it," Jackie said. "Name your price."

"All of it, every penny you stole from your father."

Cash could hear everything. He gave me a thumbs-up.

Jackie laughed, a musical up-and-down sound. But there was hate all the way through it. "A million dollars? Let's not be greedy. Let's say half. Half sounds about right."

"One phone call and you go away forever," I said.

"Think hard, Whip. The same call means you lose half a million dollars." Her tone was confident and taunting. "Living out in that dump trailer park, I'm sure you need more than a new truck. I'm talking a suitcase full of cold hard."

Cash made an insulted face as he mouthed the word "dump."

"I've got a place in the mountains," Jackie said. "I'm enjoying the view right now. We can meet here. I'll direct you."

I knew she was lying but played along. "Right into the sights of your sniper pal?"

"Vincent? He's a sweetie."

"He tried to kill me."

"Old news, Whip. We're business partners now."

"Downtown Tucson. Ten tomorrow morning."

"Make it 2:00 p.m. I've got a long drive ahead. Where at downtown?"

"I'll call ten minutes beforehand and tell you the location."

"That way Vincent can't set up a shot. I get the feeling you don't trust me at all." She gave a high-pitched sigh meant to show resignation. "Somehow I'll deal with the disappointment. I hand over a suitcase full of cash, you give me the phone, and we never see each other again, is that it?"

"That's it."

"What a captivating thought," Jackie said, and her tone changed again, now filling with menace. "If this blows up, if the police are there or anything goes sideways, anything at all, Vincent will find you and this time he won't miss."

I punched off the call. Cash bit his lip like he was thinking hard and nodded at Jimbo's truck. "If our giant friend here's telling the truth, she don't have the money. It's stashed away in Mexico City."

"He's telling the truth."

"That means Jackie's got nothing to put in a suitcase, so why would she go downtown?"

"No reason at all."

"But she wants Sterling's phone bad and, by golly, it's right here," Cash said. "That means she'll be coming to Double Wide instead and that's what you wanted all along."

I said nothing.

"And if she ain't in the mountains like she said, pushing back the time was a trick, right?"

"She's counting on us letting our guard down waiting on tomorrow," I said.

"Which means we'll be seeing her sooner than tomorrow. Like, say, tonight."

I said nothing again.

"Well, then," Cash said. "We best gear up. And there's folks we need to clear out of here in a hurry. Can't protect everybody."

I told Cash to have Sister Phil pack a bag and roust Ozzie out of bed and have him do the same. They were to wait by the Audi. He started to walk away, but something was on his mind.

"I'm not complaining or nothing, Mayor," he said. "You know me."

"Like hell."

"But you have a way of making things harder than they need to be, you know that?"

"Heard that before."

"Reckon I've said it myself."

"Like I told you, you can check out of this hotel whenever."

He put his hand over his heart. "The very suggestion wounds me."

"Good. I need you."

"Damn straight you do. A lovely adventure such as this."

CHAPTER SIXTY-ONE

Rod Santa Cruz told me to call him if I needed anything. I went inside the Airstream and called. We had a short conversation, after which I went back to the bedroom and shook Roxy by the shoulder to wake her up.

She hummed a string of unintelligible sleep sounds.

Another shake and her head popped off the pillow and her eyes opened.

"Do you trust me, Rox?"

"Huh?"

I knelt beside the bed. "I need you to trust me."

"I trust you. Of course I trust you. What's wrong?" She sat up on her elbows and yawned. Her breath held the faint whiff of Scotch. "What's going on?"

"I need you to drive Sister Phil and Ozzie to Rod's house."

"Rod's house? Whaaat?"

"They'll be bunking there tonight. I want you to stay with them until this is over."

She sat up all the way. She had no clothes on. She was a shapeless object, only the whites of her eyes giving definition to the darkness. "Wait, you're the one that wanted me to come here in the first place."

"This is going to work out. You trust me, right?"

"Stop asking me that. I hate it when people ask me that." She fingered a strand of hair behind her ear. "What's going on?"

"I need them out of here tonight, and you, too."

"Answer my question. Tell me what's going on right now. "

LEO W. BANKS

I scooped up her clothes and handed them to her. She grabbed the bundle and dropped it on the bed beside her. Her eyes stayed on me.

"You talked to Jackie," she said. "She's coming here to get it, right, the phone?"

"Cash will escort you out."

"You two worked out some arrangement. Didn't we agree to give the phone to Benny?"

"Rod understands what I have to do."

"Doesn't surprise me." She shook her head in disbelief. "You two. Freakin' twins." She rubbed her eyes with the heels of her hands and grabbed a shirt and wrestled it over her bare shoulders. "Okay, sure, I'll drive them. They didn't ask to be part of this."

She stood and wiggled her hips to get into her jeans. "When I'm done with that, I'm going to get in my car and drive right back here."

"Don't."

"You can't push me out, Prospero."

"Whatever happens, the story is still yours. You'll know everything."

"If they don't turn this place into a cemetery first."

A horn blared outside, three shorts blasts. I flipped on the light.

"Come on, they're waiting," I said.

"You think this is about the story? It hurts me you'd even say that."

The confusion must've showed on my face.

"You've got something you have to do, and I'm not going to stop you," Roxy said. "You've got private rules you follow and good for you. But I've got something to do, too, and that's be with you on this mess right through to the end. I thought you'd want it the same way."

"I'm trying to protect you."

258

"That's what I'm trying to do, too." Her voice rose, sharpened by intense emotion. "If you'd quit being such a goddamned man about it, you'd see that."

The horn sounded again.

"I don't want you coming back here," I said. "There's no point."

Anger spread across her face, but it made room for sadness, too. "There's every point in the world. If you don't get that, maybe there isn't a point to us."

"Hold on, Rox ... Don't ... You're being foolish."

She marched out of the bedroom and out the door. Without another word, she climbed into the Audi and started the engine.

Sister Phil sat shotgun and Ozzie crawled into the backseat with a blanket wrapped around his shoulders. He leaned his sleepy face out the window. "Dude, I was banking some righteous z's. I have needs, you know."

As the car began to move, Sister Phil fingered her window down. "Whatever's going on, I'm praying for your safety, Whip. I don't want to see you hurt."

She reached her hand out to me and I took it. "Do take care, Whip."

Cash drove his Malibu ahead of the Audi down my entrance road, and out.

I said to Charlie, "You sober enough to help me?"

"I'm sharp of mind and body, Mr. Mayor, an instrument of perfection. What do you need?"

I had Cash's shoulder rig with the .45 Ruger in it. I handed it to him. "You're in charge of watching Donny Jim."

He looked at the gun, puzzled. "Point of order. You realize I'm a painter. I paint houses. With a ladder and shit."

"He's doped up and hurt," I said. "You shouldn't have a problem. Just lay off the flask, okay?"

"What flask?" Charlie's eyes sparkled and he grinned with lots of teeth. He struggled to get the holster around his midsection. It was like trying to rope pudding.

"Second point of order," he said. "What do I do if he acts up?"

"You have a gun and he doesn't. Figure it out."

"Damn. Well, if I'm gonna miss my shows, I might as well have some fun."

The two sets of taillights streaked up the mountain. When they dropped out of sight, I went back into the Airstream.

The sound of the door closing felt like the end of something.

I walked to the bedroom and lifted my mattress and took out the Glock.

By its weight, I knew it was as loaded as I could get it. Fourteen in a magazine with a fifteen-round capacity. No matter how hard I tried, I could only load fourteen before the spring mechanism locked up. I'd been meaning to get that fixed.

I walked back to the front door and opened it. Down the street, Charlie sat on his porch watching Donny Jim sleep in the back of his pickup. The headlights of Cash's returning Malibu beamed along the county road.

That missing fifteenth round pressed on my mind.

What if that was the one that made the difference?

I sat in my kitchen holding the Glock between my legs and thinking about never seeing Roxanne Santa Cruz again.

The idea massed all around me, a physical force pressing against my body.

I'd felt lonely before. But not the way I felt that night.

CHAPTER SIXTY-TWO

Cash came inside and stood against the kitchen counter eating pistachios from a plastic sandwich bag. He was as cool as a creek in winter. Eyes clear, breathing steady, voice smooth. The only accommodation he'd made to the coming trouble was to turn his Arizona Feeds hat around.

"They got several ways to come at us, but they'll use the wash," he said.

"Good cover and once they climb out, they're on us."

He stared at the floor, chewing. "I'll go on down there, have a look."

"I'll keep watch up here."

Cash cracked the door open and looked outside. There wasn't much to see under the scattering clouds, and everything was quiet except for the remnants of the rain plinking off rooftops. I watched him go down the steps until the night swallowed him.

As soon as he was out of sight, my phone chirped with a text from Opal: "They love my art! Everybody's talking about it. Miss you guys. I haven't heard from you. Everything okay?"

"Never better," I responded.

I went outside and walked Double Wide's perimeter. All was quiet.

Cash was gone an hour, and nothing happened.

Roxy called from KPIN.

"How's the story going?" I asked.

"Getting there. I'll have to trim it unless Tig Watson gives me more time." Her tone was sour. "Listen, I changed my mind. I'm going to Rod's after work."

I was relieved but didn't say so. "When do you figure to get there?"

"I don't know, soon. Hour at most."

"Call me when you leave the station."

She didn't respond.

"Everything's good, right?" I said. "You're okay?

"Perfect. Why wouldn't I be?"

I kept talking. It took a while to realize that she'd hung up, and when I called back, she didn't pick up.

Cash and I swept the premises again. The wash and the immediate desert around us were clear. We kept an eye on Gates Pass for approaching headlights and saw nothing. The breeze carried the night songs of the coyotes, but now they had competition from Donny Jim.

He snored like a bear in the bed of his truck.

I had Charlie move from his porch to the front seat of the Dodge Ram and turn the truck around to have the headlights facing the Airstream.

"When the game starts, I might need light," I said. "If you hear shooting and my security lights go out, flip on the beams."

"Got it." Charlie saluted with exaggerated formality.

When an hour was up, I tried reaching Roxy again and she didn't pick up. I called the station and someone on the night crew said she'd left a half hour ago.

Feeling unease, I called Rod. "She should be at your place by now."

"Not here," he said. "She didn't call, either."

"She said she was going to your house after work."

"She's pretty pissed at you," Rod said. "But she might pick up for me. Hang tight and I'll call you back."

I paced around. Some nights the Airstream felt as big as a jetliner with plenty of shoulder room. Other nights it felt like a coffin.

Rod rang back.

"Baby girl's stubborn, Whip. Said she left something important behind at Double Wide."

"She's coming here?"

"You should be seeing her headlights any minute. She's not there in ten, call me back."

If Roxy was on her way, I was going to escort her in. I grabbed the keys to the Bronco and rushed outside. Before I got into the car, headlights appeared on the mountain, two shining eyes twisting through Gates Pass.

That made me feel better. She was on her way.

But almost immediately a second pair of lights appeared following close behind. At that time of morning, it was unusual to see one car, much less two, and both moving fast. The trailing car stayed close as the two of them rolled down the mountain.

"Something's wrong," Cash said.

"I'm going up there." I climbed behind the wheel and fired the engine. As I was about to move out, my phone rang, and I heard Roxy shouting. I couldn't make out a thing.

All I heard was a jumble of knocks, bumps, and scratches, her words coming through in indistinguishable fragments behind the chaos.

I sped out of Double Wide with the phone stuck to my ear.

"Rox, are you okay? Rox! Talk to me!"

She didn't respond.

CHAPTER SIXTY-THREE

As I sped through the saguaro forest, my headlights picked up a large object in the darkness ahead. Drawing closer, I saw Vincent's Strong's pickup at the side of the road, the front tires on dirt and angled toward the desert, much of the flatbed hanging over the pavement.

It looked like a hurry-up job, swing off the road, jam the brakes, get out, and run.

The truck was empty. Beyond it, thirty yards away on much lower ground, a wedge of light showed through the brush.

I hiked down the slope and saw the Audi with its front end pitched severely forward, its grill in a ditch. The car had smashed into a saguaro, snapped it at the stem, and the giant plant toppled backward onto the hood, creasing it with a massive concave dent.

The headlights shone, and so did the interior light from the open driver's door.

My heart thundered at the thought of seeing Roxy inside, hurt or dead. It stole the breath from my lungs, and I had to reach down to my feet to find the next one.

Swinging my arms, I fought wildly through the brush down to the Audi.

It was empty. Faint sounds hung on the air. Voices maybe, but I couldn't tell. They were there and gone too quickly.

For her car to plow all the way down that slope, she had to have been forced off the pavement at high speed.

Thinking she might be injured somewhere nearby, I scouted around and found nothing.

If they'd killed her, the body would be there. If it was a hostage they wanted, they'd have dragged her up to Vincent's truck and driven on to Double Wide.

With neither of those true, I figured she'd gotten away. I called Cash.

"Roxy's alone in the desert and headed your way. Half mile out."

"What about our guests?"

"They're following her and I'm following them."

"I love a parade," Cash said. "Three?"

"Most likely. Jackie, Vincent, and Holly. If they have Roxy, do not shoot, understand?"

"Roger that."

"Otherwise make Vincent your first target."

"If he steps inside the wire, he will know my wrath."

The clouds had cleared, but all the sky would give me was a half moon, and that would have to be enough. I started toward Double Wide. Bent low to the ground, the Glock in my hand, I moved as quietly as I could, a shadowy figure weaving among the saguaros.

The earlier rain had moistened the ground, softening my footfalls.

No snapping twigs. No crunching sound on sandy ground.

I thought of Roxy running through the same desert with killers at her back. She knew the desert. She and Rod had hunted all over southern Arizona. She wasn't afraid of it, and if her choice was run or die, she could run.

But there were three of them, six eyes all looking. They'd probably spread out, sweep wide to find her, and she might've been hurt when her car plunged into the ravine.

I moved faster. The air felt heavy, like I was running through a wet curtain. The storm was behind Paradise Mountain now, throwing off brilliant flashes of lightning as it moved south.

Breathing hard, I kept moving, looking ahead as far as I could see, looking from side to side. Roxy was nowhere. I wanted to call out to her but held back.

My security lights came into view, a halo over Double Wide.

I trudged the final steps to the trailer park's perimeter, the Airstream thirty feet ahead across Main Street, and ducked into a mesquite bosque.

The hanging branches gave good cover. Within seconds, I heard a faint bird whistle on my left, and there was Cash hustling to my side.

"Roxy?" I whispered.

"No trace." He pointed to the north end of Main Street. "Two unfriendlies come out of the desert up there and ducked into the wash. Vincent was one of them. He passed by too fast to get off a shot. The other was Jackie Moreno. Did not see Roxanne. Repeat, I did not see Roxanne. But my visuals were weak. She could be with them."

"Holly?"

"Negative. Did not see Holly either."

"You're sure Vincent and Jackie are in the wash?"

"No doubt," Cash said. "Wait or go?"

"Wait. I'm banking they don't have her."

"If they don't, she might be back in the desert. I can go back and look."

"No, we wait. They'll come out soon and we'll know."

As I spoke those words, the brush across the street rustled and Vincent climbed out of the wash behind the Airstream. He took a knee with a rifle in the ready position, and seconds later Jackie was beside him.

They appeared to speak, and Vincent stood. He was a big man, long legs, full in the shoulders. He walked around the trailer onto Main Street and turned to face my front door as if intending to climb the steps and go inside.

Cash stood and his rifle roared.

Vincent crumpled onto my bottom step, but he wasn't still.

Jackie had a handgun, and judging by the rapid rate of fire, it was a 9 mm. She squeezed off several shots in our direction, but they were just a postcard that got lost in the mail. The bullets snapped and whistled through the branches above us.

But she'd achieved the desired effect.

We sprawled facedown in the dirt.

By the time I rose again she'd disappeared into the wash and Vincent had gotten to his feet. He stumbled like he might go down, steadied himself, shot out my security lights, and vanished behind the sudden darkness.

Now the indifferent moon gave Double Wide its only light.

At the sound of gunfire, Charlie was supposed to flip on Jimbo's headlights. I waited and waited some more, but they never came on. I needed those lights shining.

Cash stayed under the mesquites while I sprinted across the entrance road behind Opal's trailer. On the way, I stopped at the junked Ford Fiesta and grabbed Ash Sterling's phone.

If they had Roxy, I might need a bargaining chip.

I emerged at the far end of Opal's trailer, right across the street from Jimbo's truck. Holly stood in front of it, her feet spread and a gun in her hand.

"Sorry, Donny Jim James," she said. "Too bad it has to go this way."

She fired a single shot through the windshield. I bent around the corner of the trailer and shot four rounds at her, at the same time yelling, "Lights, Charlie! Lights!"

Holly spun and fired at me, taking wood chips off the side of the trailer.

I waited and stuck my head out again and fired several more times. Holly's body twisted around, and she fell to one knee, rose quickly, swung her right hand across her body under her armpit, and fired a shot at me. Then she swung her arm back and fired five more rounds at Charlie.

This time the windshield exploded.

With the glass shards flying, Charlie's hand came up holding the Ruger sideways. Only the gun and the hand were visible. He fired through the open space, squeezing off round after round and screaming like somebody was sawing off his arm with a butter knife.

I fired at Holly, too, and she'd had enough. She was on the move. She ducked, looping her good arm over her head as she ran into a cluster of trees at the side of the road.

Hearing the shooting, Cash had left the mesquites and run up behind me.

He saw Holly fleeing, said, "She's mine," and sprinted across the street after her.

I ran to the truck and found Charlie lying across the seat. The side of his head was a mass of blood. I grabbed him by the shoulders and sat him up. He still held the Ruger, his fingers like steel around the grip. I uncurled them and dropped the gun on the seat beside him.

"Charlie, man, where you hit?"

He mumbled something. Part of his left ear had been shot off. He fell sideways into me. His weight was too much, but I did what I could to slow his fall out from behind the wheel and lower him onto the ground beside the truck.

Jimbo raised his head over the edge of the flatbed. "What the hell?"

"Holly thought she was shooting at you."

"Holly? Again? Shit. Bro."

"Breaking up is hard to do. Throw down your blanket."

Cash's rifle boomed in the wash, and immediately following came the sound of a handgun returning fire.

I used Jimbo's blanket to wipe the blood off Charlie's face. "Forgot about the lights," he said, and gave me a feeble grin. Blood stained his teeth.

Someone fired two shots that pinged off the front of the truck.

"You have to move, Charlie," I said. "Can you get up?"

"Can try." He groaned, said, "Jeepers creepers," and rolled onto his knees, palms flat on the ground, and began crawling on all fours toward the back of the truck.

"I ain't sticking around this place," Jimbo said, and climbed out of the bed.

"Help Charlie," I said. "Get him out of here. You two find someplace to hide."

Jimbo hesitated as if he might split on his own but decided otherwise and reached his good hand under Charlie's armpit and dragged him into the darkness behind the truck.

The Glock in hand, I looked over the open door down the street, saw nothing, and leaned into the cab of the truck and flipped on the headlights.

Only the one on the passenger side still worked.

Another shot and this time I saw the muzzle flash. It came from behind Bertie's saguaro, right outside the Airstream.

Then a voice: "Fed 'em to the javelina."

It was Jackie Moreno.

I aimed the Glock over the door, squeezed off a shot, and the slide opened with that unmistakable metallic click. The magazine was empty. I'd fired all fourteen rounds.

Cash's Ruger sat on the front seat, but before I could reach in and grab it, Jackie let loose with five fast shots. The right headlight blew up. Another bullet struck the door with a loud *thwack* and, passing through, creased my right arm at the shoulder.

The impact knocked me off balance, and I fell to the ground.

Jackie kept firing as I squirmed behind the big front tire.

"Amateur move, Whip," Jackie said. "Running out of bullets. So sad."

She stepped around the saguaro into the open, gripping the pistol with two hands as she walked toward me down the street.

CHAPTER SIXTY-FOUR

Jackie fired again as she walked, the bullet crashing into the grill.

"First I put Ash's fingers in the freezer," she said.

The shooting in the wash went on, which I assumed was from Cash's rifle and Holly's pistol. The sounds were widely spaced, as if they were trading shots from cover.

"Had a forty-eight-hour window to find his phone," Jackie said. "Touch ID disables after forty-eight hours. Did you know that, Whip?"

Two more bullets banged into the front of the truck.

"After that I had to decide," she said. "What does one do with a loved one's severed fingers? I mean, they're no good to me anymore. And gross. Can I say that?"

Laughing crazily: "Is there a disposal protocol? I Googled it. But I wanted something that was all mine. Original."

She pronounced the last word slowly, emphasizing every letter.

I poked my head out. Jackie was closer now, shaped by the moonlight.

She fired three times, the blasts coming so close together they sounded like one. The ground around me tossed up dirt and pebbles, and the tire exploded. The truck listed sideways as the air rushed out.

Silence, and a break in the shooting.

"I have something you want," I yelled. "Ash's phone."

"Whip, darling, do you really think you can bargain with me now?"

"You want it, don't you? It's in my pocket."

"I want it, and I'm going to kill you and take it." She kept walking. She fired again, and the sound of lead smashing into metal sent a shiver up my legs into my stomach.

"It's too late for you, Whip."

She wasn't going to take any deal I offered. She'd come to do a job, and she was going to do it. But if I could stall her until she had to reload, I might have a chance to get to the Ruger.

"What do you think happens if you kill me?" I said.

"Simple, I take the phone and leave."

"No. Cashmere Miller walks out of that wash and shoots you dead. Unless I tell him we have a deal. I'll throw you the phone and you walk out of here."

She fired another round that *thumped* into the flat tire.

"Hmm. Let me ponder that one."

She was about ten feet away. Behind Jackie, I saw someone run out of the desert, cross Main Street, and climb my front steps into the Airstream. The figure was a streak in the half darkness, fast moving and unidentifiable.

Jackie fired again. "After careful consideration, I reject your offer."

I said, "You can have the phone in hand and be in Mexico in an hour."

Most 9 mm handguns hold fifteen to seventeen rounds. She couldn't have many left. Jimbo's blanket was at my feet. I balled it up like a football and tossed it into the open.

She shot it and it rolled over the ground several times.

That was her last bullet. I heard the slide on her gun pop open.

With screaming pain up my right arm, I scrambled out from behind the tire.

Jackie was holding her gun up by her shoulder. She thumbed the magazine release, let the empty fall to the ground, pulled another from her pocket, and palmed it into the tube. She racked a round and fired at me as I dove onto the front seat of the truck.

She fired twice more, shredding the driver's headrest and leaving the rearview mirror hanging sideways.

"I'm throwing out the phone," I yelled. "It's all yours."

I heaved Ash Sterling's phone through the windshield space, giving it a high arc to keep it in the air a long time, then sat up with the Ruger in my left hand.

Jackie Moreno's eyes followed the phone she'd wanted for so long, and her hand reached for it, and that was when I shot her.

She fell back in the dirt, arms spread, her right hand still gripping the gun.

I walked over to her. Her eyes were wide open and blank. When I stepped on her wrist and reached down to pick up her gun, she startled to awareness.

"You tricked me," she said.

"I owed you one."

"We never get what we want on this earth, do we?" Her words barely made a sound, as if she'd already gone to some other place, far beyond.

"This is what I planned, this is exactly what I wanted," I said. "Sometimes there's nothing worse than that."

"At least those javelina had a feast," Jackie said, and died.

I stood in the middle of Main Street, dazed and unmoving. I needed time to catch up on my breathing, to bleed in peace and imagine forgiveness.

There was a noise behind me.

Vincent Strong was there.

He'd hobbled out of the wash halfway between the Airstream and Jimbo's truck. The wound from Cash's rifle had left him bent over, the right side of his body bloodstained and twisted in a grotesque way.

He inched toward me, heaving his body forward with each step, his face twisted in agony but with a hellish grin. With his right arm hanging loose, he held his rifle up with his left hand, the arm pressed tight against his ribs, finger on the trigger.

It was pointed right at me.

Holding the Ruger down against my leg, there was nothing I could do.

"I want you looking into my eyes when I shoot you," he said.

Twenty feet behind him, Roxy said, "Hey, Vincent, don't be a jerk."

With surprising speed, he swung the rifle around. But Roxy was faster, and her shotgun exploded. The force of the charge hitting him made a grotesque sound, and he went down.

In the long silence following the blast, Cash emerged from the wash. Seeing the two bodies in the street, he slung the AR over his shoulder and gave me a solemn nod.

"It got crispy down there, Mayor, but it's done." He pointed at Roxy with admiration. "That girl's got sand."

Cash went to find Charlie and Jimbo, and I walked back to Roxy.

Her lips were white, her clothes filthy and torn, and blood streaked down her face and arms from numerous small cuts. I picked leaves and twigs out of her hair.

"You hid in the desert."

"I had a head start but couldn't keep it. Couldn't outrun them." Her eyes were huge. "I know I should've told you I was coming back, but you would've said not to come. Right? I know you would've."

"It's all right."

"I changed my mind, that's all."

"Rod said you forgot something important." I motioned to the shotgun. "I'm glad you came back for it. You saved my life."

"I didn't come back for the shotgun, you dummy. I came back for you."

She laughed and dropped the gun and threw her arms around me, and the laughter became tears. She pressed the side of her face hard against my chest.

"All I could think was I'm not dying today," she said.

As she held on tight, her whole body shook, and so did my heart.

CHAPTER SIXTY-FIVE

Rod Santa Cruz arrived at Double Wide a few minutes later. He stepped from his car with a gun in his hand and let his cool brown eyes sweep the scene. He saw Vincent's body in the street, the upper half a crimson paint spill, and Jackie's down by the Dodge Ram.

He made his eyes crooked as he stared at me. "You were supposed to call back."

"Got a little busy, Rod."

When he saw Roxy's condition, the veins on his neck fattened. "Who did this?" he said in a tightly controlled voice.

Roxy pointed with her chin at the two bodies. "Take your pick."

Rod walked over to Vincent's corpse and looked down saying nothing, showing no outward emotion, and raised his foot and drove the heel of his boot down as hard as he could into Vincent's face.

The crunch and snap of his facial bones caving in made a stomach-turning sound, and Roxy looked away. Rod threw back his suit coat and returned the gun to his hip holster.

"Everybody good?"

Rod called Benny Diaz and he drove to Double Wide trailed by a crowd of other cops and forensic techs, who fanned out to walk around and mumble. Roxy spent the morning at St. Mary's Hospital for observation and fluids, and I got my arm patched up.

Next day, Roxy went to KPIN to work on the story.

I'd promised Lonesome Eddie Palmer a call. His phone rang fifteen times, and when he answered, he didn't say hello, not exactly. What he said was, "This better be fucking good."

I told him what happened.

Palmer made a noise that might've signaled happiness, but it sounded more like someone strangling a sage hen.

"You're like me, Whip. You start on something and gotta finish it. Carry it around every damn day."

"It's over now."

"Good."

With unfinished business on my mind, my next call went to Carlos Venable, owner of the Mexico City Pirates. Six years before, after I'd pitched and won the deciding game for the Mexican League championship, Carlos had told me if I ever needed anything to get in touch.

He was one of the most powerful businessmen in Mexico, but that championship meant more to him than anything. If I'd asked him to find Bigfoot, he'd have brought me the corpse in a box with a ribbon on it.

"Whip Stark, my dear friend," he said. "Where have you been?"

After some catch-up talk, I asked if he could get the security video from Enrique's Boutique in the Polanco for the day Jackie and Val had been there. I said I'd send him photos of both women.

"Is that all?" He laughed a rich man's laugh. "I'll make a call."

Two days later, my morning email harvest included Carlos's response and I jumped into the Bronco for the drive to Scottsdale. But before getting on I-10, I crossed town to St. Anthony's Church and knocked on Sister Phil's door.

When she opened up and saw me, she threw her arms around me.

"I was so happy to hear you made it okay!" she gushed. "Thank the Lord! Oh, thank you, thank you. I was so worried about you."

The reaction surprised even her, and she quickly disengaged and stepped back, blushing. She coughed a very proper cough. "Would you like tea?"

While it was brewing, she said, "All I do is try to keep busy. It's like I don't belong in my own apartment anymore, don't know whether to sit or stand. I'm having trouble regaining my old life."

"You've been through a lot," I said. "It'll take time."

"I'll offer it up. I just hope I still have a job. What'll happen to my students if Father Bob decides not to take me back?"

"He'll take you back."

"If only I could be so sure."

"You said he likes money."

"The man stuffs his pillowcase with it, if you ask me."

"I have something in mind."

She asked no questions. We sat and sipped tea and talked. I told her more about what had happened at Double Wide, the agony and the regret, and that got me talking about my father.

"I'll never be the man he was," I said.

"Oh, I don't believe that."

"You don't understand, Sister Phil."

"But I do. You're thinking you might do the same thing again." Her eyes were dark, but there was light in them just the same. "Am I right?"

I couldn't hold her gaze and turned my head. "How many do you get?"

"As many as you need. Forgiveness has no number."

In parting, she gave me another of her layaway handshakes. "If I still have a job, Whip, I want you to sit in on my Bible class."

"Maybe I will. How about afterward I take you to Starbucks?"

"Goodness, no. I'm done for the year."

CHAPTER SIXTY-SIX

At Constant Lexus, the receptionist said Val's lunch companions had already picked her up. "She has a super-important meeting with some big executives." The receptionist was brightly painted, overly cheery, and looked a week removed from the high school cheerleading squad.

"I was supposed to join them, but I'm running late," I said.

She puzzled and fingered some papers. "She didn't mention another guest."

"You know how forgetful Our Pal Val can be, and I'm afraid I'm the same way. What was the name of the restaurant again?"

"Cowboy Grub. It just opened and everybody's talking about it."

I found the restaurant on a busy corner of downtown Scottsdale. The sign was shaped like a branding iron. Inside, there were wine racks, distressed wood, and low light to make sure everyone looked presentable after a hard day riding the range with Ralph Lauren.

With weathered hats and spurs hanging everywhere, the interior decor was working cowboy, but the prices were cattle baron.

Val sat at a secluded table with three men. She put her wineglass down hard when she saw me. "Whip Stark." She stood up so quickly her chair nearly tipped over. She wore a white cable-knit sweater that captured every one of her curves and red velvet skinny pants.

The waiter had followed me to the table. "Miss Constantine, do you require assistance?"

"It's all right, Rex," Val said.

He gave her a reverent nod and kept looking over his shoulder at me as he walked away in case I jerked out a six-shooter and started fanning the room.

Val introduced me to her lunch companions. Two were company presidents. They had shiny black hair, elegant suit jackets, and good teeth. The third was a vice president. He had a bald spot and a bola tie.

No handshakes for me. They could barely manage nods.

"Let's go somewhere and talk about Jackie Moreno," I said.

Val motioned to her guests. "Maybe this isn't the best time."

"How about I pull up a chair and we talk right here?"

She dropped her eyes and looked sad. "I've lost my ex-husband and my stepdaughter, Whip. What is it you want to talk about?"

"Start with the last time you talked to Jackie."

"I told you, I've had no contact with my stepdaughter in five years."

"This is Jackie's burner phone." I held it up and pressed redial.

Val's phone was sitting out on the white tablecloth. It hummed to life. She blushed, snatched it up, and silenced it. "Could I speak to my friends privately, Whip? I'll meet you outside in a moment."

I pulled the Bronco up to Cowboy Grub's front door. Val stepped out a minute later, long-striding to the .22-caliber clicking of her six-inch stiletto heels.

The shoes were cream colored and had red platform soles. They were the same shoes she'd worn the first time we met. She climbed in and slammed the door.

"Was that really necessary?" she said. "I do a lot of business with those men."

"Why'd you lie?"

"Because Jackie's a murderer and I can't be associated with a murderer."

"But you can have a long conversation with her. What did she call you about?"

"She was upset about Ash's murder and needed an ear. I had no idea at the time she was responsible, obviously."

I pulled onto Scottsdale Road and headed north. It was 11:45 in the morning. The sweet smell of Val's perfume blew over me and mixed with the wisps of oily smoke leaking in from under the dashboard.

"Are we going anywhere in particular or just driving around?" Val said.

"Let's talk about your shoes," I said and pointed. "You bought them in Mexico City, didn't you? Enrique's Boutique in the Polanco."

"Now, that's a topic I can get into. Amazing, aren't they?"

"You said you'd just gotten back from there last time we talked."

"You have a better memory than me."

"Do you remember the date you bought them?"

"The date? Of course not."

A woman like Val would remember the date, the price, the name of the salesperson, the temperature at the time, and probably the barometric pressure.

"It was three days after Ash's murder," I said. "You and Jackie went shopping together."

She quick-eyed me. Her factory face turned gray.

I drove along. Scottsdale looked beautiful, clean and bright blue under sheltering palm trees. In a month's time, the winter visitors would be back and making their gleeful calls to friends in the glacial Midwest to boast of seventy-degree daytime highs.

"We can do this all day, Val. I've got nowhere to be."

"Okay, okay." She held up her hand to stop me. She had fingernails like daggers. "We talked, we did. She called a week before Ash's murder. We hadn't spoken since my wedding and we ended up talking a long time."

"Some coincidence. Nothing for five years and she calls a week before Ash's murder."

"Think whatever you like, Whip, but she said she was thinking of me and I was delighted to hear from her."

"Go on. What'd you talk about?"

"Everything. I told her about work, my life, the divorce, and she told me about school. We reconnected and she suggested a shopping trip. When she was a teenager, I'd take her to the Polanco to get away and she wanted to do it again, like old times. She picked the date, offered to buy tickets, and everything was set."

"The story gets better," I said. "Three days after your ex-husband's murder, you go on a shopping trip."

"I was upset, naturally, and wanted to cancel," Val said. "But Jackie wasn't bothered at all. She said Ash had messed with her life enough when she was little, and insisted we stick with the plan. She said it would be our way of celebrating."

"You weren't suspicious at all."

"I knew she hated Ash, but I never imagined she could do such a thing." Val stared out the window for a long moment. "Until she asked me to help carry her suitcases into the Bancomer. Right then I knew and was paralyzed."

"Too paralyzed to leave or call the police."

"She said if I talked, she'd kill me. Her eyes, my God, they were crazy. I had to do what she wanted." Val's voice cracked and she snuffled into a tissue. "I'm sorry, but just remembering frightens me."

She covered my hand with hers on the steering wheel, and I got a creeping sensation up my arm. "Now do you understand why I don't want to talk about it?"

The lunch crowd had exited the offices around Scottsdale Fashion Square, making the sidewalk as busy as the street. The Bronco rumbled along.

"You lie as easily as you breathe, Val."

"Whip, what are you saying?" Her words were breathy, the tone pleading.

"Let me tell you how it really went."

Val tugged at the tissue in her lap. "I'm telling the truth."

"You and Jackie were in it from the start," I said, and reached across the seat and grabbed her phone. "If the cops go through your call records, I'm guessing they'll find a bunch of untraceable calls from the 520 area code."

"I never called her, not one time."

"But she called on her burners plenty of times to set everything up," I said. "You went to Mexico City with her to get your cut of Ash's money, only she double-crossed you."

"You can't possibly believe that."

"That's why that last call was so angry. You wanted your money and Jackie still wasn't paying up. What'd she promise? Half a million?"

She let out a dismissive sound. "Ridiculous."

"I figure she kept you quiet by threatening to tell Dimitri about your affair with Titus. That would've cost you millions in the divorce. You and Dimitri had a prenup, right?"

Val's wide painted eyes stared straight out the windshield, unblinking.

"How am I doing so far?"

She didn't move or speak.

"I have to say, you and Jackie played it like pros," I said. "Jackie tells me to talk to you, and you keep putting me off, not calling back. When I finally get you in the Lexus, the acting job you put on, it was top-notch.

"But you made a mistake," I continued. "You told me you'd just been to the Polanco before you knew who I was. That's funny because I'm a pretty famous guy. Baseball player."

"Sorry, I don't follow sports." Her tissue had been put away and she'd given up on the pretend weeping. It was getting to be too much work. "What exactly did I do to earn this imaginary money? I'd love to know."

"Exactly what Jackie wanted," I said. "You built her up to me as a saint and painted Vincent as a crazy man to help set him up. But most of all you gave her Titus Ortega."

She jerked toward me in the seat. Her eyes were hot. "Don't talk about Titus to me. Don't you ever talk about Titus."

"Titus had to go because he knew what Jackie did in the Foothills, and so did you," I said. "You lied when you said you didn't. You knew Jackie was going to have him killed and told her how to find him anyway, didn't you, Val?"

"I told Jackie he was looking for a gallery, that's all. I told you the same thing. Why would I do that if I knew she was going to kill him?"

"By then you'd been to Mexico City and knew she was going to screw you," I said. "Plus, I figure guilt had set in, and you wanted me to find Titus before Vincent. Just so you know. I did find him. But he was too far gone to listen."

"I loved Titus," she said absently.

"I believe you. But you loved Jackie's money more."

Val sat perfectly still, staring at nothing.

I said, "How does it feel to give up someone you love and not get a dime out of it?"

Val waited a long time, and when she spoke again her voice had emptied of all the anger and sadness. The only thing left in it was cold steel.

"Love's a wonderful thing, Whip. But it always has an expiration date, doesn't it?"

On the street, the bicyclists were spandexed and helmeted. The men walking the sidewalks wore pressed slacks and fine leather loafers. The dogs were spared the indignity of having to walk. They were cradled in the arms of women who were coiffed, rouged, and ready for lunch.

Looking out at the parade, Val said, "Are you going to the police, Whip? I suppose you can, but I was tricked. I didn't know Jackie was going to kill Titus and I didn't know she killed Ash until I got to Mexico City. Nobody can prove I did. I'm the victim here, Whip."

She spoke smoothly and with assurance. Listening to her was getting to me.

Her voice rode bareback over every nerve in my body.

"Okay, I talked with Jackie on the phone," she went on. "Prove we conspired. You can't. And maybe I should've called somebody, but I feared for my life. Based on what we know about Jackie Moreno now, it was well-founded. Some prosecutor might try to hang me, but I'll hire the best lawyer I can find, and we'll see, won't we."

She was right. She'd have the money to slick out of it.

My brakes squealed as the Bronco stopped at the light at Indian School Road. People in the crosswalk stared. I couldn't blame them. The brakes were one thing, but the Bronco's engine sounded like a series of explosions at a paint factory on Sunday morning.

"Can I get back to Cowboy Grub now?" she said. "They have the yummiest salads."

"You might not know sports, Val, but I had a decent career, won some big games."

"How wonderful for you."

I explained my connection to Carlos Venable and the Mexico City Pirates. "I called in a favor." From my pocket I produced a printout of Carlos's email that included a screen grab from the security camera at Enrique's Boutique.

I held the photo up to her face. It showed Jackie and Val trying on shoes. They were sitting side by side on a luxurious couch with a salesman in a tailored suit kneeling in front of them. They were smiling and holding drinks in flute-shaped glasses.

"Fearing for your life, Val?"

She glanced at the photo. The skin around her eyes twitched.

"You told me you didn't want this scandal to ruin you," I said. "What do you suppose would happen if this got out?"

She got brick-faced.

"Public opinion would hang you," I said. "My Pal Val and her murdering stepdaughter shopping for shoes seventy-two hours after Ash Sterling's death? The parties, the fame, the money, it all goes away. You'd be done."

Val's shoulders heaved in a long sigh. "Now I get it. This is a squeeze."

"I prefer to call it a transaction."

"The Bancomer money has nothing to do with me. It's in Jackie's name."

"The money's not coming from her safety-deposit box, Val. It's coming from you."

She gave me a nasty stare. "Not the altar boy after all, are you, Whip."

"I want half of what Jackie stole from Ash. Five hundred thousand or I'll make sure this picture leads every TV broadcast in Arizona. How do you think your friends at Cowboy Grub will react to that?"

Her face turned porcelain except for two fire-red cheekbones. An ugly moment crept by.

"Give me your account number," she said. "I'll wire it to you."

"The money's not going to me."

I told her that two charitable funds had been set up at the Wells Fargo branch on Wilmot Road in Tucson. One was to help the children of Paul and Donna Morton and the other was in the name of Sister Joseph Philomena from St. Anthony's Church.

The split between the two accounts would be exactly fifty-fifty.

"If those accounts don't have two hundred fifty thousand dollars in them within five days, I release the photo."

Val said nothing more as I drove toward Cowboy Grub. Partway there, she demanded to be let out. I pulled to the curb, and she jumped to the sidewalk with the car still moving.

Her perfume had overwhelmed the smoke leaking from the dash. I preferred the smoke.

Soon as I pulled away, I found a car wash and paid for the super-deluxe-holy-crap clean job to get her smell out of the Bronco.

CHAPTER SIXTY-SEVEN

The DNA tests on the knife that killed Cristy Carlyle came back. The material in the grooves along the handle was indeed blood, and it belonged to Carlyle and Earl "Bumpy" Topp, who'd cut himself in the attack.

Nothing on the knife came from Sam Houston Stark. As I'd known all along, he wasn't a murderer. Sam had been wrongly convicted and died a death row inmate.

I told Dietz to call a press conference and ask that the case be reopened.

"Can't do it," she said. "That would have to come from people that make a lot more money than me."

"You're refusing?"

"I'm telling you the way it is, Stark."

I reminded her that she was the one who killed Topp, ending the best chance we had to get the right man convicted of Carlyle's murder.

She didn't like that. "Are you suggesting that was my intention?"

"Am I being subtle here?"

Even in my anger, I knew there was a possibility I wasn't being fair to Dietz. The encounter might've happened exactly as she'd said. Bumpy Topp came at her with intent to kill, and she had no choice but to put him down.

Topp had attacked me and pizza guy Tom Mohegan in the same manner.

Dietz said something that shocked me.

"I understand you're involved with a TV reporter. Roxanne Santa Cruz, I believe. She's been covering this, am I right?"

"That's right."

"Have her call me. I'll go on camera and explain what I did and didn't do, and what the DNA showed. That's all I can do. Your father didn't do this, and whether you believe it or not, the truth matters to me."

"You surprise me, Dietz."

"Now I want you to do something for me and it's important."

"Anything."

"Lose my phone number."

Roxy did a story on the Foothills murders and began preparing pieces on my father's case. Tig Watson okayed a multipart series in which she planned to name Bumpy Topp the real killer.

The trouble with local TV was that it was local TV. The reach was limited, and by the time her stories aired, I was afraid they'd be viewed like a newspaper correction.

No matter where they played it, and corrections rarely made the front page, the original story stood tall as ever. With luck, maybe Roxy's stories would start a bonfire and go national.

That was the best we could hope for to clear a good man's name.

CHAPTER SIXTY-EIGHT

On a lovely mid-December morning, I drove out of Double Wide with Titus Ortega's paintings in the Bronco. I'd forgotten about them and Abigail Whitcomb had been calling.

Opal Sanchez sat beside me. She wore a black derby hat that pressed her long black hair against her bubble cheeks, framing her face. Her fingernails were painted black and sprinkled with gold stardust.

Nothing definite came of her New York trip, only fine words of praise and a promise to see more of her paintings later on. Opal was disappointed, and I wanted another gallery owner to see her work.

Ozzie Fish sat in the backseat, his long blond hair done up in a man-bun. He'd returned home to his apartment twice, and both times when his mother left to visit her boyfriend in Phoenix, he hitchhiked back over the mountain.

The mother had problems, and Ozzie wasn't one of them. She barely knew he existed. The way things looked, Double Wide would be getting another permanent resident before long.

Halfway along on I-10, I stopped at a fast-food joint and bought three pancake and egg breakfasts to go, a coffee for me, orange juice for Opal, and a Yoohoo for Ozzie.

When Opal walked back outside, her pockets were overflowing with stolen salt and pepper and ketchup packets.

"Come on, dude," Ozzie said. "You got enough ketchup for, like, years."

Opal didn't speak or budge, except to flash her middle finger over the seat. Ozzie laughed, and we ate in the Bronco and continued to Kokopelli Station in Tempe.

Abigail liked Opal's paintings, bought two, and asked her to bring more when she had them. It was a pleasant meeting, after which we stopped at the cemetery to visit Sam.

The engraved headstone was finally there.

On it was a quote from *Hamlet*: "*Good night sweet prince: And flights of angels sing thee to thy rest!*"

Opal read the words out loud. "That's beautiful. Who said that?"

"Shakespeare."

"I heard of him."

She wanted to know all about Sam, and on the way back I talked and talked. I must've needed to, because I told her everything about my life growing up, how Sam supported me from my first day in baseball, how he loved me and never quit on me when everything looked bad.

She listened amid the bird cheeps and rodent squeals of the video game Ozzie was playing in the backseat.

Soon, Opal started sniffling, and I couldn't understand why she was crying. After all, she'd never met Sam.

When I asked, she said, "He sounds exactly like you, Mr. Whip."

I was honored to be compared to Sam Houston Stark, but I didn't need the blubbering, so I changed the subject, and we made it all the way to Double Wide without more waterworks.

ABOUT THE AUTHOR

In his career as a reporter, Leo W. Banks won thirty-eight statewide, regional, and national journalism awards. His 2018 novel, *Double Wide*, won two Spur awards from the Western Writers of America—for Best First Novel and Best Western Contemporary Novel. *True West* magazine called it the Western crime novel of the year and the New Mexico–Arizona Book Awards named it Best Mystery for 2018. He grew up in Boston and lives in Arizona.

CPSIA information can be obtained
at www.ICGtesting.com
Printed in the USA
LVHW111603140820
663221LV00003B/631